THE FAITHFUL ALLY

THE
FAITHFUL ALLY

ERIC LINKLATER

THE REPRINT SOCIETY LONDON

FIRST PUBLISHED 1954
THIS EDITION PUBLISHED BY THE REPRINT SOCIETY LTD.,
BY ARRANGEMENT WITH JONATHAN CAPE LTD., 1956

PRINTED IN GREAT BRITAIN BY RICHARD CLAY AND COMPANY, LTD.,
BUNGAY, SUFFOLK

A Story of His Highness
Zafrullah bin Ismail bin Said
Sultan of Namua, Lord of the Island Sea
who retained also his grandfather's
Title of Honour:
Faithful Ally of Queen Victoria

*With a playgoer's gratitude
and a
friend's affection
to Sir*
RALPH RICHARDSON

One

MR. JAMES MORLAND, Adviser to the Sultan of Namua and Commissioner for Tribal Territory, watched with pleasure three brown-skinned gardeners uprooting a large bed of cannas. He was a humane, enlightened man, lenient in judgment, patient with the savage errors of primitive people; but he could not tolerate the excesses of tropical vegetation, and when he was out of humour would give violent orders that laid waste the gardens of the Secretariat. Grenadillas and hibiscus, poincianas and jacarandas and multi-coloured giant coleus fell in a brilliant carnage to appease his anger, and under his recurrent ban bright coppices and flaming borders were pruned and excoriated till they looked as bleak as a municipal park in the north of England after a wet spring.

The cannas, a furnace of colour, were cut down and their roots dug up. They had filled an oval bed in the centre of a lawn, and Morland told the gardeners to turf it over. It was impossible to grow good grass, but the coarse herbage of the country could be kept tidy by daily mowing and rolling, and green did not assault the eye like scarlet. A lawn, however bright, was not flamboyant.

He turned towards his office and looked with disapproval at the vine whose leaves and blossom festooned the veranda. That would have to be dealt with before long, he thought, and said good morning to his chief clerk. It was just eight o'clock, but already, under a dazzling sky, the air was hotter than the high noon of an English summer.

'I want to speak to Mr. Kershawe,' said Morland.

7

He went into his own room and sat down to read the typed copy of a report he had begun to write the day before. There was a new Governor at Fairweather, the capital of British New Brabant—a youngish man, dry and puritanical and ambitious—and though Morland approved of him on the whole, and even liked him, he resented, as was natural, the additional and often unnecessary work that always followed a new appointment. The Governor had decided that the Year Book required more than annual revision: it had to be rewritten. 'And let us try,' he had said, 'to create something which, though factual and accurate in all its facts, may give a little pleasure to people who are accustomed to reading for pleasure.'

Morland, a little fretfully, considered his opening paragraphs:

The Sultanate of Namua lies on the north shore of the great island of New Brabant, its coastline barely five degrees south of the equator, and divides the British administration in the east from the Dutch territories of the west. Its climate, though hot and humid, is made tolerable by the sea-breeze that plays lightly for most of the year, savagely for two or three months; and by the winds that pour gratefully down, though often carrying fog, from the high, central cordillera.

Small in comparison with the whole island, the Sultanate is nevertheless as large as Portugal, and most of it, as it rises in sharply broken steepness to an alpine backbone, is almost inaccessible except by aeroplane. The highlanders are short in stature, and of uncertain temper. Their villages, widely separated by profound gorges and precipitious heights, are also divided by mutual and immemorial fear and animosity, and the process of pacifying them by the introduction of law has been arduous and is still far from complete.

The cost of administration and the greater part of the Sultan's private income are derived from the oil-wells of Te Aku, an island in an archipelago that lies between eighty and a hundred and twenty miles from the coast and is, according to tradition, the earlier home of the ruling house and some of the coastal tribes—now inter-bred with Polynesian and Malayan adventurers—from which, in the seventeenth century, they invaded the adjacent shore of New Brabant.

Port Philip, the capital or administrative centre of Namua, is pleasantly situated but its development has been hindered by lack of resources. . . .

So far, he thought, it was inoffensive, but he had perhaps approached too abruptly the closely related subjects of the Sultan and finance. The Colonial Office of an earlier day had persuaded the Sultan's father—a mild man who collected butterflies—to accept a division of the revenue from Te Aku which was probably unfair to His Highness and certainly unjust to Namua. A large proportion, debited to defence, went into the exchequer of British New Brabant, and Namua suffered in consequence. Morland had no wish to enlarge the present Sultan's income, which he considered more than sufficient, but he urgently desired a larger revenue for his country; and in his next paragraph he had underlined, a little too heavily for policy, its natural claim to the profits of the oil-wells.

Reluctantly he decided that his statements must be more gently phrased, and while he was wondering how to modify the challenge of the words without impoverishing the meaning of what he had written, his chief clerk came in and said, in

9

clipped and careful English, 'Mr. Kershawe, sir, is now on the line.'

There was, in fact, no line between them. Kershawe was a District Officer whose parish, called Maipani, lay high in the mountains to the south-west, and communication was by radio-telephone, when it worked. Measured on the map with a ruler, Maipani was only ninety-six miles away, but to march there, over the hill-tracks that the tribes were paid to keep open, took eight days in the dry season. No one attempted to march in the wet months.

'Kershawe?' said Morland. 'What's the situation this morning?'

Obscured by a teasing, buzzing noise, a faint and desiccated voice replied. 'A good lot more of them arrived yesterday, sir. About forty or fifty, as near as I can judge, and they say others are coming. They were banging away on their drums last night, but only for an hour or two. I saw Samarai about midday, and he was just the same. Pretending to be quite confident, and perfectly bland. They follow him about wherever he goes, but so far there's no real sign of antagonism. They're all very cock-a-hoop, but they keep well away from us.'

'You're not worried, are you?'

'Oh no, sir. There's nothing to worry about.'

'I'm sure you're right, Kershawe. I'm quite sure of that. The reinforcement I've sent you, the six constables under Sergeant Kula, ought to arrive tomorrow, but I don't want you to advertise their presence. Don't use them to display your strength. I'm coming up myself on Friday, in the courier plane—'

'I'll be glad to see you, sir.'

'But I don't want you to receive me with any ceremony. I don't want to create the impression that we're taking this business too seriously. We've got to show ourselves perfectly calm and easy, and so long as we're not provocative I don't believe there's any risk of violence. You know what our policy has always been. . . .'

Ninety-six miles away, or eight days' march, Kershawe sat by his desk in a long thatched hut of native architecture, and putting his hand over the microphone said to his companion, who sat on the top of the rough-hewn steps which led to the hut, 'He's given out the text, and now he's starting the sermon.'

Kershawe, a short, swarthy young man, lean with exercise and burnt by the sun, was responsible for the maintenance of law, and some degree of order, over eight hundred square miles of mountainous country whose tallest peaks rose to nine thousand feet. Here and there, on lesser heights chosen for their difficulty of approach, were small, crowded villages whose inhabitants lived on the produce of the gardens they had cleared from scrub or forest, and pastured a few score lean pigs that were regarded rather as wealth than sustenance, and only slaughtered on ritual occasion. Cannibalism had officially been suppressed, but was still a lively memory and an occasional indulgence.

The armed force at Kershawe's disposal consisted of a native corporal and six constables. He also employed a clerk and a medical orderly, educated men from the coast; an interpreter, from the same village, who spoke two or three of the hill dialects; and a couple of houseboys. His only white companion within five days' march was an Australian who kept a trade-store and had a licence to recruit labourers for the big plantations in the lowlands. Tom Penny was a man whom other men, wanderers like himself, would usually claim to have known in Thursday Island or Pago Pago, in Cloncurry or Rabaul, in Kalgoorlie or Tobruk. He had shot kangaroos for a living, and been a barman, a gold-miner, a sea-cook, and a gambler. At fifty-one or fifty-two he said life had gone past him like a flash. But now in Maipani, where he found peace and quietness and no distractions, he had settled down, or so he declared; and he had indeed lived there, apparently contented, for more than a year. He was a little man, bald-headed and as red as a ruby, with bright blue eyes and hands deft at any craft.

Kershawe had spent two years in the district, and he also thought his life had been peaceful. There had been crimes of violence, every now and then, in the hill-top villages, and he had often had to march with a couple of constables by mountain-tracks to arrest a sullen or bewildered murderer, to quell some minor riot, to sit in judgment and hear a charge of rape or pig-stealing. He had lived a busy, strenuous life, but in two years he himself had never been in grave danger. An angry woman had thrown a knife at him, a half-wit had tried to shoot him with a broad-bladed arrow; but he had never had to order his constables to open fire, or draw his own revolver. In Namua, as in all British New Brabant, there had been for nearly fifty years a fastidious disapproval of manslaughter as an aid to pacification, and every officer in the service had been taught that a calm display of confidence was not only preferable, in a moral judgment, to gunfire, but more effective and much more economical. Those who, like Kershawe, were untroubled by nervousness, quickly accepted the teaching, and the others did not survive their period of probation.

But now the simplicity and peace, the relative peace, of Kershawe's life were threatened by an emotional, visionary belief, which had already spread like smallpox through a score of villages, that British administration was soon to be swept away and replaced by a miraculous benevolence. A perfect, indiscriminate, and wholly undemanding benevolence. The villagers infected by this belief had already abandoned the cultivation of their gardens and congregated in an upland valley within two or three miles of Kershawe's headquarters, where daily they listened to the ranting promises of a man called Samarai, who had either inspired the maniac faith which possessed them, or been thrown up by it as a boulder from the sea-bed may be thrown up by some deep, invisible commotion. . . .

'I can't hear you,' exclaimed Morland tetchily.

'No, sir, my batteries are almost done for, I'll have to get new ones. But I can hear you.'

He listened patiently while Morland repeated his insistent command that nothing should be done to reveal anxiety, or prompt a suspicion that authority was seriously impressed by the rising; and when Kershawe said that he could probably, with little risk of bloodshed, secure the arrest of Samarai, Morland from his office exclaimed, 'That you must not attempt! That would be disastrous, however it fell out. You would only make a martyr of him, and you might turn a wave of harmless hysteria into a really dangerous movement. No, no! There must be no display of force. We must stand aside— calm and unimpressed—and then, after the collapse of their hopes, help them rehabilitate themselves.'

'Very well, sir, I see the point of that,' said Kershawe, 'but I hate to think of their gardens all going to ruin, while we do nothing.'

He turned to Tom Penny, still sitting on the top of the steps, and asked, 'Do you want to speak to him, before he rings off?'

'Look at those two bastards,' said Penny, pointing to a couple of natives who had appeared from the other side of the hut and now, a dozen yards away, stood staring at him with the dull curiosity of cattle. They were sullen of aspect, naked but for some rough ornaments and little pockets of red cloth between their legs, and one, with a sheaf of arrows slung from his shoulder, carried a six-foot bow, the other a pair of long

13

spears. The archer, who was the taller and younger, had a half-healed wound that ran the length of his left thigh.

'Look at them,' said Penny, 'and tell me where they come from.'

'They're none of ours.'

'Too true they aren't. If you ask me they've come over the border out of Dutch territory. Our Mr. Samarai's winning friends and influencing a hell of a sight too many people for my liking.'

He spoke to them in the Maipani dialect and asked where their village was; but they showed no sign of understanding, and did not answer. He spoke again, in another dialect, and the shorter man, as innocently as a child, yawned.

'Well, beat it!' Penny exclaimed, waving his hand. 'Get to hell out of here, you're spoiling the air.'

The taller native stooped to pick a fly from the wound on his leg, and then, as if they had exhausted their interest in the foreigners, they turned and went uphill with a quick, lithe, half-running step.

'I've just seen some new arrivals, sir,' said Kershawe to the telephone, 'and I'm quite sure they're not our own people. Penny thinks they've come over the border. I've got Penny here with me, sir: would you like to speak to him?'

He listened, and said, 'He wants to know what trade you've been doing.'

'Tell him I've retired. Say I'm living like a gentleman. I haven't seen a customer for a week, and I've forgotten what they look like.'

Kershawe spoke again to the telephone, and then, in a good imitation of Morland's voice, told Penny, 'You must exercise patience, my dear fellow, and realize that in the islands trading conditions have always been somewhat precarious, but profits are correspondingly high—'

'Tell him to take a running jump!—No, wait a minute. Don't ring off. Ask him what's the dirt about the Sultan and his new girl-friend. Say that up here, alone with nature and the cannibals, we're still interested in crime and high society.'

Kershawe made him a sign to be quiet, and asked, 'Is there any news of the Sultan, sir?' He winked to Penny, and repeated his question. 'No, sir, I've got no particular reason for asking. Except that we're interested, of course.'

He listened to Morland's reply, and took off the head-phones. 'He's rung off. He's got no time for gossip, he says.'

'Superior bastard, isn't he?' said Penny.

Two

THE yacht, which was incongruously named *White Heather III*, made a picture of extraordinary elegance as she approached the roadstead from the north-west. She was a three-masted schooner, and the off-shore wind, before which she leaned with a negligent grace, was just strong enough to fill her flattened sails to the plumpness of oyster-shells; and in the last hour of tropic daylight they shone like nacre. The sea was deep blue to within a cable-length of the shore and to half a cable from Battery Island, that sheltered the roadstead from the west and north; and the white hull of the yacht, and the white feathers at her bow, were of equal purity and a dazzlement to the eye.

With calm assurance she held her course for the island until it seemed, to those who watched her from the Yacht Club, that she must surely strike; but then, as debonair as a figure-skater, she came about and filled on the other tack. Now, smartly, her topsails were sent down, and tacking again she glided through the unruffled sea to her usual anchorage between the island and a fishing village, a mile west of Port Philip, where three or four hundred copper-skinned natives lived an equable, noisy, amphibious life in palm-thatched houses built on stilts over the water, or in the narrow dark canoes that were moored about them.

The watchers in the Yacht Club were almost silent until they heard the rattling descent of the anchor-chains—at that distance a thin, dry sound—and then, as if recognizing that this contact with the land had made inevitable their participation in the scandal which was housed aboard *White Heather*—a scandal that had exercised their imagination and their tongues for the past fortnight—they all began talking at the same time; and though some disguised their feelings under a tone of disapproval there was, in the sudden flowering of conversation, a general affirmation of pleasure at the prospect, and even those who deprecated the yacht's arrival did so with relish in their voices, and betrayed their consuming interest in the situation by the warmth with which they deplored it.

It was not a large company. The Yacht Club was a modest building with whitewashed walls and a concrete floor, with a roof of corrugated iron and a membership that consisted of Government officials and their wives and daughters, a few of the senior traders, two or three bankers and a couple of shipping agents, and employees of the Anglo-Namuan Oil Company who flew in, perhaps once a month, from the desolation of Te Aku, the islet a hundred miles away that looked like the last crust of a sterile, vanished continent, and whose wells gushed only petroleum. It was the oil of Te Aku that had bought *White Heather* and let the Sultan maintain her in the severe elegance of perfection.

The watchers stood on the veranda of the Club—its timbers creaked and there were ants in the crevices, but from the garden below rose the scent of frangipani—and there was a little gust of approval, not all of it hilarious, when a woman whose determined expression and stalwart bearing were reinforced by a strident voice declared, 'She may be as guilty as hell, and I've no doubt she is, but that won't stop me meeting her. I've got my own standards of behaviour, and they're more rigid than most people's, but they don't exclude curiosity. I want to see what she looks like, and hear what she's got to say for herself; though I don't suppose I'll believe it. Wouldn't you go to see a circus if it came?'

17

'Not if the ringmaster was an avowed enemy and all the clowns secret agents,' said the man she spoke to, a lean irascible Scot in the Public Works Department. But his rebuke made no impression on Mrs. Marly.

'I'm not frightened,' she answered. 'Whatever she does to Americans, I don't think she'll try to convert me.'

It was twenty-five years since Mrs. Marly had first come to Namua, a pretty, brown-haired girl with candid blue eyes, an expression of cheerful confidence, and the tennis-racquets with which she had lately won a tournament at Scarborough. A quarter of a century in the tropics had given her a massive body, but her shoulders were still square, her back upright, and in the energy of her movement there remained the aggression of a good match-player. Her neck had thickened, the youthful daring of her chin had become a fatly padded truculence, but her eyes, set deeply between sun-wrinkles, were bright as ever and her hair had acquired a dashing Nordic hue.

Her husband, a taciturn, inconspicuous, but kindly man, was the wealthiest of the island traders. They were childless, and persistent in hospitality. Mrs. Marly smoked cigars and drank three or four whisky and sodas after dinner. In the Sultan's absence she dominated—but not without opposition —the social life of Namua, and though she hardly needed official standing she had acquired it when her nephew, James Morland, was appointed Adviser to His Highness and Commissioner for Tribal Territory. Morland was a bachelor who entertained very little, but when he did give a dinner-party his aunt stood beside him to receive his guests. He disapproved of her manners, but they had common ground in the warm interest that both took in his career.

Now, turning her back on the sea, she looked about her and loudly exclaimed, 'Where are the young Pembertons? Ah, there you are! Come along and have a drink. We're not going to leave here till we know if the Sultan and his refugee are coming ashore tonight, so we might as well make ourselves comfortable. Are you going to join us, Henry?—Dr. Playfair, Mrs. Pemberton: I can't remember if you know each other.'

'Yes, indeed. You don't suppose Mrs. Pemberton could escape my wicked eye?'

'She's only been here three days, and I thought you were too busy ever to leave that disgusting laboratory of yours.'

'I've been here for six months, and a fresh complexion draws me like a magnet.'

'Well, you can sit beside her, but don't talk about your revolting work. Shall we take that table by the window?'

The table, of plain scrubbed wood, had one leg shorter than the others, and the cane chairs, of native workmanship, were narrow and uncomfortable. But Mrs. Marley sat herself down with so firm and decisive a composure that the others dared show no unease. 'Boy!' she called in a commanding voice.

The servant who came wore only a wrap-around garment, from the waist to a hands-breadth above the knee, of yellow cotton with a black border. His colour was a polished brown and his hair grew in a dense and wiry mass, twice as big as his face, above a bony forehead. He listened patiently while Mrs. Marly discussed what they should drink, and Mrs. Pemberton looked at him, and looked away, and looked unwillingly again; for she still found it embarrassing to be waited on by a man so nearly naked. Out of doors, under the heat of an incandescent sky, men who wore nothing but a lap-lap and the livery of the sun seemed proper enough. Out of doors it was the women who embarrassed her, with their bare breasts dancing plumply as they walked. But indoors it seemed to her that male servants, standing close beside her in nothing but a cushion-cover, were even worse. She was twenty-two, and till now she had never been out of England.

'Do you think they'll open the Palace?' asked Dr. Playfair when the boy had gone.

'It's always open, though he hardly ever uses it. But that would make it awkward; very awkward indeed. What I mean is, you can be tolerant and broad-minded about a woman aboard a yacht, but put her in the Palace and—well, it changes the whole situation, doesn't it? If you call on her there, it means you approve of her being in the Palace. And I certainly shouldn't.'

'I'm fascinated by the thought of meeting her, wherever she is,' said Dr. Playfair. He was a tall, red-faced, ingenuous man with narrow shoulders and thin, fair hair brushed closely to his sunburnt scalp; and his interest in life was unaffectedly cheerful. He was a parasitologist, on loan to the island government, and he was happy to have found, in the tissues and intestines of the Namuan highlanders, several varieties of hookworm and filaria previously unclassified. 'I have never known,' he continued, with something of wistfulness in his voice, 'a woman who could properly be called an adventuress.'

'Don't you believe it,' said Mrs. Marly in her bluff, party style. 'We all are.'

A little nervously Mrs. Pemberton said, 'I suppose I'm being stupid, but what I can't understand is why, if Mrs. Nottingham—'

'I prefer to think of her as the Countess Tratteanu,' said Dr. Playfair. 'There is an ambience about the title in which her story seems more plausible.'

'Whatever her name is, she seems to have upset everyone she's met—the French as well as your government, and that American photographer—and to bring her here, in his yacht, is bound to get the Sultan into trouble too. Well, why has he done it?'

'We haven't seen her yet,' said Mrs. Marly, 'but I'll be surprised if she's downright ugly or grossly deformed.'

'Perhaps he wanted to annoy the Governor,' suggested Dr. Playfair.

'That's quite possible.'

'From all I've heard of him,' said Pemberton, 'it could be just another silly escapade.'

William Pemberton was ill at ease in the small, apparently self-satisfied community, confined by its own interests, of the Yacht Club. He had been told that the officials he would meet were among the best in the Colonial service, and that in Namua, as throughout the British half of the island, the native policy of the administration had for fifty years been singularly enlightened. But in the three days that he and his wife had spent in Port Philip he had heard no conversation of more than departmental interest, except personal gossip in the Club; and that, in which he could not join, he had found so dull as to be almost meaningless. His own world, a provincial university where he was a lecturer in anthropology, was as circumscribed as that of Namua and had made him intolerant of other societies.

He had not much grace of manner to recommend him— he was inclined to be aggressive and he spoke with a Lancastrian accent which, though presumably genuine in origin, had become an affectation—but his intellectual ability was at least respectable, and in his devotion to his work there was a sombre enthusiasm. He was thirty-three years old, and unacademic in appearance: he looked more like a professional footballer than a scientist.

'The Sultan's a playboy, and always has been,' he said. 'Isn't that the truth of it?'

'It's very far from the truth, as you'll soon find out if you're lucky enough to meet him,' said Mrs. Marly, and temporarily silencing him with the coldness of her glance, pierced the end of a small cigar and brusquely demanded a match. She frowned judicially, and blew a jet of smoke from pursed lips. 'The Sultan,' she said, 'is five-eighths of a great man, and that's more than you usually find. You can't look down your nose at that! He's as handsome as a statue, he's got personality and a first-rate brain—'

'And what use does he make of it?'

'He's badly handicapped,' said Dr. Playfair. 'He wears the swaddling-clothes of benevolence. He's cabined and confined in a constitution which, I believe, hasn't yet been written. He lives under the protection of the Colonial Office, and though he had the vision of a Newton and the talent of a Metternich he couldn't show a hair of them.'

'He doesn't always see eye to eye with the Administration: that's true enough,' said Mrs. Marly. 'My nephew the Commissioner has sometimes had to speak to him quite sharply. But Jim would be the last man on earth to deny his *quality*. And as for charm! My God, what charm!'

She looked up to the ceiling, as though impatient of life's common level; she shrugged her great shoulders, and puffed a windy gout of smoke. 'But you've got to be a woman, of course, to appreciate that.'

Mrs. Pemberton, all innocence and pretty as a hedge-rose, yearned to the prospect of knowing such a man. Her youth leaned out of her eyes like a girl from a high window. 'I do hope he'll stay here,' she sighed.

'He's a rich man,' said her husband impatiently, 'and that's enough to make women interested in him. But he doesn't earn his money and he doesn't spend it for anyone's advantage but his own. Economically speaking, he's just a parasite.'

'Now you're trespassing on my preserves,' said Dr. Playfair, 'and I doubt if you know much about them. There are more parasites than are dreamt of by those who have only seen a tapeworm in a bottle—'

'I shan't listen!' exclaimed Mrs. Marly with a ladylike grimace.

'There are good parasites and bad parasites,' said the Doctor. 'There are parasites that enrich the life of their host, and parasites that diminish the vitality of beasts and men who might otherwise do us a great deal of harm; and sometimes we interfere with them, in the cause of science, when in the cause of humanity we ought to leave them alone. I have in my laboratory a nicely pickled hydatid cyst, of quite uncommon size, that the Civil Surgeon removed from the liver of that fellow Samarai—'

Pemberton, leaning forward, interrupted him. 'Do you mean the man who started this religious mania?'

'There's precious little religion about it,' said Mrs. Marly.

'But that's who you mean?'

'Yes,' said the Doctor, 'and if it hadn't been for modern surgery he'd have died six months ago, and a good thing too. A fluke called *Taenia echinococcus* was doing a very useful job of work in him, and it was a great pity that my friend the Civil Surgeon thought it his duty to remove the structure. As he now agrees.'

'I don't,' said Pemberton. 'I'm very much interested in this outbreak, and I'm looking forward to investigating it. It's a great stroke of luck to have a trained anthropologist on the spot; and a wonderful chance for me, of course.'

His wife regarded him with admiration, and Dr. Playfair concealed his expression behind a handkerchief of yellow silk into which, with the clamour of a trumpet-voluntary, he blew his nose. Then he called for another round of drinks, and Mrs. Marly said to Pemberton, 'You needn't bother to go chasing after Samarai, who's up in the mountains somewhere. I can tell you all about his goings-on. I've seen the same sort of thing in New Guinea, years ago, and there's nothing in it but mass hysteria and bone-idleness.'

Mrs. Marly, with a generous contempt, began to speak of the habits of the natives as she had observed them, with a minimum of understanding, for more than twenty years, and Pemberton listened sullenly, resenting all she said, but incapable of undermining her confidence or preventing her loquacity. He had gone to the Pacific in consequence of a paper he had written, of some originality, on the *Kulturkreis* theory, which had won him a Guggenheim Fellowship; and he hoped to find evidence that would substantiate Thor Heyerdahl's belief in a westward translation of culture from Peru, and thereafter—for his ambition had no limits—to link Heyerdahl with the diffusionist thesis of Perry and Elliot Smith. But a story he had heard, perhaps too highly coloured, of a savage apocalypse that was uniting the mountain tribes of Namua in passive revolt against the Administration had roused a new and temporarily quicker interest, and he had decided to break his journey to watch the course of events and discover, if he could, the nature of the impulse that had inspired so persuasive a revelation.

In Port Philip he had been disappointed by the composure of the inhabitants and the untroubled air of the Secretariat. There was general acknowledgment that the rising was a nuisance, because it would upset the economy of the country—it would have to be paid for—and everyone agreed that Samarai was a pernicious influence whose proper place was the penal settlement on Te Aku. But no one seemed to worry about the possible growth or consequences of the rebellion, and to Pemberton's deep annoyance there was singularly little interest in its psychical origin. Now, through the smoke of Mrs. Marly's cigar, he had to listen to her flat and prejudiced account of the tribesmen—to stories of their laziness, incompetence, and cruelty—and hear his own protestations brushed away. He tried to tell her that in the primitive mind were deep abysses which deserved the most delicate and scrupulous exploration but she pooh-poohed so fanciful an idea. She knew all about savages—or as much as any reasonable person would want to know—and neither Pemberton nor anyone else could teach her more. Her mind was inviolable, and Pemberton was deeply offended by her refusal to understand that what he said was uncommonly interesting, and he himself, in the circumstances, an important person. It was the more exasperating because his wife, beside him, was manifestly enjoying herself and laughing too loudly for his liking. It would do her more good, he thought angrily, to listen to him than to Playfair's idle flattery.

Playfair, with a transparent affectation of simplicity, had asked her if she was used to being the prettiest girl in the room, and Mrs. Pemberton, to his delight, had answered seriously, 'It hasn't been much of a distinction lately. When I got married and went to live in a university town I thought all the men would be terribly clever and all their wives terribly distinguished-looking. But they weren't. Well, some of the men looked distinguished, but they weren't interested in anything but their own careers; and some of the women were clever, and they just made me feel stupid and out of place.'

Playfair pointed to this woman and that, sitting at nearby tables—it was dark outside, the lights had been turned on, and the company, all in white suits or dresses, had in their pale unblemished clothes a superficial family likeness—and whispered a little tale of rival precedences. 'Now she's the leading intellectual here, and you can't possibly feel stupid in her company; and there's our reigning beauty, and if you stay for more than a week she'll try to poison you. She'll have to, poor thing, or die of jealousy. But take a chance, Mrs. Pemberton, and I'll look after you. I'll devote all my time to you—my spare time, at any rate.'

Young Mrs. Pemberton felt a wonderful return of the well-being that had gradually ebbed away from her as the great aeroplane in which she had left England crossed a strange blue sea, a red and stranger desert, and India beneath the stars. As the earth turned below, while she flew through the clouds above, it seemed that she had left behind her a comfortable and friendly shore and was swimming out into a vast unknown sea where there was no footing and nothing familiar that she could cling to, as if it were a raft, and get her breath again. The heat of the tropics had surprised and discomfited her, and in Singapore she had been vaguely frightened by the pressure, as it seemed, of a countless and quite incomprehensible population. Her husband, incapable of understanding her distress, had given her no sympathy; but in Port Philip, where he was ill at ease in the Yacht Club, she had been reassured by the small and unassertive company, and now in the genial air of Playfair's admiration she felt almost at home despite the foreign perfumes on the evening breeze, and the nakedness of a passing servant.

But her pleasant conversation was cut short by a common stir of interest in the room, and the secretary of the club, a man who concealed constant anxiety behind a hearty manner, came in and looked about him, from group to group, with a prolonged and conspicuous deliberation. Then, having made up his mind, he approached Mrs. Marly's party and stooping above her table said gravely, 'There's a message from the yacht. The Sultan's ill, and wants to see a doctor. I don't think you should say anything about it—'

'Have you told my nephew the Commissioner?'

'No, not yet.'

'You ought to do that at once.'

'Yes, I shall, but I've got to find a doctor first.'

'There's no use coming to me,' said Playfair. 'It's not my job.'

'Watkins is out and won't be back till late,' said the secretary, 'and Marshall's in bed with a bit of a temperature.'

'Well, tell him he's got to get up.'

'His wife says she doesn't want to disturb him unless it's absolutely necessary.'

'But you can't expect me to go!'

'Why not?' demanded Mrs. Marly. 'You *are* a doctor.'

'Of a rather limited and narrow sort. And if the Sultan hasn't a sense of humour—'

'He's got a wonderful sense of humour,' said Mrs. Marly. 'Though I don't see how that matters.'

Pemberton laughed coarsely and said, 'Tell him you're a specialist, and that'll give him confidence.'

'He may be in pain,' said Mrs. Pemberton.

'I've wasted a lot of time, trying to get hold of Watkins or Marshall,' said the secretary anxiously. 'It isn't my responsibility really, but I've got to do something, and if you won't go I don't quite know what.'

'Oh, all right, I'll risk it,' said Playfair, and stood up. 'But I hope to God it's nothing serious.'

'My car's at the door,' said the secretary. 'I'll run you down.'

'And don't forget to tell the Commissioner,' said Mrs. Marly.

Three

FAIRWEATHER BAY, where now stands the small capital of British New Brabant, was given its name by Captain Cook in the year 1770; and hardly a visitor since then had roused as much speculation and stirred so lively an interest as the lady who, known at first as Mrs. Nottingham, was presently re-introduced, by her frightened and revengeful companion, as the Countess Tratteanu.

She had come from Saigon in a small and dirty ship whose Chinese owner traded under the Panamanian flag, and her companion was an American photographer called Leroy Cooney. He was a tall, good-looking, and energetic young man whose profession took him on many comfortless, hazardous journeys to countries which, because their conditions of life were unusually squalid or exceptionally violent—because they were in the throes of revolution or ruined by an earthquake—deserved the shocked attention of more prosperous communities; and in his profession he was well known for the resource and determination with which he found and photographed, for the weekly magazine that employed him, scenes of uncommon pathos or nerve-racking horror.

His health and spirit remained unimpaired by strenuous travel and the spectacle of moral and physical disaster, for his fine physique was matched by a confident and sunny mind. He was not indifferent to the suffering he had seen—he gave generously of money, food, and even his clothes in every country he visited—but he saw nothing ineradicable in the misery of the world, and therefore it did not appal him; it did not overwhelm or even sap his spirit. He believed, quite simply, that the world would gradually be cured of its ailments, of material poverty and vicious foibles, as American culture spread and penetrated less happy lands, and a new habit of industry transformed their primitive or misgoverned people into contented customers.

Early one morning this robust and sanguine young man went to Government House—a modest, single-storeyed building whose tall flagstaff dominated seven acres of well-kempt park and gardens—and in a state of pitiable agitation demanded to see His Excellency. The Governor was on tour, but his Private Secretary asked Cooney to breakfast and over the table—his visitor, too nervous to eat, drank several cups of coffee—heard with cynical amusement the story that Cooney told with shame and dismay.

Mrs. Nottingham, he said, was a Communist agent, previously known as the Countess Tratteanu. For several months he had been aware of her real identity, though till quite recently he had had no reason to suspect her of undesirable political beliefs, still less to suppose that she was politically active. But several times within the last few weeks—his voice revealed a growing indignation—she had criticized the French administration in Cambodia, and American policy in Korea, in a way that compelled him to believe she sympathized with the enemy. And last night, after a bitter argument that seemed to grow out of nothing at all, he had asked her point-blank whose side she was on; and she, in a fit of temper, said she preferred faith and efficiency to doubt and muddle.

'And from that you inferred that her sympathies lie with the Communists?'

'Why, sure. I heard the way she said it.'

'Is Tratteanu her real name?'

'It used to be.'

'But surely she's English? I've met her, and no one who hadn't been born and brought up in England could speak in that tone of voice.'

'She's English all right, and so was her first husband. His name was Nottingham. But two or three years ago she married this guy called Tratteanu.'

'A Rumanian?'

'He went to school in France and lived mostly in Paris. But the family was Rumanian, and so was he.'

'Where is he now?'

'He died in Luang Prabang six months ago. He got cerebral malaria and was out in twenty-four hours.'

'And she gave up her title, and resumed her former name, because of her Communist sympathies?'

'No, sir. The way I read it, they were both Communists but they didn't want to advertise it, so they used the title to keep under cover. She only called herself "Mrs. Nottingham" after Tratteanu died because she thought she'd be safer with a British name and a British passport.'

'Is it valid—the British passport?'

'It's up to date. I've seen it.'

'What was Tratteanu doing in Luang Prabang?'

'Haven't you ever heard of him? He was well known. He was an Orientalist, he'd written a couple of books and was aiming to write another. They were all in French, though, and I never got very far in them. But what he was really doing, I guess, was being a Communist and spreading poison wherever he could.'

'And you say she is still politically active. How do you know that?'

Cooney crushed on a fruit plate a cigarette he had newly lighted, and passionately exclaimed, 'Because last night she went to work on me! That was after we'd had our argument, after she'd owned up to Communist sympathies. She began telling me that Communism was what Asia needed. That it was only the Communists who could bring peace and restore order. She said Asiatics didn't understand democracy, not in the way we Americans do, and didn't want it. She said all they wanted was a recognizable social hierarchy and a guaranteed price for paddy. She told me I ought to get rid of preconceived ideas and learn to think for myself. She said that to me, a good American! She tried to convert *me*! Well, for Christ's sake, isn't that being active?'

The Private Secretary happily decided that this was a story which, when he went on leave, would be his contribution to many a dinner-table; but he maintained his appearance of gravity and said, 'Surely Mrs. Nottingham's Communism is rather an individual brand?'

'I guess she knows the Party line. Maybe they've got a new slant on things in the Far East.'

'I haven't heard of it, and frankly I doubt it. But tell me, Mr. Cooney, what you want me to do?'

'Well, you ought to know, better than me! She's dangerous, and you've got to get rid of her some way. But I don't want any publicity about this. I've got a job and I've got my public, and it wouldn't do me any good if it got about that I've been living with a dame who's an active Communist.'

'Your relations with her have, in fact, been intimate?'

'You've seen her. Well, she isn't the sort you'd take around like your little sister, is she? Especially when you find her in a place like Luang Prabang, all alone and desperately unhappy. She didn't know what to do next, and when I came along I felt real sorry for her. So I took her down to Saigon—I was doing a big job in Indo-China—and pretty soon we got shacked up. It was only natural.'

'I don't think,' said the Private Secretary, 'that we should make any move at all until H.E. comes back. Mrs. Nottingham isn't likely to do much harm in the next day or two—'

'She's still at the Grand,' said Cooney. 'I checked out first thing this morning and got me a room at the Imperial. She won't have another chance to work on me.'

His ingenuous face wore a look of stern and healthy resolution. His brown hair, cut *en brosse*, was, it seemed, vibrant with indignation. Only the impatience with which he smoked his sweet-smelling cigarettes betrayed his continuing shame and nervousness.

'Then we'll keep this to ourselves,' said the Private Secretary, 'till I've had a word with H.E. about it. And then I'll give you a ring and make an appointment for you.'

'That suits me,' said Cooney, 'and I'll keep my trap shut as long as you say. Well, thanks a lot. It certainly was a relief to get that off my chest.'

If Cooney had behaved as discreetly as he promised there would have been no scandal, and Mrs. Nottingham, who was a reasonable woman, might have been persuaded to leave the island as inconspicuously as she had arrived. But so buoyant was Cooney's feeling of relief that at half-past ten, at a fly-blown table on the veranda of the pretentiously named Imperial Hotel, he ordered a gin-sling to celebrate his happiness, and by half-past eleven had drunk four. Ted Ives, the editor of the local newspaper, found him talking quietly to himself and smacking his right fist into the cup of his other hand as if he were recapitulating a physical victory.

Ives was a young Australian, lean and weather-dried, with a harsh, excited voice, pale, restless eyes, and an angry mouth. He had chosen his profession because it offered so many opportunities for destruction. Whatever was closed to view he liked to break open, and it gave him much pleasure to pull down what was set above the common level. He sometimes professed his belief in the future of humanity, but he had no faith in its present virtue. He would often support a popular cause, but he could never suppress for very long his hatred of its leaders. He was clever, and in his own way honest. He had held good jobs in Australia, but even there, where neither reverence for institutions nor adulation of public figures is characteristic of its inhabitants, it was felt that he went too far in the opposite direction. He had come to Fairweather after being unemployed for some time, but misfortune had not taught him prudence and he had quickly incurred the disapproval of the Administration and doubled the circulation of the *Fairweather News and Gazette*.

While Ives drank beer, Cooney had two more gin-slings, and there woke in him—it woke and grew beyond restraint —the true American reverence for the press, the innate feeling that a newspaper man not only had a duty to discover, but the right to be told, all things that happened. Self-pity moved him also, an expanding commiseration with the grotesque ill-fortune that had put him to bed with a Communist; and in Ives he recognized the man who could set him right with his own conscience. So presently he repeated all he had told the Private Secretary; but in more detail.

Ives knew how to make the most of a story, and the next issue of the *News and Gazette*—it was published twice a week —carried on its front page a sensational narrative of Communist intrigue in the Pacific, now happily frustrated by the idealism of an American photographer. There were two portraits of Mrs. Nottingham that Cooney had taken, which created an impression of cold and enigmatic beauty, and short biographies of her and Count Tratteanu that plausibly suggested they were *intellectuals*, and implied thereby that they were rootless, irresponsible, and naturally disaffected. Ives, who had the capacious memory of a good journalist, knew the name of Tratteanu and discovered that the Count had been, not only a scholar, but eccentric, and at one time had lived in a lamasery: for such behaviour, he suggested, there could only be a sinister motive, and 'Mrs. Nottingham' might well be a victim of her late husband's guile. But that, he said, was no excuse for mercy. She was a dangerous woman, and in a leading article he demanded her immediate deportation.

On the day of publication the yacht *White Heather III* came into Fairweather, and the Sultan, in ebullient humour after a rough voyage from Cairns in Northern Queensland—he had been fishing for marlin off the Barrier Reef—went ashore and instructed the manager of the Grand Hotel to make preparation for a party. Some forty guests were hurriedly invited, and by seven o'clock about sixty had arrived. There was much talk of the contents of the day's paper, and the Sultan, when he was shown a copy, laughed heartily at Ives's story but was greatly interested in Cooney's photographs. He asked where Mrs. Nottingham was, and the manager told him she was dining in her own room. The Sultan sent his compliments, and an invitation to join his party.

She kept him waiting for forty minutes, and her entrance was dramatic. The Sultan's hospitality was lavish and the party noisy, but within a few moments all the shrillness and hoarseness and clatter of voices died away, and Mrs. Nottingham shook hands with the Sultan in as complete a silence as awaits a symphony concert when the conductor's baton has commanded attention.

With perfect calm, and apparent simplicity, she said, 'This is most kind of you, I was feeling lonely tonight.'

'I've been much exposed to journalists myself,' said the Sultan. 'For most of my life I've been a martyr to public interest, and I wanted to tell you that you have at least one sympathizer in Fairweather.'

A few people ostentatiously left the party, and rather more went quietly away. Some laughed and applauded sycophantically, and the majority, having looked for long enough with a hard curiosity at Mrs. Nottingham, and wondered at her boldness, shrugged their shoulders and let the waiters refill their glasses. The party went on, a little smaller than it had been but gradually becoming noisier, and in the midst of the noise, as if in the still centre of a typhoon, the Sultan sat and talked with Mrs. Nottingham.

The manager of the hotel was a White Russian who had once owned a half-share in a restaurant in Shanghai. He had escaped with little more than his life when the Communists took the city, and retained a bitter hatred of the policy, and all its agents, that had twice despoiled him. He took advantage of Mrs. Nottingham's preoccupation to search her room, and presently went to the Commissioner of Police and delivered a package containing a dozen photographs of smiling Chinese peasants, each above a caption that proclaimed glad contentment with Communist government, and a like number of pamphlets. One of them was in Malay, another in the Dayak language of Borneo, both of which the Commissioner could read. They described, with offensive naivety, the wholesome satisfaction of life under the rule of local soviets, and they closely resembled some pamphlets which the Principal of the New Brabant Teachers' Training College had lately discovered in the desk of one of his pupils; who was now in jail.

When, on the following day, the Governor returned from a tour of the interior, he found his Attorney General, the Commissioner of Police, and the Sultan all waiting to see him. The Commissioner had arrested Mrs. Nottingham at daybreak, and the Sultan, in a towering rage, demanded her immediate release. The Attorney General, who looked very tired, was inclined to think the Commissioner had acted precipitately, but the Commissioner, a stubborn man of great gallantry but rather less percipience, was not merely unrepentant but stiffly self-satisfied.

'Section 43 of the Defence Act has never been repealed,' he said, 'and I'm well within my rights. I'm responsible for security—'

'Not entirely,' said the Governor.

'In practice I am, sir. I didn't ask for anyone's authority when I arrested those Chinese three months ago.'

'The fact that you once jugged the right men—by mistake, I presume—doesn't give you a warrant to fill your jail with anyone you take a dislike to,' exclaimed the Sultan.

'They were Communists,' said the Commissioner stolidly, 'and so is this woman.'

'I'm not sure she is,' said the Attorney General. 'She claims to be, but she knows very little about Communist dogma. I spent an hour with her this morning, and though she rather boasts about her faith, she didn't impress me as being a very good disciple. Her late husband—'

'Count Tratteanu?'

'Yes, sir. He was a scholar, and I've a little amateur knowledge of what he was expert in. He wrote a very good book on esoteric Buddhism. Well, it's common knowledge that he was a Communist member, but they let him in because of his reputation, not because he was orthodox. A man like that couldn't be. He once said that what appealed to him in Communism was the renunciation of self. Mrs. Nottingham says he was quite unworldly; and by that I think she means good. I rather fancy that she began to call herself a Communist to please him, and never took the trouble to learn much about it.'

'That sounds very nice indeed,' said the Commissioner, 'and I might believe it if it weren't for the pamphlets she had in her

36

room. Pamphlets very like those that someone, not long ago, gave to a boy at the Training College.'

'Mrs. Nottingham denies all knowledge of what was found there.'

'It's no trouble to a woman to tell lies,' observed the Commissioner.

'Perhaps it isn't,' said the Sultan, 'but I'd like to take you outside and punch your nose!'

'You're welcome to try, sir.'

'Come, come, gentlemen,' said the Governor. 'That sort of behaviour isn't going to help us. Now what I want to know, in the first place, is Mrs. Nottingham's nationality. Is she, in law, English or Rumanian?'

'English,' said the Sultan. 'By birth and custom and natural law she's English.'

'I've got documents that prove she isn't,' said the Commissioner. 'She was legally married to Count Tratteanu, and he was a Rumanian citizen.'

'I haven't had time, so far, to form a considered opinion,' said the Attorney General, 'and I may want to seek advice in the matter.'

'I'm not asking you to commit yourself,' said the Governor, 'but try, by tomorrow, to give me your own view.'

'I'll do my best, sir.'

'And now'—the Governor with an air of distaste held by thumb and forefinger a copy of the *Fairweather News and Gazette*—'tell me whether she did, in fact, make any serious attempt to convert this man Cooney. What does he himself say?'

'Answer that one,' said the Sultan to the Commissioner of Police.

'I'm afraid I can't, sir.'

'Why not?'

'Because I don't know where he is, sir.'

'Oh, nonsense,' said the Governor. 'People can't disappear in a place like Fairweather.'

'I went to his hotel this morning,' said the Sultan, 'with the simple intention of saying what I thought of him, and thereby persuading him—as I hoped—to defend himself. But he wasn't there. He'd packed up and gone.'

'Without paying his bill?'

'He'd left twenty-five dollars in an envelope, which the manager said was fair enough.'

'But where has he gone?'

'Three pearling-schooners and the *Wonsan* went out on the morning tide. He may be in any one of them. The manager told me he was drinking a lot yesterday, and had a quarrel with Ives. I suppose he realized that he'd made a fool of himself, and decided to disappear.'

'Can you do anything about this?' asked the Governor.

'I'll try, sir,' said the Commissioner, 'but I'm not very hopeful.'

'But without Cooney you can't possibly substantiate your charge—or what I suppose is going to be your charge—that she's been trying to subvert people.'

'She had Communist pamphlets in her possession, and she was travelling with a British passport though she is in fact a Rumanian citizen. I think that's enough, sir.'

'Is it?' asked the Governor.

'I'm not sure, sir,' said the Attorney General.

'You'll have to release her,' said the Sultan, 'and the sooner the better.'

'May I, without being offensive,' said the Governor, 'ask if you have a personal interest in the case?'

'I have the tradition of my house to consider,' said the Sultan. 'A tradition fortified, I may remind you, by treaty with England. I am the Sultan of Namua, and wherever I go I carry the memory of my grandfather and that generosity of his which received the recognition of Her Majesty Queen Victoria.'

He stood up and regarded the Governor—a smaller and thinner man—with a deliberate arrogance; and then, suddenly smiling, he leaned and whispered to the Attorney General, 'As to the matter of bail, my credit is good in Fairweather, and you can have any sum within reason.'

Mrs. Nottingham was released that evening, and three days later the Sultan gave another party at which both he and Mrs. Nottingham went out of their way to placate and charm the Commissioner of Police. At a late hour the Sultan and the Commissioner sat together with a bottle of brandy between them, and the Commissioner, who was normally an abstemious man, had to be taken home by the Attorney General.

Daylight, the next morning, came sullenly through a warm and viewless haze. Fairweather, on the south-eastern corner of New Brabant, is more subject to sudden fog than Port Philip in the centre of its northern shore, and few of its inhabitants were perturbed by the weather though a good many of them suffered from the after effects of the Sultan's party. Among the latter was the Commissioner of Police, who, for the first time in three years, arrived late at his office. Slowly he signed some routine orders and reluctantly read his daily reports, one of which gave details of the ships entering or leaving the port within the last twenty-four hours. With consternation he saw that *White Heather* had put to sea at 2 a.m., when the weather was still clear; and telephoning to the Grand Hotel he discovered that Mrs. Nottingham had also gone.

There was no ship in harbour that could give chase—the Governor's yacht was in dry dock—and two light aeroplanes that might have gone up to search were earthbound by the fog. *White Heather*, with the Sultan and Mrs. Nottingham aboard, had disappeared, and nothing more was heard of them for nearly three weeks.

But in the next issue of the *Fairweather News and Gazette* there was a story, even more sensational than that preceding Mrs. Nottingham's arrest, which described the unexpected departure of the yacht—after what Ives called an orgy—and accused the Sultan of abducting a notorious woman whose continuing freedom was a menace to the safety of the islands. The scandal spread, as quickly as aeroplane or submarine cable could carry it, from Fairweather to Penang, from Port Philip to Rabaul—it quickened the quiet lives of Kershawe and Tom Penny in the highlands of Maipani—and as for the outcome of a major battle, or the result of the Derby, many people who sustained, within romantic landscapes and vistas of tropical luxuriance, an existence of respectable monotony, waited with growing impatience for news of the yacht and its reckless voyagers.

Four

A LITTLE tetchy because he had to undertake a general
practitioner's job—a little nervous because he doubted his
capacity for it, and more than a little excited by the prospect
of meeting the Sultan and Mrs. Nottingham—Dr. Playfair
was driven down to the beach by the secretary of the Yacht
Club, and on the beach firmly opposed the secretary's suggestion that he too should go out to the yacht, where perhaps
he could make himself useful.   Dr. Playfair, who did not much
like the secretary, saw no need for a division of his privilege,
and had no desire for a witness to what might well be a display
of incompetence.   He had called at the hospital and the
matron had given him a bag containing the usual appliances,
remedies, and instruments, and he was determined to face his
challenge alone.   With some unkindness, then, he bade the
secretary wait for him, and from a narrow, swaying jetty
stepped into a smartly appointed, cushioned motor-boat, and
was quickly ferried across the dark sea to the yacht.

The accommodation-ladder was brilliantly lighted, and at
the top of it stood two brown-skinned sailors, a steward, and
the captain; whose complexion was dark as a Malay's though
his accent was Scotch.   The sailors saluted, the captain shook
hands, and the steward said, 'This way, please.'   Dr. Playfair
went below, and in a saloon painted and upholstered in ivory
and apple-green he was welcomed by a woman of remarkable
beauty who wore silk pyjamas a little darker than the green of
the cushions.

She said, 'Are you the doctor?   How good of you to come!'

Playfair smiled as foolishly as if he were a medical student again, told her his name, and listened without much comprehension while she described the Sultan's illness. He talked aimlessly, and felt his hands grow moist. It seemed to him that his closely brushed hair lay as untidily on his scalp as if he had been walking bare-headed in the wind; and he put up his hand, unnecessarily, to smooth it. But by degrees he grew able to enjoy what he saw.

Her carriage was erect, and the symmetry of her features, the calm of big, heavy-lidded eyes, gave her an expression of almost severe tranquillity. Her face had a sculptured, classical beauty, but her breasts an Oriental luxury, and her long thighs, the outline of which was clearly visible beneath her thin trousers, were like an illustration to some extravagant tale of improbable pleasure. Her hair, a natural pale yellow, grew rather thinly and was brushed back from her forehead into a modern *chignon*. Her voice was cold and level, a school-teacher's voice. Her white leather sandals exposed small, well-shaped, and carefully tended feet with rose-pink nails.

'So it isn't very serious?' said Dr. Playfair, and regarded her —as he hoped—with confident and friendly eyes.

'I don't think so,' she said, 'but it's painful, of course, and he's got a temperature.'

'It's several years since I've done any general practice, but I expect I can deal with this. The men who should have come weren't available—one is ill and the other's away somewhere— so I said I would do what I could, if it wasn't too difficult—'

'I'm sure we can trust you!' She smiled gravely, and with a sinuous turn of her body said, 'This is the way.'

The Sultan lay on his side in a broad bed, and to Playfair presented a scowling face and a slightly bloodshot eye. He wore yellow pyjamas which were ruffled by the draught from an overhead fan, and his first words were, 'You're the doctor, are you? Well, don't pay any attention to what she's been saying about me. I've got a boil on my bottom and there's nothing else wrong with me. Can you deal with that?'

'This is Dr. Playfair,' said Mrs. Nottingham. 'He's a specialist, so you're in good hands. Perhaps you'll be able to get up for dinner after all.'

She shut the cabin door and left them, and the Sultan said, 'Though you wouldn't think it to look at her, that woman's capable of talking like a perfect fool. Do you have much to do with women?'

'Not professionally.'

'No, I didn't mean that. But it doesn't matter. Take a look at this, will you?'

He pulled down his trousers and lay with his face to the pillow, and Playfair said, 'Oh dear, that's very nasty. You're more of a stoic than I am, I'd make a great fuss if I was suffering as you must be. That's much worse than a boil, that's a carbuncle.'

'Can you do anything about it?'

'Yes, quite easily, it's ripe as a cherry—but it may hurt a little—and then I'll give you some penicillin to clean up the infection. I'll wash my hands first.'

He took off his coat and washed his hands, and admitted that he was enjoying himself. At close quarters he had found Mrs. Nottingham a little daunting, but now he was delighted by his remembrance of her and the knowledge that she was still near at hand. He was also aware of a gratifying sensation of power: he had been fearful of a fractured bone, but he could deal with a carbuncle. By God, he could! And while he cleaned its hot and tender crater he saw, not the Sultan's gluteal fold in which it lay, but Mrs. Nottingham's calm eyes and the exuberance of her bosom.

He soothed and dressed the wound, and padded it with

cotton wool. 'And now,' he said, 'I'll give you an injection of penicillin, and then you'll be convalescent.'

The hypodermic needle was new and sharp, and the operation was deftly performed. 'What sort of a specialist are you?' asked the Sultan.

Hesitating a little, Playfair answered, 'I'm a parasitologist.'

'Who sent you here?'

The Sultan sat up, balancing on his uninjured rump, and glared at the doctor in sudden anger. Playfair explained, but clumsily, the circumstances in which he had undertaken a job outside the narrow march of his ordinary employment, and the Sultan interrupted him to ask, 'Did Morland say you ought to come?'

'No, Morland wasn't there.'

'It's the sort of thing he might have done. You couldn't accuse him of wit, not in his ordinary habit, but he doesn't like me, and sometimes that quickens a man's mind. He once told me to my face—'

The Sultan winced, and groaned and stood up. 'I'm more comfortable than I've been for a couple of days, but I can't sit straight yet.'

'You'll feel better tomorrow.'

'Morland, God damn him, once told me I was a parasite on my country—and now, when I want a doctor, someone sends you! Well, if it wasn't Morland, it's a good joke, I suppose.'

'I assure you—'

'All right, I believe you. But I still resent the fact that he might have done it.'

The Sultan looked moodily at Playfair and said, 'You can't have been long in the service, or I'd have met you before.'

'I'm not in the service. I came out from home six months ago, and I'm going back in a week or two. I've been doing some work on hookworm infection.'

44

'On hookworm and me,' said the Sultan. 'Well, it was Morland's predecessors who made me what I am. They stripped my father of his power, and took away from me the few scraps of authority that he managed to keep. And now when I've nothing to do because they won't let me do anything, they send a parasitologist to come and clean out my boils.'

'It was a carbuncle. And I do admire your fortitude! I couldn't have stood the pain of it as you did.'

'I could do more than they think if I had a chance. I could make something better of Namua, something better of New Brabant, if I weren't paralysed by those dismal little bureaucrats who talk about progress, and try to enlighten pagans with the ethics of the suburbs and the backwash of a provincial liberalism.'

The Sultan, hobbling to and fro in his cabin—a few steps this way, a few steps that, in his yellow pyjamas fluttered by the fan—was a handsome, prepossessing figure despite the flickering grimaces of ill-temper and pain that distorted his face. He was tall and well built, his colour was the glaze of the sun on ivory skin. His features were regular, but a little heavy, and his eyes, large and widely separate, were a luminous dark brown. But Playfair was thinking: He's between forty-five and fifty, he's got a temperature and his blood pressure may be too high. He shouldn't be so excited, and I ought to keep him quiet. He needs a sedative and a good night's sleep.

There was a knock at the door, and Mrs. Nottingham asked if she could come in.

'I found the thermometer in my cabin,' she said. 'I thought you might want it.'

'I do,' said Playfair, and shook it, and told the Sultan to put it below his tongue.

'He's looking better already,' said Mrs. Nottingham. 'You'll stay to dinner, won't you?'

45

Playfair took out the thermometer and said, 'I don't think I should. His Highness has a temperature well over 102, and he ought to go to bed.'

'I don't call that a temperature!' declared the Sultan. 'I've had malaria, half a dozen times, and my temperature's been up to 105, and that didn't kill me. I'm feeling fairly comfortable—on one side, at any rate—so get the steward to put a cushion on my chair, and tell him there'll be three for dinner.'

He closed the door firmly behind Mrs. Nottingham and told Playfair, 'Forget what I was saying, and for God's sake don't speak of it to her. I'm not really a bad-tempered man, and when I'm in decent health I don't bear a grudge against any-one. It was the poison in my blood that was talking, not me. Staphylococci, aren't they?'

'The infective organism is a staphylococcus,' said Playfair.

'And he can talk a great deal of nonsense. So wipe it off the slate, and we'll go and have dinner.'

The Sultan put on a dressing-gown of a patterned yellow velvet, and taking Playfair by the arm led him into the saloon. 'My dear,' he said, 'you were perfectly right. He is a specialist of superlative skill, and I am well on the road to recovery. I think we should drink champagne tonight.'

'He can always find an excuse for having champagne,' said Mrs. Nottingham.

'My religion compels me to. I'm a Mahomedan, though a very poor one, and the Prophet forbade us to drink wine of any sort. And I never do without some good reason.'

He rang, and a steward brought two bottles in an ice-bucket, and set glasses on a side table.

'Is that cold enough for you?' asked the Sultan. 'Well, sit down and tell me what you think of Namua. Tell me what's been going on.'

'We've all been talking about you for the last three weeks. You and Mrs. Nottingham have been our only topic.'

'I knew it would start an appalling scandal,' said Mrs. Nottingham, 'but I was desperate, I didn't know what they were going to do to me.'

'His Excellency the Governor was almost as much at sea as you were.'

'He's so cold and unsympathetic,' said Mrs. Nottingham. 'I couldn't trust him! So I went to His Highness and threw myself on his mercy. I literally went down on my knees to him. And he was kind and generous beyond belief. You must tell people that, Dr. Playfair. Tell everyone. Please do!'

'But my sudden attack of nobility,' said the Sultan, 'didn't go to my head, thank God. It went to my bottom, where it festered and turned into a carbuncle. And you can tell people that, if you like.'

'You can make a joke of it,' said Mrs. Nottingham, 'but it was no joke to me.'

'Have you met the Governor?' asked the Sultan. 'He comes out of the same litter as our friend Morland, don't you think? Though he behaves more pompously, as befits his position. When I went to see him, to tell him he'd no right to keep Elizabeth in his filthy jail, he had the insolence to ask me if I had any personal interest in the matter. I had, of course. I'd been talking to her for two and half hours the night before, and he'd be a poor sort of man who didn't feel a personal interest in her long before that.'

'Flatterer!' she said.

'Be quiet, this is my story.—Well, I wasn't going to take him into my confidence—no fear!—so I got on my high horse and reminded him of the great tradition of Namua. You know we pride ourselves on giving asylum, don't you?'

'I know the story of your grandfather,' said Playfair.

'He was a great man, and my father was a delightful person, though not so effective. It was the Governor who reminded me, by his damned impertinence, that I was born of their blood. So I made up my mind to let him have a demonstration, and when Elizabeth told me she was really worried about the possibility of being deported as an undesirable alien — which she isn't, of course — I told her there was plenty of room aboard *White Heather*. A couple of nights later we slipped out of Fairweather and left the Governor, or so I hope, feeling like an orphan in a storm, bewildered and bereft. — Is that a boat alongside? I don't want to see anyone else tonight.'

'No, dear, you're much too tired.'

'Where have you been since you left Fairweather?' asked Playfair.

'We've had a very pleasant cruise, and went as far as Bali. My family has had dealings with Bali for a long time. My father had two concubines from there. They were sisters, they came of a very good family, and we're still friendly with their relations. So we went and called on them.'

'It was a delightful and most unusual experience,' said Mrs. Nottingham.

'It must have been,' said Playfair, and turned to see who stood at the door.

The steward came softly in and spoke to the Sultan in a quiet, confidential voice. The Sultan, frowning, reflected; and then said to Playfair, 'You're my medical adviser, and I put myself in your hands. Our friend Morland has come to see me — that was his boat we heard — but I'm doubtful if my health is good enough to stand the sort of interview that I anticipate. What do you think?'

'Oh no!' said Mrs. Nottingham. 'It would put you in such a bad temper.'

'I'm asking him,' said the Sultan.

'I agree with Mrs. Nottingham,' said Playfair. 'I agree, that is, that you shouldn't talk business tonight. You ought to be in bed, and you're certainly not fit for any serious discussion. Morland will have to wait.'

'Tell the Commissioner,' said the Sultan to his steward, in the language of Namua, 'that Dr. Playfair says I am too ill to see him, and assure him of my deep regret that I must decline the pleasure of his company. And for God's sake make haste and bring dinner! I'm as hungry as a shark.'

He refilled their glasses from the second bottle and said to Playfair, 'I've been talking entirely about my own affairs, but from now on I'm going to listen to you. I want to hear what you think of Namua. How much have you seen?'

Some two hours later, when Playfair was on his way back to the beach, it occurred to him that he had talked too much. The Sultan had, indeed, encouraged him. The Sultan had the faculty of active listening. And though Mrs. Nottingham had not added much to the conversation, she had enlivened it, she had kept it flowing, by her mere presence. For such a woman tempted a man to talk, she incited him to be witty if he could, and make some parade of his qualities. Was I showing off? thought Playfair. I believe I was. But not offensively, I hope. Oh dear, I wish I hadn't tried to impress them. But I did, of course. It was such a good dinner, it made me feel I ought to live up to it. And I suppose I drank too much. No more than the Sultan, but he must have a better head than mine. At any rate I didn't take his money. I'm glad of that. . . .

After Mrs. Nottingham had said good night and gone to her cabin, the Sultan had asked him, 'What's your fee, Doctor?'

'My fee?' repeated Playfair.

'For your professional services. I'm accustomed to pay for what I get.'

'But I'm not a general practitioner. I couldn't possibly charge you for what I've done.'

'You're a fool if you don't.'

'If I had come in my professional capacity—'

'Ah yes!'

'So you will not, I hope, compel me to accept payment. Because, sir,'—Playfair, with clumsy sincerity, made a little bow—'because, sir, I am not of Morland's party. . . .'

The wavering light of a torch came down to meet him as the boat ran slowly alongside the jetty, and in a querulous voice the secretary of the Yacht Club said, 'You've been a devil of a long time, Playfair! I thought you were never coming.'

Playfair, who had forgotten all about the secretary, said, 'I'm so sorry, you really shouldn't have waited.'

'But you asked me to! And I thought I might be needed.'

'I didn't expect to be so long.'

'Is he seriously ill? Morland was very short-tempered when he came back without having seen him.'

'The Sultan didn't feel up to serious conversation. He's running a temperature.'

'What's the matter with him?'

'You mustn't ask questions like that. What a doctor hears at a patient's bedside is strictly confidential.'

'I'm so sorry, Playfair. I didn't mean to be offensive.'

'Not at all, not at all,' said Playfair, and tripping over a stone fell to his knees in the sand. 'It's very kind of you to have waited. Very, very kind.'

The secretary helped him up, and asked, 'Did you meet Mrs. Nottingham?'

'A wonderful woman!' said Playfair. 'And when I say that, I'm speaking not as a doctor, but simply as a man.'

Five

AT the age of forty-seven the Sultan still dearly loved a party; or, at any rate, the beginning of a party. He retained, almost intact, a belief that the mere weight of numbers might express, as it were, from some fortuitous gathering of quite ordinary people an occasion of extraordinary and unpredictable pleasure. He hoped that somewhere, in the throng of strangers who so often came to his parties, he would find a new companion, man or woman, who by unexpected wit or unfamiliar beauty could release him for a little while from tedium, and even, if fortune were richly kind, discover for him a fresh purpose in life—or adequate compensation for its lack of purpose.

This enduring faith in the reviving power of conviviality was a token, not only of his robust physique, that never suffered from an excess of conviviality, but of the frustration he had suffered under the benevolently progressive policy of the Colonial Office. He was a man who, in less enlightened times, might have been an imaginative and adventurous autocrat, and perhaps an efficient autocrat; but before he had developed his innate strength to rule he knew that his growing strength would be wasted, because he would never be allowed to use it. He did not, at first, feel any resentment against the circumstance of his age or the intangible authority that had clipped his wings. He had a handsome allowance from his father, and the assurance of a fortune when his father died. He had an instinct for enjoyment and a natural gift for hospitality; and when he began to give parties he found in them a pure and generous satisfaction. But as he grew more aware of his power to entertain, he gradually acquired a feeling that he was entitled to the profits of entertainment; and because in his youth he was uncommonly handsome as well as carelessly rich, he found a good many young women who thought as he did, and increasingly the contingency led to trouble.

After three years at an English public school he went to Cambridge, where in spite of recurrent disagreement with the authorities he took his degree, and presently settled in London to read for the Bar. His reading was negligible, but his parties were notorious; and his father was persuaded to recall him to Namua. There he won, though briefly, the favour of the Administration by joining an expedition to the almost inaccessible country about the headwaters of the Sipi river, and, when its leader died of exhaustion, bringing it safely home again. His father, a mild and affectionate man, rewarded him with the ill-advised gift of a house in Singapore. The parties he gave there, after surprising the colony by their opulence, offended it by the catholic variety of the guests and the Prince's exuberant freedom from the prejudices of caste and colour. The scandals which accompanied his entertainment in London were repeated more loudly in Singapore, and again he was recalled to Namua.

He was rescued, after a dull year or two, by the outbreak of the war of 1939, and having been given, somewhat grudgingly, a commission in the Indian Army, he revealed his gallantry, when opportunity came his way, in Arakan and Burma; where he was twice decorated. These years of hard service were, in another sense, the most peaceful he had known, and when the war came to an end he seemed for a little while to have found equanimity and a taste for quieter pleasures. His father was ailing, and he was persuaded to marry. A suitable bride was found—she was the daughter of a seriously minded Malayan prince, and had been educated at Roedean and the London School of Economics—and when the doctors told him that his father would be dead within the year, he consented to immediate marriage and had the satisfaction of seeing his father die happy.

The marriage, however, did not prosper, and the Sultan had once confided in a friend: 'I have nothing against Roedean. It appears to be an excellent school. I could be happy with a dozen girls from Roedean. But never, never again shall I share my bed with a graduate of the London School of Economics!'

The Princess retired to some property she owned near Penang, and the Sultan went to England to superintend the building of a yacht. Thereafter he spent much of his time at sea, and though he continued to give parties they were less extravagant and seldom grew rowdy. This was because he no longer led the revels and incited high spirits to leap higher, as he had been used to do, but was content to be the observer, or the seeker: watching for opportunities of enjoyment that his guests, by their assembled weight, might tread out of their ordinariness as individuals—and ever looking for some new companion who by the novelty of his wit or the freshness of her complexion could give all the world a lick of new paint. . . .

'I have had a very good night,' he said to Mrs. Nottingham on the morning after Playfair's visit, 'but I'm not inclined to go ashore yet, so I think we should invite a few people to come aboard this afternoon. Not many. About twenty or thirty perhaps. And Morland, who'll insist on seeing me some time today, can be put off till five o'clock, when he won't be able to monopolize me and his voice will be muted by the throng.'

'Are you frightened of him?'

'Not in the least. But I hate being bored.'

'I feel perfectly calm. You've made me so happy that I can't imagine anything capable of spoiling my happiness.'

'I hope nothing will. But I promise you Morland will do his best.'

'What can he do?'

'You're a fugitive from justice.'

'From injustice. You said so, that night in Fairweather.'

'They're often the same thing.'

'Not in your eyes. That's why you gave me sanctuary.'

They were on deck, taking their morning tea in the brief coolness of the morning, and leaning towards him, as if yielding to a sudden yet grave impulse, she kissed him on the lips. He let his hand fall on her thigh, but with no more emotion than the simple pleasure of feeling rough silk move against a hard, smooth surface. 'You shouldn't come on deck without slippers,' he said.

'I like to feel the planks when they're wet with dew.'

'And you like to show me what good feet you have.'

'I must do something in return.'

'You've paid your passage. You needn't worry about that.'

'But you're not as fond of me as you thought you were going to be.'

She spoke calmly, without complaint or cajolery in her voice, and he answered as coolly, 'I've had a boil on my bottom, and for the last two or three days I haven't been fond of anyone. Least of all myself.'

Lightly she caressed his hair, and sighed; then stood, and walked to the rail. The sun had risen and the smoothly glistening sea was turning blue, the hillside under a cap of mist was bright green. So clear was the air that the great, down-curving leaves of the coco-palms stood out in high relief against the hill, and across the water the shrill, chattering voices of women and children in the brown, stilted houses of the fishing village on the nearby shore came as clearly as the clock

54

chiming in the saloon. The men of the village, in their narrow dark canoes, were already far out at sea.

Slowly she turned and asked, 'Who are the women you're going to ask?'

'Is it your turn to be nervous?'

'No, I'm not afraid of them. They won't feel very charitable towards me, and some of them may show their dislike. But only to begin with, and because I'm new. If we stay here they'll get used to me quite quickly, and then they'll just gossip about me as they do about each other.'

'But with a sharper tongue. Some of them will be jealous of you,' he said complacently.

'That won't make much difference. Jealousy's natural to women, it's in our blood.'

'What nonsense! I've known women who never had an unkind thought.'

'Only sluts. Sometimes the shameless, unredeemable slut isn't unkind, but that's because she can't be bothered with opinions of any sort.'

'Rubbish.'

'Thoroughly nice and respectable women, with weak husbands and children to defend, are usually seething with jealousy.'

'Sometimes,' said the Sultan angrily, 'you say extra-ordinarily silly things.'

'So you've told me before, but I don't believe you. You've got a romantic belief in women.'

'I must have been fortunate in those I've known. More fortunate than you.'

'You've never kept one very long.'

'Do you think I'm to blame for that?'

'No, my dear. I'm sure it was their fault entirely.'

'But you're free from all the weaknesses that cripple others. Is that what you want me to believe?'

'I think I'm more honest than most; perhaps that's the real difference.'

'It's a dangerous quality, without tact to control it.'

'It has its advantages. And if you would listen to me sometimes—'

'If I listened to you long enough I'd be bitted and bridled, and saddled and schooled, and a safe, easy ride for any young lady after ten lessons. Isn't that what you're aiming at?'

'You'd always need good hands.'

'I'm not going to be taught or directed, or governed or reformed, by anyone—though she'd hands like Paderewski.'

'But why are you so angry? What are you angry about? I said nothing—'

'It's the way you said it. You don't make conversation, you make announcements.'

'I'm sorry.'

'And so am I. Perhaps it was thinking about Morland that made me bad-tempered. And now I'm going to have my bath, and at breakfast I'll forget you're the most exasperating woman I've ever known—and only remember you're the most beautiful.'

'Before you go—'

'Well, what?'

She cupped his face in her hands and kissed him. 'That's all,' she said.

Throughout the day the sky was windless, and the early flamboyance of the sun was quickly dulled by its own excess. At midday the heat was intense, but the air was no longer bright. A vapour rose from the hot sea in which life wilted and all colour was obscured. The roads about Port Philip were empty of traffic, the fishing village slumbered by the waterside, and in the Secretariat pale officials analysed trade reports and wrote memoranda on paper that grew soft and damp beneath

56

their sweating hands. But soon after four o'clock there were half a dozen women, smart and composed in newly ironed party frocks, waiting by the jetty on the beach for the Sultan's motor-boat, and during the next half-hour some thirty people who would otherwise have gone listlessly to the Yacht Club, to drink iced lager and quietly grumble, went eagerly—forgetful of the heat and brisk with anticipation, brisk in well-laundered shirts and dresses—to the hospitality of *White Heather* and their long anticipated, often discussed first meeting with Mrs. Nottingham.

She disappointed the women. They had set too high their hope of being shocked, their hunger to dispraise. They had expected someone who, within a screen of the couturier's art, would reveal a spirit as brutally acquisitive as a tiger's claws. They had looked forward to seeing, in clothes more expensive than they could afford, a type of womanhood they must all deplore and a fatal attraction that none might deny. And when they were introduced to a calm and coldly handsome woman in a linen frock more simply fashioned than their own, they thought her dull and wondered why the Sultan had ever taken an interest in her. Their husbands, though equally surprised, were more observant and more appreciative, and several of them pretended to be on very familiar terms with Dr. Playfair, who stood beside Mrs. Nottingham as her press-agent might stand beside a visiting *prima donna* of the films. Dr. Playfair looked very happy, though uncomfortably hot.

At five o'clock the Sultan said to those about him, 'I've told the captain to take a turn out to sea, and we'll make our own breeze. It's the only way to get cool.'

'But you can't go yet!' exclaimed Mrs. Marly. 'Jim isn't here!'

'It's five o'clock.'

'I suppose he's still working. Someone's got to work.'

'That depends on what he's doing, and why. So many of

us—not I, thank heaven—feel an absurd, exaggerated reverence for work, work for work's sake, without ever considering what its product is, or where it goes. It's hardly too much to say that work has become the opium of the people.'

'Give me a light,' said Mrs. Marly, and waved a cigar in impatient fingers.

'I'll let him have five minutes' grace, but no more.'

The diesel engines were already mildly thumping, and half a dozen thin brown sailors stood on the forward deck. The anchor chains came wetly in, and the captain was about to ring for slow ahead when Mrs. Marly sharply exclaimed, 'There he is! He's on the beach now.'

The accommodation-ladder was lowered again, and with glum admission of his disappointment the Sultan watched the motor-boat come out towards them. Morland climbed slowly up the ladder, and the Sultan went to meet him.

Morland with obvious vexation said, 'I hadn't realized you were giving a party, sir. I expected to see you alone.'

'I have my commitments,' said the Sultan. 'The obligations of friendship can't be ignored. But come and have a drink, and if you want a private talk with me—'

'That's what I've come for.'

'We'll find a quiet corner presently. Now what will you have?'

Morland, though above middle height and erect of carriage, was meagrely built and gave an impression of delicacy. His strength, however, was wiry and enduring, and a hot, humid climate suited his constitution and kept him in excellent health. He had a pale complexion under black hair, and a beaked nose, out of proportion to his other features, gave him distinction of a rather ungainly sort. He was much respected by his colleagues for his knowledge of the country and devotion to the service, and because he could be generous to those in whom he found a similar devotion he had inspired a good deal of wary affection among his juniors. Those of his own rank, most of whom were older than he, thought he showed too ambitious a temper and was too zealous for his own advancement. The Sultan admitted his virtues, but had never pretended to like him; and to Morland the Sultan was an extravagant anachronism with whom, as a man, he had no sympathy whatever. He worked unremittingly for the welfare of the Sultan's state and people, and the Sultan admitted that Namua had never been better served. 'If you believe,' he would add, 'in progressive government, and are satisfied that Morland's nose is correctly oriented.'

The reviving breeze of the yacht's passage out to sea induced in his guests a livelier mood, and most of them were now gathering round the buffet which had been set up on deck. In the flux and reflux of thirsty traffic the Sultan found it easy to detach himself from Morland and join Mrs. Pemberton, whom Mrs. Marly had brought with her; and Mrs. Pemberton made no concealment of the pleasure it gave her to stand, a little apart from the throng, and talk to him on the slightly throbbing deck of his urgent ship.

She told him about her husband, and the importance of his work. She told him about her family, and where they lived. He learnt something of her schooldays, the name of her best friend, and the endearing peculiarities of her headmistress. She knew nothing of his life and interests, so she talked of her own, and because she was excited she talked with a charming animation, and the Sultan found sufficient pleasure in her manner, in the changing light of her expression, to disregard the small content of her words. She told him that her first experience of foreign travel had been disappointing till now; but now in the warmth of the yacht's fresh wind, and a sun-dazzled sea for circumference, why, 'This is life made perfect,' she said.

'But of course! This is the dream of everyone who isn't ashamed to dream. A well-found schooner in the South Seas—what more could you want?'

'Nothing at all. Not at this moment. But why did you call her *White Heather*? You ought to have a more romantic name.'

'You don't think *White Heather* romantic? But my dear girl, it's the very symbol, almost the synopsis, of a great romance! Come down to the saloon and I'll show you.—But I can't go so quickly as that, I'm still half a cripple. Some staphylococci came to call on me.'

They went slowly down the companionway, the Sultan with a heavy hand on the rail, and leading her forward in the saloon he showed her, set into the bulkhead, a small, gilt, oval frame in which, behind glass, a sprig of what had once been white heather—but now its bloom was the colour of tea-leaves—was fastened by an old-fashioned tie-pin to faded blue velvet.

'Disraeli is supposed to have picked that,' he said, 'and Mrs. Disraeli gave it to my grandfather.'

'Were they friends?' asked the innocent Mrs. Pemberton.

'There is no suggestion of a sentimental attachment,' said the Sultan gravely. 'Mrs. Disraeli wasn't a young woman when my grandfather met her. But he was, for a little while, a popular figure in England, and the Queen had received him. That diamond pin was a gift from her.'

'What made him popular?'

'He had saved and sheltered and fed the whole complement of a 16-gun sloop of the Royal Navy. The sloop had gone ashore on a reef two hundred miles east of here, where there was a sultanate, now extinct, whose ruler was something of a pirate. My grandfather, in his ships, happened to appear on the scene just as the pirate sultan was about to attack the sloop, which couldn't defend herself because all her guns had been thrown overboard to lighten her.'

'What was your grandfather doing?'

'He was leading what was later described as a punitive expedition; though the truth is he was making a quite unprovoked, and what he hoped would be a surprise attack, on a rival power. He did attack, and because he was a good leader and had the advantage of superior numbers, he defeated his rival with—according to the captain of the sloop—"very great slaughter". Then he went to help the shipwrecked sailors. But the sloop was badly damaged, and though they got her off the reef, she sank. So my grandfather took the captain and all his crew back to Namua, where they lived with him—very happily, it's said—for about three months till another ship came to pick them up. And a year later my grandfather received a silver-framed photograph of Queen Victoria, inscribed in her own hand *To our Faithful Ally*, and an invitation to visit England. Where, as I said, he was very well received.'

'And got a piece of white heather from Mrs. Disraeli.'

'Disraeli said he had picked it himself, but that I have always doubted. He had certainly been staying at Balmoral, but I can't imagine him tramping the hills. It was probably some stalwart gillie who found the heather. But Disraeli brought it to Hughenden and gave it to his wife, and she gave half of it to my grandfather. And when he decided that what he really wanted was an English-built yacht he called her *White Heather*, and she was the first of them. The second was sunk by the Japanese—but her captain saved *that*—and this is the third. Do you still think I could have found a better name?'

Mrs. Pemberton was young enough to say, 'How wonderful!' with a true sound of wonder in her voice, and frank enough to let doubt darken her admiration when she felt a doubt. 'I was wrong,' she said. 'It's a very romantic story!

But did your grandfather kill a lot of people—and did Queen Victoria and Mrs. Disraeli know he had?'

'I don't suppose they gave it a thought.'

'How many did he kill?'

'In the course of a long life I daresay he was responsible for the death of three or four hundred—all of them armed men who, if they'd had the chance, would have been delighted to kill him. It's a small total when you compare it with what a man could do today, but his weapons were simple and he had to get close to his enemy before he could use them.'

'But three or four hundred! He must have been very unhappy when he was old, and thought about them.'

'Not a bit of it. Our modern sense of guilt was only introduced by modern weapons; and my grandfather, not having had the advantage of them in time of war, didn't feel their disadvantage in time of peace.'

'And your father: was he the same?'

'Dear me, no. My father was a gentle person who collected butterflies. He pulled down the old barbaric palace where my grandfather lived, and built a really charming, civilized house. Perhaps you've seen it?'

'Only the outside.'

'I must take you there—'

'I'm intruding, I'm afraid,' said Morland, and came into the saloon with the obvious purpose of intrusion. 'But I really must have a talk with you, sir.'

'You've had your orders, have you?'

'I've received certain instructions.'

'Then I'd better hear what they are.—Will you forgive me if I desert you, Mrs. Pemberton? Or, to be accurate, ask you to desert me? I won't be very long, and then I'll tell you about the house my father built.'

He walked stiffly with her to the door of the saloon, and

stiffly returned. Carefully, with a groan as he went down, he sat himself on a cushioned chair and said, 'I haven't been very well for the last few days.'

'I'm sorry to hear that, sir. Was that why you came in here?'

'No, I was coming here in any case. This is my own country, Morland.'

'You could have saved both of us a lot of trouble if you had disembarked your passenger somewhere else.'

'I have no intention of disembarking her.'

'That's what we'll have to discuss, and I think, sir —'

'Did you send that fellow Playfair to see me last night?'

'No, sir.'

'You're sure?'

'Quite sure.'

'Well, he's a good man, whoever thought of it, and I like him. Now what do you want to tell me?'

'I think you ought to see this letter, sir. It's from H.E., and it puts the whole matter very clearly.'

He took from a long official envelope three closely typed pages, unfolded them, and gave them to the Sultan.

'He's a wordy fellow, isn't he?' said the Sultan, and settled himself to read.

Six

'THERE'S a cigar-box on that small table. Help yourself, Morland, and give one to me. Would you like a drink?'

'No, thank you.'

The Sultan lit his cigar and said, 'I do dislike official letters. They're so unctuous and flabby, like a cold omelette.'

'The meaning of that one is clear enough, however.'

'I see that you are "to use every endeavour to impress upon His Highness the gravity of the situation". Do you yourself think it grave?'

'I do, sir.'

'The point at issue, of course, is the Governor's authority, and I'm not disposed to admit that his authority is as large as he pretends.'

'As representative of the Paramount Power—'

'You know perfectly well, Morland, that my position under the Paramount Power has never been satisfactorily defined or positively determined; and when the paramount power is British that can't surprise anyone. From time to time we've made certain agreements that have, on the whole, been mutually beneficial; though sometimes New Brabant has come off better than Namua. In the matter of the oil revenue from Te Aku, for instance—'

'That's an old question, of course, but I admit your father agreed to a very generous division.'

'On the understanding that certain privileges that he valued would be acknowledged and respected: privileges that became mine when I succeeded him.'

'As a general statement, I accept all that. But in this particular case—'

'In this case a privilege inseparable from my title is being impugned. Why, only a few minutes ago I was telling that pretty girl whom you drove away about my grandfather—telling her of what he always regarded as a personal commission from Queen Victoria and a personal treaty with her—and now a threadbare little bureaucrat thinks he can dislodge me from the tradition of asylum that my grandfather established, and destroy its generosity!'

'That letter, sir, is signed by His Excellency the Governor.'

'I said so, didn't I? A threadbare little bureaucrat.'

'You are making this very difficult for me—'

'I intend to make it impossible.'

'But surely, sir, you must admit that privilege of any sort has geographical limits. Suppose, for the sake of argument, there was a new Act of Parliament that acknowledged and defined your right to give asylum: it couldn't possibly extend that right beyond your own frontiers.'

'Where are my frontiers? I am by inheritance Sultan of Namua, Lord of the Island Sea, Faithful Ally of Queen Victoria. And can you measure the Island Sea?'

'No, I can't. Nor can anyone else. But it certainly doesn't stretch as far as Fairweather.'

'Are you quite sure? In the reign of Queen Victoria the power of Britain could be stretched, if need be, as far as any harbour where a British ship was lying. And my ship was in Fairweather.'

'You can't behave today as Britain used to sixty or seventy years ago.'

'But I did.'

'You can't behave like that and get away with it! That's what I mean.'

'And that is what only time will declare. I think I can.'

Morland, his cheeks twitching with anger, got up and said, 'I'm trying hard to be patient—' and turning, saw Mrs. Nottingham at the door of the saloon.

'You ought to come on deck, both of you,' she said. 'The sky has cleared and there's going to be a beautiful sunset.'

'Come in, my dear. This is Mr. Morland, whom you haven't met before, though you know who he is.'

She advanced upon him with an air of kindly assurance, her chin lifting a little—to greet him with a steady gaze—as she smiled and held out her hand. 'Of course I do, and I've been looking forward to meeting you, Mr. Morland. Do come on deck, and let me give you a drink.'

She held his hand too long—she seemed reluctant to let it go—and Morland, with some appearance of discomfort, retreated a step or two and said, 'I'm afraid we're too busy for that. There's a difficulty we have to resolve without loss of time.'

'You had better read this,' said the Sultan, and gave her the Governor's letter.

'That's confidential, sir!'

'It's all about her. She can't be kept in ignorance of what's going on.'

'There's a right and a wrong way of doing things, and this is the wrong way. I had hoped that you would explain to Mrs. Nottingham—that you would advise her—'

'To go back to Fairweather and stand my trial?' she asked. 'I haven't read all this, but it isn't really necessary, is it? There's so much of it, and most of it seems to be repetition.'

'From a legal point of view—'

'But I'm here because His Highness's point of view is humanitarian. And whatever you may say in your official capacity, Mr. Morland, I'm sure you admit in your heart that a humane man is a better judge of right or wrong than any lawyer.'

'I think,' said the Sultan, 'I shall leave you to argue it out between you.'

'No, sir, that's quite impossible! I won't—I won't have it. You can't shuffle out of your responsibility. I must have your decision before you go.'

'Then I shall assert my privilege,' said the Sultan. 'I am, I know, Sultan of Namua only by sufferance. It is merely a convention that I'm Lord of the Island Sea. But there is still a shred of reality in my claim to be the Ally of Queen Victoria.'

'Morally speaking?' asked Morland spitefully.

'Yes, morally. Though, let me hasten to add, I recognize a distinction between private morality and public morality.'

'What man doesn't?' asked Mrs. Nottingham; but the Sultan ignored her.

'Public morality—morality in government—implies tolerance and generosity in government.' Stiffly, and with a little mutter of pain, the Sultan got to his feet. For a moment he hesitated, and then, with authority in his voice, and unexpected feeling, he said, 'In the days of her great Queen England was a harbour for the outcast and the rebel. The refugee from tyranny and oppression turned instinctively to England: to the liberality and freedom of England. And here in Namua, ever since my grandfather gave asylum to the crew of an English ship, we have followed English example—the example of Victoria's England—and so long as I exercise the lightest scrap of authority, or command the least remnant of privilege, I shall continue to follow it, and give refuge to the distressed.'

'That is to say, to Mrs. Nottingham.'

'At the moment, yes. You may tell the Governor that she is under my protection, and I do not wish her to leave my territories.'

67

Morland turned to Mrs. Nottingham and said, 'It is my duty to tell you that though His Highness's intention may be charitable, he has made a very bad decision. It may be a calamitous decision. And you, of course, are not bound to accept it. My advice to you is to return to Fairweather—where you will receive all possible help and be legally represented—and stand your trial.'

'And what would happen if I did? Would they deport me, and expect me to go and live in my late husband's country?'

'You can hardly ask me to anticipate the verdict of the court.'

'You don't offer much inducement, do you? No, Mr. Morland, I think, on the whole, I prefer to stay where I am.'

She walked to the Sultan, and took his hand and stood beside him.

Morland said harshly, 'I must ask you, formally, to surrender yourself to justice. If you refuse—'

'Oh, but that's most unfair! I don't refuse anything, but you can't expect me to ignore His Highness's wishes, can you? I'm his guest. I'm deeply indebted to him, and I'm certainly not going to do anything of which he doesn't approve.'

'I think that settles it,' said the Sultan. 'And now can we go on deck?'

'I'm bitterly disappointed, sir. Not for my own sake, but because this decision of yours—this ridiculous, romantical decision—is going to cause trouble that may well threaten your position here. You know perfectly well that you can't settle this business simply by saying no! Yours isn't the only principle at issue. And I should like to point out that H.E. has gone to great trouble, and is prepared to take more trouble, to avoid causing you anything in the nature of humiliation if only you'll meet his wishes.'

'He is not a man to whom I should care to be indebted,' said the Sultan. 'You, I know, are doing your best to look after my interests, and I'm grateful to you. I really am. But I prefer to use my own judgment.'

'You've chosen a particularly bad time for that,' said Morland.

'I'm sorry to cause inconvenience.'

'The habit's growing. I'm flying to Maipani tomorrow to try and deal with a man who's making a nuisance of himself— a confounded nuisance—and who wouldn't be in the country if it weren't for your judgment.'

'Who is that?'

'Samarai. Three years ago I wanted to deport him, but you objected. You took him under your protection. And now he's upset the whole of Maipani, and some of the neighbouring districts too, by telling them that God's coming in a heavenly aeroplane to take them under His personal care. That, sir, is a direct consequence of your exercising your own judgment.'

'I heard in Fairweather that he'd started preaching again. He was always keen on religion, that's why I took an interest in him. But we've heard nothing for the last two or three weeks, of course. Is he getting dangerous?'

'I really want to watch the sunset,' said Mrs. Nottingham.

'Go along, my dear, and I'll be with you in a few minutes. But I must hear about Samarai first. . . .'

On deck, oblivious to the splendour of the lapsing sun, Pemberton stood with two members of the Yacht Club whom he had cut out from the throng about the buffet and penned, with the efficiency of a sheep-dog, against the starboard rail. Pemberton was a little uneasy, somewhat excited—it would be an exaggeration to say he was nervous, but he was on the edge of nervousness—because at dawn tomorrow he was flying from Port Philip to the highlands of Maipani, and nearly everyone to whom he told his plans replied, 'Well, that'll give you something to remember! I've done it once'—or twice, or thrice—'and I wouldn't go again for a month's pay.' Or sometimes: 'I'd come with you, I'd come like a shot, but I promised my wife I'd never do it unless I had to.'—And Pemberton felt his recurrent need to explain, to anyone who would listen, that he was a person of importance in the academic world, and Namua was uncommonly fortunate to have him in its midst and find him prepared to undertake a dangerous flight to put Namua on the scientific map.

'You've got to admit,' he said, 'that it's an extraordinary coincidence. There aren't so many genuine anthropologists in the world—I mean men who've been properly trained and who've got the right ideas—and it isn't often that one of us gets a chance to see a case like this, of a primitive people, a Stone Age people, reacting to some new concept of the supernatural. But I was just on the doorstep, so to speak, when I heard of this man Samarai, and I realized at once it was up to me to investigate. And I won't spare myself, you can depend on that. I've got a feeling I'm going to see something very remarkable, and I'll give the intellectual world a remarkable account of it.'

'It is what happens very often in Wales,' said one of his listeners in a joyfully rising, sadly plunging intonation. 'We have many revival meetings there that come to nothing in the end, and this man Samarai is a revivalist preacher, and that is all you can say about him. I wouldn't walk a mile to hear him.'

'You might learn something,' said Pemberton, wantonly offensive, 'if a good anthropologist went to work on a Welsh chapel.'

This assertion led to argument which had nothing to do with Samarai, and in the meantime, on the other side of the deck, Mrs. Pemberton was walking with Mrs. Marly.

Mrs. Marly had already told several women what she

thought of Mrs. Nottingham, and now she was saying, once again, 'It's her effrontery that staggers me! She arrives here in the Sultan's yacht, and naturally enough we assume they're living together. She's not the first woman I've seen aboard this ship, and she won't be the last; and they all pay their passage in the same way. But the others didn't talk about it. They didn't advertise their profession. They didn't *proclaim* their intimacy. But almost the first thing she told me was that she'd had to dress his carbuncle twice last night and twice today. Well, I call that sheer effrontery.'

'Perhaps they're married,' said Mrs. Pemberton. 'There may have been a secret marriage.'

'He's got a wife in Penang,' said Mrs. Marly. 'I admit they've been separated for years—she was a good-looking girl, too: rather cold, rather aloof, a little bit like Mrs. Nottingham, now I think of it—but she's still his wife. There was no divorce.'

'Isn't he a Mahomedan? Mahomedans can have several wives.'

'I daresay he's got more scope than a Christian, but he's too sensible to take advantage.'

'Well, if they're not married, I think he's just being kind to her.'

'You can't pretend his kindness is disinterested. She has her attractions—including that of considerable experience, I should say.'

They turned, and saw Mrs. Nottingham come on deck; and Dr. Playfair, quickly removing himself from those to whom he was talking, hurried to meet her.

'Look at that,' said Mrs. Marly. 'You've got to give her credit of a sort. She can bring them to heel, can't she? I could do it too, when I was young. But that's a long time ago. My God, what chances I threw away! If I'd had the knowledge

71

I have now, with the figure and complexion I had then—but that's an old tale of sorrow, isn't it? And I shan't bore you with it. Let's go and have a drink.'

At the buffet they joined Pemberton and his pressed listeners, and Playfair and Mrs. Nottingham stood nearby. Presently, with Morland behind him, the Sultan came out and called loudly for champagne.

'My self-esteem has been hurt,' he said, 'and nothing but champagne will medicine it. Morland tells me that I alone am to blame for this trouble in the hills, because some years ago I saved Samarai from being deported.'

'But the Civil Surgeon did worse than that,' said Playfair. 'He saved Samarai's life.'

'I'm very grateful both to him and to you, sir,' said Pemberton. 'And before long the whole scientific world may be grateful too.'

'Do you hear that, Morland? Instead of regarding me as a local nuisance, you may have to recognize me as a universal benefactor.'

'My budget will still have to bear the cost,' said Morland.

'There's far too much fuss being made about this man Samarai,' said Mrs. Marly. 'The whole thing will just fizzle out.'

'But it must be properly investigated,' said Pemberton.

'What is there to investigate?'

'Human nature, for one thing. The more we know about savages, the more we know about you and me.'

'Don't you believe it!' Mrs. Marly blew an indignant plume of cigar-smoke and said, 'Good heavens, man, do you think there's any common quality between me and those naked, head-hunting cannibals on the mountains?'

'Quite a lot, I'd say.'

'I don't see the humour of that remark.'

'It wasn't meant to be humorous. It's true.'

Mrs. Marly turned her back on him, and asked the Sultan if he was going into residence at the Palace.

'No, I don't think so. We're very comfortable here, aren't we, Elizabeth? But I was telling Mrs. Pemberton she must go and see it.—My father, Mrs. Pemberton, once went to the United States, where he took a great fancy for their Colonial architecture. So when he came home he built a new palace on the model of Thomas Jefferson's house of Monticello.'

He turned suddenly to Mrs. Nottingham and asked, 'When you were living with that young American friend of yours—Mr. Cooney, wasn't it?—did you ever talk about Jefferson?'

There now stood round them nearly a score of people who, when they heard the Sultan speak of that scandalous association, could hardly believe their good fortune. They drew their breath—sharply, with a shiver of delight—and pressed a little closer. In a taut silence of exquisite anticipation they waited for Mrs. Nottingham's reply.

But again she disappointed them. She showed no embarrassment, in her voice there was no tremor of unease. She was, perhaps, a little puzzled as she repeated, 'Jefferson? No, we certainly never spoke of him.'

'But surely, to comfort Mr. Cooney when you so alarmed him by admitting your association with Communists'—again his audience sighed, trembled, felt in their blood a pleasant chill—'surely you should have reminded him that Jefferson believed in peace, commerce, and friendship with all the nations of the world?'

'I'm afraid I don't know much about Jefferson.'

'But you should! Everybody should. He said a lot of things I don't agree with, but also he said, "I tremble for my country when I reflect that God is just". Oh, it's very shocking that

73

you don't know about him. But ignorance is growing in the world, isn't it, Playfair?'

'Spreading like a blight,' said Playfair cheerfully. 'The more we find out, the less we know.'

'Let's walk on the other side, Mrs. Pemberton. I have sown dismay among my friends, and now I can't bear their reproachful eyes. I think I shall take my glass with me.'

He held it out to be refilled, and walking with a little limp, led her away, the glass high in his right hand like a rose to be sniffed.

'Don't ask me about Jefferson,' she said.

'Of course not. You are excused what would, in others, be the grossest faults. Shall I take you to see the Palace tomorrow?'

'But we're going to Maipani tomorrow. I don't want to go, but I've got to.'

'What an adventure for you.'

'Is it as dangerous as people say? The flight there, and this man Samarai?'

'There's no danger at all. You fly up to the mountains, but the aeroplane's a good one and the pilot knows his way. And Samarai's a very interesting fellow. I know him.'

'I'm feeling horribly nervous about it.'

'Don't regret that. To be nervous beforehand is a good way to get the full flavour of experience. Of a first experience.'

'I'd much rather go sailing.'

'Why not? There's a breeze, and it's freshening.'

He drank his champagne and limped away to find the captain. Orders were shouted, and the crew came running from the fo'c'sle. They were lithe, brown-skinned men who ran swiftly on bare feet. They wore white shorts and singlets, and their lively muscles rippled the smooth skin of their legs and arms as they heaved on the halliards and hauled aft the sheets. The tall sails rose on the masts and filled with the evening breeze. The deck tilted, and the stewards hurried to clear away bottles and glasses and dismantle the buffet. The engines were stopped, and instead of the muted thump of the diesels the rushing, shearing sound of the cloven sea was heard.

The sun, a molten globe, balanced on the straight horizon and the sky above it was a diaphanous, bright gold. The Sultan went to the wheel, the sheets were eased off, and as the schooner's head fell away from the wind her deck slanted a little more and the women of the party with bent knees and fluttering cries hurried to the weather side. The breeze freshened, the sea grew darker, and here and there a ruffle of white water caught the light of the afterglow and grew sharply luminous.

The Sultan sailed his ship full and hard, and standing at the wheel he appeared to have indeed the gift of mastery and the craft of governance.

Seven

O N the eighth morning after the party in the yacht, before the sun had risen high enough to show itself above the mountains of cloud that were piled above the solid mountains which enclosed the valley, Kershawe, the District Officer in charge of Maipani, sat with Morland on the veranda of his new bungalow. He had built it with pride in his labour, he was ingenuously pleased with its achievement, and he and Morland were living in it though it was still far from being finished. The doors were unpainted, there was no glass in the windows, and at night the lamps attracted a drift, then a cloud, of soft and clumsy moths, of thinly buzzing insects, that dimmed the pale electric globes with the fluttering curtain of their wings. But in spite of its deficiencies the new bungalow was vastly preferable to the old building, a hundred yards away, which Kershawe had abandoned when its thatched roof, too long a breeding-ground for small snakes and spiders, had begun to sag in the middle and threaten to bury him beneath a mattress of rotten timber, dead palm-leaves, and the nests of its un-countable population. His new veranda, moreover, com-manded a view of the whole settlement; of the air-strip, broken-backed in the middle of its run, and the score of buildings that made his capital.

The air-strip ran north and south, and to the east of it, on a descending slope, were the new bungalow and the old one, Kershawe's office, the store-sheds and a hospital, and Tom Penny's bungalow and store. On the other side were the police barracks and married quarters, the three long huts of the jail

—only distinguishable from the barracks by their perimeter of barbed wire—and another store-shed. South of the air-strip, on rising ground, was the largest of the buildings, the Rest House. They were all of sombre hue, with grey walls and a brown thatch, but here and there grew red or yellow flowers— there was a gardened strip of scarlet beside the jail—and small green patches of cultivation shone in the warm and misty light like weed-patches in the grey, transparent, swift-running water of an English chalk-stream. It was of these gardens which he had planted, and steadily enlarged, that Kershawe was thinking while Morland talked to him.

It was Morland's belief—often justified but always exasperating—that he could hammer home, into the minds of his subordinates, a principle or a policy by infinite repetition; and during the week he had been in Maipani his constant thesis had been the necessity of patience and forbearance in all their dealings with the dissident tribes. He himself was convinced that the disorder of the people's minds would be cured, in time, by mere exhaustion, but to interfere with them would inflame their temper and might make them dangerous. He was uninterested, or only superficially interested, in the nature of their infatuation, and he saw no reason to look for deeper motives in Samarai, their leader, than vanity, hysteria, or a propensity for making mischief.

'We have always avoided violence,' he said. 'For half a century that has been our policy, and events have proved it an efficient policy. We inherited a principle, and we've found it expedient.'

'Yes, I know,' said Kershawe, and detached his attention from a plot of sugar-cane, behind his old bungalow, that half a dozen convicts were weeding under the yawning supervision of an armed constable. 'One of the first things I heard, when I joined the service, was that in all New Brabant we had only

77

once sent out a punitive expedition, and it took five years to repair the damage it did and restore confidence. But in spite of that there are times when force is necessary; or a threat of force. And I think this is one of them.'

'You're wrong,' said Morland.

'We've allowed seven or eight hundred people to assemble, and there are more coming all the time. A few weeks ago we could have got rid of them easily enough, but—well, we didn't. And now it'll be rather more difficult. But we ought to do something before it becomes impossible.'

'What do you suggest?'

'You can't reason with them in their present state of mind. You've talked to them, and so have I, and it's had no effect. So the only thing to do is to give them an order, and show them they've got to do what they're told because we're the stronger side. Tell them to go home and back to work, and if they refuse fire a volley over their heads and put the fear of death into them.'

'And if it fails to produce the proper effect?'

'Then fire another, a bit closer.'

'And if they ignore that?'

'They won't. They've all got fear in their minds, it's natural to them. There's fear in every one of them, like a dog sleeping in the shade. And it isn't hard to wake it.'

'That's perfectly true, and we've always tried not to frighten them. We've tried to cure them of fear, and give them confidence instead.'

'They've shown no confidence in me for the last month, and not much in you since you came here.'

'None at all. But they'll come back to us when they discover that Samarai has misled them. They'll come back to us, and we'll have to feed them.'

'That'll make a hole in our budget,' said Kershawe glumly.

'Yes, it's going to cost a lot. But I'm prepared for that.'

Kershawe got up and walked to and fro, his boots loud on the hollow veranda. 'If I could find a way to bring him here alone—I mean Samarai—we could arrest him,' he said, 'and if we had him under arrest they would be helpless. They couldn't try to rescue him, because we would make it quite clear that he would be the first victim.'

'If you did that,' said Morland, 'you wouldn't be inviting trouble, you'd be demanding trouble. Don't you see the danger of frightening them too much—frightening them beyond endurance? You would drive them crazy.'

'By laying hands on Samarai? He isn't a god.'

'They believe every word he tells them. They're perfectly convinced that within the next few days a miraculous aeroplane, an aeroplane from heaven, is going to arrive with such a cargo as no one has ever seen before. An aeroplane loaded with every luxury you can think of; kerosene lamps that don't need kerosene, axes that never get blunt, lap-laps in bird-of-paradise colours, lolly-water and chewing-tobacco and fat pigs for everyone, and a ton of canned peaches. All that is coming to them by grace of Samarai. And if I arrest him they'll go crazy with fear. Fear of losing what they've set their hearts on.'

'There are four of us, including Pemberton. We've got a sergeant and a corporal and twelve constables. We could look after ourselves.'

'There are nearly eight hundred natives here, and if they attacked we should have to shoot to kill. That's a thing I've never done in the sixteen years of my service, and I'm not going to develop bad habits now.'

'So all we can do is to sit and count what every day's going to cost us in food and lost labour?'

'When you're dealing with people as primitive as these,

you've got to be patient. It takes a lot of patience to make a civilization.'

'And they won't thank you for it when they've got it.'

'A few of them may,' said Morland.

Kershawe pointed to two figures who, on the long slope of the hill beyond the police barracks, were walking towards the settlement. One of them was Pemberton, the other the native interpreter, a man called Oala.

'Have you heard Pemberton talking about that?' he asked. 'Pemberton thinks we're civilizing them out of all desire to live. He says they prefer to be savages. That's the way he likes them too.'

'His wife doesn't,' said Morland coldly. 'She told me it was worth coming to Maipani for one thing and one thing only: and that was to learn gratitude for having been born in England.'

For a little while they watched in silence the approach of Pemberton and his companion, and Morland asked, 'Can you see what Oala's carrying?'

'It looks like a bow.'

They stopped near the head of the air-strip, and Pemberton, taking the bow and a sheaf of long arrows from Oala, went uphill to the Rest House. Briskly he climbed the steps to its veranda, and they could hear him calling for his wife.

'Pemberton's enjoying himself,' said Morland.

'But she isn't, and I wish he hadn't brought her.'

'She doesn't like Maipani, but she might have got into trouble if he'd left her alone in Port Philip. She can't get into trouble here.'

'I hope not,' said Kershawe.

Pemberton, his wife beside him, came out of the Rest House and down the steps. He was still carrying the bow and the sheaf of arrows. They walked towards the new bungalow, and

Morland and Kershawe got up to welcome them. Morland, who in his ordinary habit was shy of women and protected himself and his dignity against them with a cold assumption of indifference, had in the remoteness of Maipani allowed himself to show a little awkward affection for Mrs. Pemberton. She was very young, and looked younger than her years. She was very pretty, and because she was so manifestly unhappy among the mountain pagans, her prettiness invited some display of protective kindliness. She was, moreover, so dominated by her husband that she was unlikely to misunderstand and overrate the attention of another man: of one, especially, who was in some degree her host and had an obligation to be kind. So Morland had permitted himself the luxury of being amiable, and now, wishing her good morning, his voice rang with a bluff *bonhomie* that was assumed and yet not false.

'How are we today?' he asked with avuncular concern, and she, slowly climbing the steps, took his hand and said wearily, 'It's hotter than ever, isn't it? These clouds press down and down, I feel as if I'm carrying the whole weight of them.'

'They're opening already. You can see right down the valley, and there'll be a clear sky in an hour or so.'

'And then the sun will be worse than the clouds.'

'Oh come, Mrs. Pemberton, you're being too hard on Maipani. The climate up here's much better than it is on the coast. It's quite exhilarating when you're used to it.'

'I should never get used to it. Can I have a cold drink, please?'

'But of course,' said Morland, and shouted, 'Boy!'

A houseboy came out, a little, snub-nosed, impassive man dark brown in colour and naked to the waist. He wore a scarlet lap-lap belted with a black strap, and in the black busby of his hair was stuck a scarlet flower. Mrs. Pemberton looked at him with a wary eye, and Morland said, 'What about you, Pemberton? Would you like some beer?'

'No, it's too early for beer. I'll take a squash. And just look at this bow, Morland.'

'Yes, in a moment.' Morland, speaking rapidly in pidgin, told the houseboy what was wanted, and took from Pemberton a roughly made but powerful bow. It was nearly six feet long, and strung with cane. 'Yes, it's a good one. It's a war-bow.'

'Try the pull of it. It must be nearly sixty pounds.'

'It's heavy, but not as much as that. Where did you get it?'

Mrs. Pemberton interrupted to say, 'Do tell William to be careful with those arrows. I'm sure they're poisoned.'

'That's not likely. In spite of the stories you hear, I don't believe they've got an effective poison.'

'They don't need one,' said Kershawe. 'Their arrows are so dirty that a wound goes septic at once. And that's just as useful.'

'Put them down, William, please!'

Pemberton paid no attention to her, but examined the arrows, each in turn, with a collector's interest. He was in vigorous health—his face and arms and knees scorched by the sun, his khaki shirt dark with sweat—and his mood was equally robust. He enjoyed an outdoor life, and liked an opportunity to live more roughly than need be. He could walk thirty miles a day and dine happily, in a tent in the rain, off a tin of bully beef and some biscuits. The savage tribesmen of Maipani fascinated him, and he went among them as confidently as a farmer among his cattle. He could finger their feathers and adornments as inoffensively as a farmer pulling and assessing the healthy loose hide of a bullock, and with infinite patience he questioned them—through the police interpreter, Oala—and listened eagerly to their confused and often foolish statements. Within two or three days of his arrival he was on familiar terms with nearly a score of them, and could tell Kershawe that some of their foreign visitors lived three days' march across the Dutch frontier. He was quite shameless in the persistency with which he begged or bartered ornaments, and at night, with unabated vigour, he would write long notes of all he had seen and heard.

He was less attentive to, and less patient with his wife; and the people and the landscape that made him happy, had made her miserable. As he grew red, she turned pale, and the prettiness of her youth was already a little sharpened, as if by a low fever. But her eyes seemed the larger in consequence, and when the houseboy in the scarlet lap-lap brought out a tray of drinks, and Morland gave her a big tumbler of lime-squash, he put it into her hands as if she were a child, and patted her shoulder.

'These are the ordinary fish-bone barbs,' said Pemberton, holding up two of the arrows, 'but here's a pattern I haven't seen before. It would take a surgeon to get this one out. And here's an ingenious bit of work—you see how it's made? Someone's taken an ordinary European table-knife and filed it sharp on both sides to make a double cut.'

'I once saw a man who'd been hit in the stomach by one of those,' said Kershawe. 'The abdominal muscle split like a ripe plum.'

'Did he die?' asked Mrs. Pemberton faintly.

'Not as quickly as I expected. They take a lot of killing, in the ordinary way. The only thing they've got no resistance to is sorcery.'

'I don't know how you go on living here! It's a horrible country, and I want to get out of it as soon as ever I can.'

'Now don't start that all over again,' said Pemberton. 'We came here to study an outbreak of religious mania, not knowing whether it was going to be good or not. Well, it's first-class, and I'm not leaving till I've seen everything there is to be seen, and what happens next.'

'The aeroplane comes in this morning. I could go back to Port Philip and wait for you there.'

'He won't get through today,' said Pemberton. 'Not with all this cloud.'

'Won't he, Mr. Morland?'

'Yes, of course he will. I've seen him come through worse than this. The sky's breaking, the valley's almost clear, and he knows the country. He'll be here in half an hour, don't you worry about that. But do you really want to go?'

'Yes.'

'There's no danger, I assure you. You mustn't listen to Kershawe, because he enjoys violence and likes to think about it. But these people don't murder each other every day, you know.'

'Unless someone steals a pig,' said Kershawe, 'or runs away with his neighbour's wife.'

'Then, I admit, there's usually an attempt to pay him back. But things have improved enormously in the last few years.'

'Nothing can improve the mountains, or the gorge below,' said Mrs. Pemberton. 'I nearly died when we flew in.'

'We've heard all that before,' said Pemberton.

'Don't be unsympathetic,' said Morland. 'We all admit, we who live here, that flying up to Maipani for the first time is something of an experience.'

Mrs. Pemberton sat up, and clutching the arms of her chair said earnestly, 'It was the clouds that frightened me to begin with. There were clouds all the way, great clouds that swallowed you, and when you came out of the clouds you saw nothing but the ridge of a mountain or the edge of a precipice. And then we came down, down through more clouds, and there we were in this ghastly valley with the mountain-tops

84

three thousand feet above us and the river three thousand feet below, and the air-strip was only a little shelf on the hillside. We came further down, and there was another mountain in front of us, and we tilted over, and tilted over, and how we landed I'll never know, because I shut my eyes and said "God take care of me!" And how we'll ever get out I don't know, but I'd rather risk it than stay here another week.'

Pemberton, leaning against the wooden rail of the veranda, stared at his wife with sullen disapproval, but Morland, now clearly avuncular and a little worried, said, 'Would you like some brandy instead of your squash? Brandy's a much more comforting drink.'

Mrs. Pemberton took his question seriously, for not only was she unused to drinking spirits, but she had been brought up to regard them as dangerous; and it was with the air of one making a grave decision that she answered. Yes, she would take a glass of brandy.

'There is some, isn't there?' asked Morland.

'I'll go and get it,' said Kershawe.

Morland stood up and looked at the sky again. 'You'll feel more confident when you see Blakeley come in and land. When you see how cleverly he does it. It isn't every pilot I'd trust, but Blakeley's been doing it for eighteen months now, and he's never had an accident.'

'I've seen the wreckage of two planes that didn't make a good landing.'

'But that was a couple of years ago. We manage things better now.'

'I wouldn't like to land on the strip they're clearing for the aeroplane from heaven,' said Pemberton. 'It's on a slope of about one-in-six, as near as I can judge.'

Kershawe returned and said, 'It'll take a heavenly pilot as well as a heavenly plane to make a landing there.'

'They're not always very practical,' said Morland, and from the bottle that Kershawe had brought poured with a critical eye a medicinal dose for Mrs. Pemberton. 'Were you over there this morning?' he asked.

'Yes,' said Pemberton. 'That's where I got my bow and arrows.'

'You were lucky to get them. They don't often part with their war-bows.'

'It's Samarai I've got to thank. He fixed it for me.'

'Were you talking to him?'

'I tried to, but he wouldn't answer. He never will. He talks English to me, and all he says is, "I will not speak to those who will not believe".'

'That's something he learnt from the missionaries, I suppose.'

'But he got the bow for me,' said Pemberton. 'I was trying to buy it from a stubborn-looking chap who just shook his head and said no, whatever I offered. And then Samarai came over and had a word with him, and the next thing was I got it as a present. Free, gratis, and for nothing.'

'What did Samarai tell him?'

'I depend on Oala, of course, but according to him Samarai said that after three days they wouldn't need their bows and arrows any more, because the aeroplane was going to bring them plenty of guns and ammunition. White men's guns.'

As a soldier on outpost-duty, hearing a twig crack in the darkness, will on the instant become taut and still, listening for the enemy's movement, so both Morland and Kershawe suddenly grew tense and for a second or two were motionless, as if alert for the next footstep. Then Morland, his voice sharper than it had been, asked, 'You heard that yourself? You heard him promising guns?'

'I heard him say something, and according to Oala that's what it meant.'

86

'And in three days' time?'

'I'm pretty sure of that. *Kenné ma*, he said, and *kenné* means three, doesn't it?'

'We ought to move at once,' said Kershawe. 'We've got to get hold of him somehow or other, and the sooner the better.'

'I think,' said Morland, now relaxed and patient again, 'you may be forgetting something. For a moment, I admit, I was a little startled too. But Samarai's guns can't be any more substantial than the rest of the cargo they're expecting, so I don't see what we have to worry about. Unless, of course, you believe in miracles yourself?'

'If he's promising guns,' said Kershawe, 'it shows what his intentions are. I don't believe in cargoes from heaven any more than you do, but I'm quite sure we ought to put hand-cuffs on Samarai.'

'You can't do it,' said Pemberton. 'They'll all go mad if you lay a finger on him.'

'That is almost exactly what I've been telling him,' said Morland.

'These people,' said Pemberton, 'are enjoying themselves— really enjoying themselves, and enjoying life—for the first time in years. And it's Samarai who's made them happy. If you touch him, you'll drive them crazy.'

'Does that convince you?' asked Morland.

'I certainly don't accept the statement that they never enjoyed themselves till Samarai came and filled their heads full of nonsense. I know these people fairly well—'

'And you've done everything you could to make them happy,' said Pemberton. 'You've given them security, or a fair measure of security. They can walk about the country without constant fear of being assassinated. The young women don't expect to be raped as soon as they go a hundred yards away from their own village. You've put down sorcery—or, at any rate, you've managed to discredit some of the sorcerers, and make their business difficult.'

'I've done all that.'

'And because you've cut down murder, and reduced the incidence of rape, and compelled a few village sorcerers to grow sago instead of casting spells, you think you've served the people well. You're proud of having added to their expectancy of life.'

'That's perfectly true,' said Morland. 'The mass of the people here do live longer because of what we've done for them.'

'And the longer they live,' said Pemberton, 'the more life bores them. Because that's what security really means to them: it means boredom! You've taken away the fear that made life hard, and watchful, and full of meaning. The fear that made life worth living because every day was a new day. In the olden times—which only means the day before yesterday in these parts—people were nearly always planning a victory or plotting revenge.'

'Wasting time and energy, living in a dream of destruction,' said Morland.

'But they'd something to think about, something to believe in,' said Pemberton. 'Suppose a village was raided: well, those who survived spent the next six months meditating the payback. Months of purpose and preparation and confederacy. Nervous months, full of lust and intention and images of the sudden assault and orgiastic slaughter. But you've put a stop to that. You've given them security, but nothing they can take an interest in.'

'We've given them work, and in some places the missionaries have had considerable success. They've given the people new ideas.'

'In the old days,' said Pemberton, 'a man whose brother had been murdered, or whose best pig had been stolen, or his daughter assaulted, could go to the village sorcerer and get immediate satisfaction. But nowadays you expect him to listen to the missionaries. And though the missionaries promise specific rewards for being good, people have got to wait a long, long time, and even the best of rewards lose their flavour if they aren't going to materialize till you die of old age. The missionaries have been beaten hands-down by Samarai, because what he promises is coming now; or in three days' time. And their belief in Samarai doesn't only show a simple willingness to believe in miracles: it shows a general desire—a passionate desire—for something better than the benefits of security, or the far-distant payment, when you're dead, for being good while you're here. Samarai has made life exciting again. As exciting as it used to be when they could go out and murder a neighbour and acquire a new spiritual strength—as well as a full belly—by extracting, roasting, and eating his kidneys.'

Mrs. Pemberton, who had drunk her brandy with enjoyment—small petals of a rosy colour showed upon her cheek-bones—had listened to her husband with dreamy inattention, but his last sentence penetrated her indifference and reached some part of her understanding that was peculiarly sensitive.

'Oh no!' she cried. 'Oh no, William, not his kidneys?'

'Why not?' said Pemberton. 'You've eaten sheep's kidneys often enough.'

'But that's quite different.'

'Is it? I'm not so sure. For most of the time these people are just as vegetarian as a sheep.'

'But they're human beings—and sheep don't eat other sheep.'

'They haven't got the teeth for it, or else they might.'

It seemed to Morland that the rose-petals on Mrs. Pemberton's cheeks were taking on a darker hue, and with a bachelor's fear of family dispute he hurriedly interposed with the inquiry, would she like a little more brandy? To which she promptly replied, 'Yes, please.'

He turned to Pemberton and said, 'I think you overstated your case, but there's something in what you say. We've been changing the whole course of these people's lives—for their ultimate benefit, we believe—but so far we haven't found the proper sort of compensation for what we've taken from them. The excitement of violence, that is, and the stimulus of fear. And so, from time to time, you get an outbreak of mass hysteria, and a fraudulent apocalyptic like Samarai plays havoc with our economy. I've seen this sort of thing before, and that, perhaps, is why I'm less impressed by it than Kershawe. There was a smaller but similar outbreak in Tampé, soon after I joined the service, and the population stopped work in expectation of a miraculous ship: a ship loaded in heaven for their exclusive benefit.'

'Even savages, you see, keep up with the times,' said Pemberton. 'It used to be a ship, and now it's an aeroplane. And Samarai, whose father was a village sorcerer, has improved on his equipment with something he learnt from the missionaries. That boy was with him again today.'

'He comes from a village just over the border,' said Kershawe. 'I discovered that yesterday.'

'I don't see that the boy's presence makes any difference at all,' said Morland. 'He's a youngster whom Samarai has taken a fancy to: that's all. One doesn't approve of associations of that sort, but in our present circumstances it's of no importance.'

'The boy didn't appear till the beginning of this week,' said

Kershawe, 'and since then he and Samarai have always been seen together. But he's not an attractive boy, even by their standards, and once when I saw him he looked as if he'd been drugged.'

'I expect he had been,' said Pemberton. 'He isn't here for Samarai's amusement, he's to be the sacrifice.'

'Who told you that?'

'An old man called Kapa. I've spoken to him twice before, he's one of the friendly sort. And today he told me that this boy, who's a foreigner, he said, is going to be killed as a sacrifice; but not quite killed, as far as I could make out. For on the third day, which is the day of the aeroplane's arrival, he'll come to life again. But for what purpose old Kapa wouldn't tell me.'

'I'm not surprised,' said Morland, 'and if I were you I wouldn't take old Kapa's story too seriously. The boy may be badly treated, but he won't be killed. I got Samarai two years for murder just after the war, and he isn't likely to do it again. Most of these people take a prison sentence very lightly — they're well fed, they sleep a lot, they enjoy the company — but Samarai hated every day of it. He was miserable, a wreck of a man, at the end of eighteen months; when we let him go. So I'm pretty certain he hasn't got murder in his mind.'

'There's something odd about that boy,' said Kershawe. 'Old Kapa said quite plainly he was going to be killed. The rest of his story, the resurrection part, wasn't so clear. And when I tried to get details he turned suspicious and wouldn't answer.'

'If you knew all the village dialects you could listen to a hundred stories,' said Morland, 'and under the disguise of different words they would all have the same characteristics. They would all be very improbable and quite untrue.'

'I'd like to put that to the test,' said Pemberton.

Mrs. Pemberton, sitting up in her chair, asked, 'Do you hear drums, Mr. Morland?'

'It isn't concerted drumming, it doesn't mean anything. It's just a man playing for his own amusement, I expect.'

'He may have heard the plane,' said Kershawe. 'No, not the heavenly aeroplane, Mrs. Pemberton. Just the weekly courier.'

'Oh, I hope he's coming!'

'We all do,' said Morland. 'We've been out of touch with Port Philip since Tuesday now, and we can't speak to them till we get new batteries. I want to hear what's been happening in the Test Match.'

'Listen,' said Kershawe. 'That's him, isn't it?'

'Yes, there he is. Coming out of that cloud, Mrs. Pemberton. He's too high for a landing, he's taking a look at the valley first.'

The mountains of cloud that had lain closely on the solid mountains now loosely floated, and their upper sides were burnished by the sun that glared from the clear sky above them. In the valley, like sheep's wool caught on a wire fence, there were only long wisps of vapour, a glimmer of white against its shadowed sides, but to the west an alpine height of cumulus still showed, like caves within its cliff, deep holes of darkness.

The aeroplane flew along the line of the valley, a thousand feet above the landing-strip but two thousand feet below the mountain-crests on either side. It climbed steeply, and turned to starboard, and disappeared in a white flocculence.

'You'll see him again in two or three minutes,' said Morland.

'How long will he stay?'

'Not more than an hour. The air gets very bumpy later in the day.'

'And then he won't be back for another week.'

'The days will go very quickly. Maipani doesn't seem nearly as wild and unfriendly as when you first arrived, now does it? And after another week you may even be sorry to leave.'

'No, it doesn't seem as bad as it did. I think I can face it if I have a little brandy now and then.'

'I'll see to that myself, Mrs. Pemberton. And now let's go and meet Blakeley, and hear what news he's brought.'

Eight

THE air-strip bisected a small depression, a natural shelf with a gently declining floor, in the vast southern slope of the valley, that elsewhere fell steeply from its high ridge to the edge of a volcanic fault from which the descent to the river Maipani was in many places precipitous. West of the landing-ground the mountainside rose gradually to an open, barren declivity, seamed by small, dry water-courses, and about three miles away relapsed into a rough glen down which ran a high-land stream. It was here that the visionaries of Samarai's apocalypse—the savagely simple believers in the aeroplane from heaven—had settled and established themselves in crude lodgings woven of broad leaves and branches. The stench of their habitation filled the glen, and to the noise of intermittent drumming and the constant clamour of human voices was added the squealing and grunting of several hundred pigs. Every believer who could afford it had brought a pig, and those who were ostentatious in their faith had brought two or three. The pigs, which were small, fierce, and noisy creatures, were more than provender—their owners had carried bags of sago for their daily fare—and there was devotion in their slaughter as well as the promise of a good meal. A few were killed every night, but the greater number were reserved for the ritual feast that would conclude the vigil.

Beyond and above the glen an attempt had been made to prepare a landing-ground for the heavenly aeroplane. Two or three hundred small and wind-shrivelled trees had been felled, and here and there, with prodigious labour, an obtrusive rock had been excavated and trundled away. The ground so cleared was evidence of a faith that could command willing labour, but it offered no hope of a successful landing to any human pilot or a machine that had been built within the limitations of earthly skill. The work they had done, however, had given the tribesmen a livelier interest in air-traffic, and as soon as they heard in the clouds above them the engine-hum of the approaching courier, a couple of hundred abandoned their labour and ran to watch Blakeley's arrival.

They ran, over rough and broken ground, with remarkable speed. They moved with the effortless strength of deer, and because Blakeley made a much wider circuit than Morland had anticipated, several score of them arrived at the air-strip in time to see him land.

They did not resemble the noble savage of romantic legend. They were, for the most part, of humble stature, and many of repellent appearance. The men were naked but for a few feathers and streaks of paint and a dingy red cotton bag between their legs; the women, unpainted, wore nothing but a girdle of tape and a strand of tape that divided their buttocks. Their eyes were alert, their mouths agape; their common expression was sullen and suspicious, their common response to the stimulus of anything strange or unexpected a snarl of wary defiance. The sombre and burnished skin of the men rippled and flowed with the flexure of their muscles, the breasts of the younger women were sharply pointed: porcine dugs. The air about them was distasted with a feral smell.

The aeroplane from Port Philip came out of the clouds a few hundred feet above the edge of the precipice, and on a downward slant flew swiftly along the line of the valley. When it was nearly opposite the air-strip it banked so steeply that from the west the whole of its wing-span could be seen, and then, flattening in its flight, it charged the hillside as if intent on destruction. But it cleared the lip of the land and touched down, bouncing twice, on the uphill runway, and ran to the break in the strip, beyond which it taxied almost smoothly towards the Rest House; and turned in its tracks to face the gorge again.

From the one side came the savages, running silently to surround and gape at the machine, and from the other, with a slower pace, Morland and Kershawe and the Pembertons: she with a hand on Morland's arm, shrinking from the wild approach of the pagans. A few constables kept an open space about the machine, an inviolable area round Morland and his companions; but Mrs. Pemberton, to her embarrassment, attracted almost as much interest as the aeroplane. The nakedness of the staring women infected her with shame, and drawing apart from Morland she walked alone.

A sliding window was opened in the transparent nose of the aeroplane, and through the gap a noble visage smiled, a hand came out and waved benignly.

'My God!' said Kershawe, 'it's the old man himself! What in hell does he want here?'

Morland, stiffening like a sheepdog when a neighbour's collie jumps the fence, went slowly forward, and the Sultan cried cheerfully, 'Good morning to you all! Can you look after a couple of visitors for a week?'

Morland, in a voice that was quite expressionless, said, 'Good morning, sir.'

'Blakeley's a very good pilot,' said the Sultan, 'but I don't really like his aeroplane. This door's loose, and when we canted over just now I thought I was going to fall out.'

The door was opened, and Blakeley pushed out an aluminium ladder. Slowly the Sultan descended, and simultaneously in the after part of the machine, the somewhat distraught, the slightly disarrayed figure of Mrs. Nottingham appeared at another door.

Kershawe, muttering incoherently, turned away to hide his anger, but Mrs. Pemberton ran towards her and with grateful hands welcomed another woman to Maipani. 'I'm so glad to see you!' she exclaimed. 'Are you going to stay?'

'I'm afraid I shall have to,' said Mrs. Nottingham, and looked with extreme disfavour at a score of naked savages who, stooping beneath the tail of the aeroplane, had arrived in time to gape at her descent. 'We've had a very rough flight,' she said, 'and I've had to share my quarters with two servants, several bags of seed-potatoes, and some rolls of barbed wire.'

'Are you all right, my dear?' asked the Sultan, ducking beneath a wing.

'Far from it,' she said.

'But look at the view! Isn't it superb? And as soon as we've got our luggage out and had a drink, you'll enjoy it as much as I do. My dear Mrs. Pemberton, what a pleasure to see you again! Have you lost your heart to Maipani?—And Morland, my dear fellow: you realize, of course, that this is a very important day?'

'I'm not sure what you mean, sir.'

'But you ought to! It's my birthday, Morland, and down in Port Philip they'll be firing a salute. But last night, quite suddenly, I decided to come and celebrate it here. We had exhausted every spring and source of gossip in Port Philip. We went to Te Aku for a day or two, and I met some old friends who entertained me very well. But Mrs. Nottingham disliked it, and one has to admit that where the world produces wealth—oil or coal or that enchanting metal which nowadays we never see—it produces nothing else to make life agreeable. So I conceived the happy project to come here and see my old protégé Samarai, let Mrs. Nottingham enjoy the scenery, and amuse ourselves among our simple highlanders. Are they behaving themselves?'

'They've broken regulations by leaving their own territories without permission, but there's been no fighting. And I don't anticipate any serious disturbance.'

'Neither do I, or I wouldn't have come.—How are you, Mr. Pemberton? I hope you've made some interesting discoveries. —Elizabeth, my dear, look at the shadows on the hill over there. And you see that little village? It would be no more than six miles away if you were a buzzard, but if you were a constable or a district officer it would take you all day to walk there, and you would be very tired when you arrived. Our savage highlanders are really very timorous, and except on rare occasions take some trouble to avoid each other.'

Mrs. Nottingham had recovered her equanimity and repaired her *maquillage*. She said, 'I've never seen such enormous clouds before, and I had no idea that an aeroplane could land in a place like this. If I had known, I certainly wouldn't have come.'

Morland had been surprised and angered by the Sultan's arrival. To him, as to the less disciplined Kershawe, the Sultan's decision to take a holiday on the coast of a crisis was a wanton aggravation of his anxiety, an example of total irresponsibility. But after sixteen years of departmental experience and four years' personal association with His Highness he had learnt to hide his feelings, and now, though not without effort, he showed a mannerly interest in Mrs. Nottingham's criticism and told her, 'Before the air-strip was made we had an eight days' march from the coast.'

'And you prefer,' she said, 'to be frightened for an hour than exhausted for a week?'

'Decidedly so.'

'Mrs. Nottingham,' said the Sultan, 'is frightened of nothing. She is quite fearless.'

'If that's what you believe,' she said, 'I'm a better actress than I supposed.'

'You are better in all things than your modesty can possibly tell you,' he said; and then, his voice changing sharply, 'Do tell your policemen to be more careful with my luggage. That's a case of champagne they're throwing about, and those parcels, that don't appear to be of any value, are very important: they're ice. They ought to be taken to the Rest House at once, and put in the coolest corner that can be found.'

Morland watched with increasing disfavour the unloading of the Sultan's baggage. As well as the parcels of ice, wrapt in dripping sackcloth, there were several hampers of food and cases of wine, and in addition to the five large suitcases that he and Mrs. Nottingham had thought necessary for their comfort were two unwieldy bedding-rolls belonging to the cook and chief steward of the yacht *White Heather*, who had accompanied their master. They, in respectable white clothes, stood a little apart from the watchful throng. They were disdainful of the pagans, they were superior to the constabulary, and within the hierarchy of the Sultanate they held positions of established privilege. They gave no help to the unloading of the cargo other than little brusque commands to be careful with such-and-such, and put so-and-so there.

Morland looked for Kershawe to tell him to arrange the transport of the baggage to the Rest House, but Kershawe, too angry to trust his discretion, had gone to Tom Penny's bungalow. Penny, his trade ruined, philosophically spent his days shooting green pigeon, drinking Japanese bottled beer, and reading old copies of the *Sydney Morning Herald* which, in his normal routine, he seldom bothered to remove from their wrappers. The arrival of the aeroplane had not dislodged him from the fascination of out-of-date news and the comfort of a solitary glass.

Though it was beneath his dignity to do so, Morland gave orders to take the Sultan's luggage to the Rest House, and the

Sultan, waving benignly to the savages, who made no response, said to the Pembertons, 'Come along and have a drink, and then you'll tell me about everything you've seen.' He turned after a few yards, and shouted, 'You're coming, Blakeley, aren't you?'

'Yes, sir, I'll be with you in a couple of minutes,' said Blakeley. 'But don't open a bottle on my account.'

He was a small, thin, fair-haired man whom the casual observer would hardly notice. He had no gift of words, no appetite for fame, and praise of his outstanding skill embarrassed him. He piloted his aeroplane from Port Philip to rough and narrow, remote and high-pitched landing-fields among the mountains of Namua, and found in difficult, cloud-girt navigation and the control of his machine against unruly air-currents the same sort of satisfaction as a steeplechase rider takes in a brave horse, a succession of fences, and the mastery of his own hands and mind. In a country where many drank too much, he drank nothing; and his emotional life was placidly governed by a long-term engagement to a teacher of Latin in a girls' school in Melbourne.

After a few minutes he followed the Sultan and his party to the Rest House, and arrived in time to hear His Highness lauding, with a nice assumption of solemnity, the benefit to bodily health and the mind's equipoise of a glass of champagne taken early in the morning. One of the bags of ice had been opened, and a bottle pushed in to cool. The wine, said the Sultan, should be so chilled that its bubbles seem, to a sensitive person, like an April breeze escaping from the last frost of winter. 'But this morning,' he added, 'we can hardly wait so long. I'll give it ten minutes in the ice and apologize for imperfection.'

Morland refused to drink, Blakeley had lime-squash and a ham sandwich to sustain him on his return flight. Pemberton, surcharged with news of the apocalypse and views of the native mind, was encouraged by champagne to unload his burden, and found in the Sultan a willing listener. Mrs. Nottingham and Mrs. Pemberton, drawn together by isolation, took Blakeley into their company and talked to him of their sensations in the clouded air with the sudden familiarity of women talking to a doctor who has seen them through some strange and enervating malady. They discovered the gaiety of convalescence, and Blakeley, responding as blandly as if he were indeed a fashionable gynaecologist, assured them that he had never had passengers who behaved better. Passengers or patients? It was all one, they were united in the transient intimacy that both may enjoy with their conductor. And Morland, watching and listening, sourly recognized—what he had often seen before, without liking it—the Sultan's ability, in almost any circumstances, to release the party spirit, the bottle-imp of geniality.

Then Blakeley said he must go, before the mountain air grew rough, and Mrs. Nottingham decided to unpack, and Mrs. Pemberton offered to help her. Pemberton sat down to write his journal, and the others went with Blakeley, and beside the aeroplane found Kershawe and Penny and Sergeant Kula of the Constabulary standing among its unloaded, miscellaneous cargo of seed-potatoes, barbed wire, paint and nails, window glass and axe-helves and canned fruit, that had filled such space as had not been needed for the Sultan's luggage. Kershawe, saluting the Sultan, exchanged a few words with him, but curtly, without even a pretence of interest, and turning to Blakeley said, 'I can't find the new batteries I asked for. Didn't you bring them?'

'I saw them put aboard last night,' said Blakeley, 'but some of the cargo had to be taken out this morning, to make room for what the Sultan needed.'

'A case or two of wine,' said the Sultan. 'That was all I brought, in addition to a suitcase. You can't call that excessive?'

'We weren't overloaded, sir. I made sure of that,' said Blakeley.

'But to keep within your load you dumped my batteries,' said Kershawe angrily, 'and now we'll be out of touch with Port Philip for another week.'

'Can't you re-charge your old ones?'

'They're as dead as dry bones. I asked for new ones three weeks ago, and I told you last Friday I couldn't wait any longer.'

'I'm sorry—'

'It's my fault,' said the Sultan. 'Quite obviously it's my fault, and I must take the blame. I am truly sorry, Kershawe, and I only hope I can offer you compensation for any inconvenience I may cause. We'll be without communication for a week, but I brought with me some of the older amenities of life.'

'Before the week's over we may need wireless more than champagne,' said Kershawe.

'When I first came to New Brabant,' said Morland sharply, 'we had neither one nor the other, and never felt the need of them.' Tactfully he led the Sultan aside, and minimizing the value of Kershawe's opinion, explained how it differed from his own. Kershawe was a good officer, he said, and doubtless his lack of judgment would be repaired in time. . . .

'You bloody clot!' said Kershawe to Blakeley. 'Why the hell didn't you keep an eye on what they were doing?'

'You didn't see the bloody circus this morning,' said Blakeley, as hot as Kershawe. 'Luggage all over the place, champagne and whisky and a hundredweight of ice, and that damned woman saying, "Take care of my suitcase! Don't put it on the barbed wire!" and the Sultan going about like Buddha eating Devonshire cream, telling everyone he wasn't going to be a scrap of trouble, and half the hangers-on sulking, half of them panicking. Christ, if you'd been there you'd have come away without your pants.'

'It's all right for you, you can make excuses and go back to Port Philip. But we've got to stay here.'

'I'm sorry, Kershawe. I told you before, and I'll say it again. But I'm not to blame. And I'll bring your batteries next week.'

'You'd better. I don't want any passengers, I just want batteries.'

'Well, shut up and forget 'em till next Friday,' said Tom Penny, and clapped him hard on the back. 'It won't do you any good going about with a chip on your shoulder, and what the hell! We don't want to talk to those leather bottoms down in Port Philip. They never listen anyway.'

Penny had kept in the background when he saw Morland and the Sultan coming: he had reason to avoid the Sultan, and he seldom talked with Morland, whom he distrusted. But he was fond of Kershawe and often showed his liking by roughly abusing him. Within very narrow limits Penny was a serious man, and he seriously believed that Kershawe had a natural virtue—in the older sense of the word—which an English upbringing, an English education, had regrettably obscured. He had done what he could to abrade and wear away the unfortunate veneer by rowdy criticism, and Kershawe, whose nature was equally combative, usually replied with pungent comment on Australian levellers; they got on very well together. Now, after facing Penny for a moment with as much anger as he had confronted Blakeley, he shrugged his shoulders and said, 'All right, let it go. We'll manage, I expect. But I still say you're a clot, Blakeley.'

'I do my best,' said Blakeley. 'I'll bring your batteries next week, but don't blame me if I forget your mail. And now I'm going.'

He shouted to the Sultan, who with Morland had turned about and was approaching them again, 'Goodbye, sir. I'll pick you up next Friday.'

'Goodbye, goodbye, my dear fellow! And thank you so much!'

'Has he got the out-going mail?' shouted Morland.

'It's all aboard, sir.'

Blakeley climbed in and started his engine. The propeller slowly turned, and cut a shuddering circle from the enclosing air. The engine roared, diminished its harsh cry, and slowly picked it up again. The pagans, their brief interest in the aeroplane long since exhausted, had returned to their populous glen, and the runway was open. Sergeant Kula and a plump constable pulled away the chocks, and after a moment in which it seemed to be breathing deeply the aeroplane raced down the rough slope, bounced where the strip broke in the middle, and was airborne. It cleared the edge of the gorge, and banking steeply against the loom of the opposite mountain turned to the west. It levelled on its course and rose steadily into the hot blue sky.

'I wish I could do that,' said the Sultan, and turning to Penny held out his hand. 'The last time we met, at the bar of the Ocean Hotel in Port Philip, you told me that if only I had had the good luck to be born on the banks of the Murrumbidgee I might have become a worthy and useful man. Is that still your opinion?'

'No, sir,' said Penny. 'I mean, yes, sir, after a fashion. I was drunk at the time, but I wasn't trying to be offensive.'

'Nor were you. We had a very enjoyable conversation which I, perhaps, remember better than you. But don't let that worry you. I've had innumerable conversations with countless people of which I can't remember a word, and don't want to.'

'If you ask me,' said Penny, 'we all talk too much.'

'We do indeed,' said the Sultan, 'and evolution is to blame. Our tongues have inherited the strength of our lost tails, and with great ingenuity we often use them to swing from branches which aren't there.—Are you still upset about those batteries, Kershawe?'

'I'm not really worried, sir.' He turned to Morland and said, 'But Penny's been telling me something about that boy, Samarai's boy, that you ought to hear.'

'What is it? Village gossip or something definite?'

'Penny's heard the same story that Pemberton was told; or something very like it. But he knows more than Pemberton.'

Nine

TOM PENNY, sitting on the veranda of Kershawe's bungalow —the Sultan on one side, Morland and Kershawe on the other—looked happily at the pair of bottles in front of him, and with comfort in his voice, with the philosophy of a man who acknowledges his debt to life and spends his credit as it comes, said to His Highness, 'There are three things happen, sir, after you pass the age of fifty. The girls lose their looks, the police become schoolboys in uniform, and bottles get smaller and smaller. There's nothing you can do about the cops and the popsies, but you can defeat the malignity of little bottles by taking two at a time. And that's how I maintain my youth and high spirits, sir.'

The Sultan had insisted on being told immediately all that was known of Samarai's adoption, or apparent adoption, of an unknown boy from across the border, and on their way to the bungalow Morland had repeated with unconcealed impatience, as a credulous traveller's discovery, Pemberton's story that the boy was to be sacrificed in some improbable ritual. Pemberton, he said, was too willing to believe anything that would add colour to his investigation.

The Sultan made no comment, and they climbed the steps to Kershawe's veranda. Kershawe called his houseboy and told him to bring beer, but only Penny wanted to drink; and now, pouring a full glass with a careful hand, he leaned above the table like a red sun threatening to suck dry a wayside pool by the mere heat of his countenance.

He drank and said, 'I've got this advantage, that both my

boys are natives of Maipani. The others here are coast boys, and so's Oala. They don't pick up the gossip of the place like my boys, and because I haven't got an official position my boys aren't afraid to talk. My word! I wish I could make 'em shut up sometimes.'

'What have they been telling you?'

'About this boy of Samarai's, and about Samarai too. He's been talking big the last couple of days.'

'What is he saying?' asked Morland.

'Have you ever seen them kill a boy and bring him back to life again?'

Morland made a gesture of distaste—a gesture that combined a chairman's disapproval of some tedious amendment with a maiden lady's recoil from impoliteness—and answered, 'It's hardly likely that anyone would attempt such a thing in my presence, or that I should permit it. I have, I confess, seen a village sorcerer pretend to kill a dog, and then revive it. But there was a trick in it, of course. The dog was only stunned.'

'How long did it live?' asked Penny.

'A day or two, I think. I can't remember.'

'They don't ever live more than a few days,' said Penny. 'There's no trick about it, Morland, except the trick of doing exactly what they say they're going to do.'

'Have you seen it?' asked the Sultan.

'Too true,' said Penny. 'My oath! I'll never forget it, though it was more than thirty years ago, when I first came to New Brabant. I was seventeen at the time, and we were washing for gold on the Sipi. The only other river I'd ever seen was the Murrumbidgee, and it was usually dry. But the Sipi came down with a roar between high stone cliffs, and the natives were as wild as the scenery. But we got on with them all right, and the girls were a lot better-looking than these she-goats up here. That's how I came to see what was going on, and hear what it meant. It was a boy of fourteen or fifteen they killed, and after they fetched him back to life they never left him alone till they heard what he had to say. He didn't say much for a day or two, but the third night he told them they had to attack another village. That was what they wanted to do, but they couldn't make up their minds. It was a bigger village than their own, and he told them the proper way to go about it, which was just the opposite way to what you'd think. And he told them the right time to attack, and the attack was successful. And then he died.'

'How did they kill him?' asked Morland. 'In the first place, I mean.'

'The sorcerer hit him on the back of the neck with a bloody great club.'

'And stunned him!' said Morland. 'He only stunned him.'

'If you've only been stunned,' said Penny, 'you don't walk about carrying your head like this.'

He pushed back his chair, with a shrill complaint from the planks of the new floor, and stood up and faced the others. He let his head droop sideways and fall to his right shoulder in a grotesque and horrible position. He had a long neck and its muscles were uncommonly flexible for a man of his age. His head lay on his shoulder as if his neck had been broken, as if the column of his spine had been snapped and could no longer support the weight of it. His eyes half-closed and his mouth slackly open, he walked a little way with a tottering, stiff, unbalanced gait; then suddenly resuming his normal bearing, he returned to the table and drank another glass of beer.

'That's how the boy looked,' he said, 'and that's the way he went about for the next couple of days.'

'I saw them do it to a dog,' said Morland uneasily. 'It's the same trick essentially.'

'You'll have a chance to check up before long,' said Penny. 'This boy's going to be sacrificed three days from now.'

'Pemberton spoke about three days,' said Kershawe, 'but according to his story the boy's going to come to life again after three days.'

'I know what my boys told me, and Pemberton—well, Pemberton doesn't live in Namua. He just comes here to write a book about it.'

'I daresay Pemberton made a mistake,' said the Sultan, 'but you're in danger of making another. Don't be misled by "three days". It doesn't necessarily mean seventy-two hours. It often means nothing more definite than "sometime soon".'

'And the whole story,' said Morland, 'is as unreliable as their notion of time. I don't believe a word of it. Samarai isn't the man to commit murder and face the consequence of murder. I know him. He isn't a stupid man, he's a calculating man. He knows perfectly well what the cost of killing that boy would be —and what could he gain by it? Nothing at all.'

'Everyone who took part in the sacrifice, everyone who stood round and watched it, would be committed to him,' said Kershawe. 'They would all be guilty, and that would give him an even stronger hold over them.'

'That's right,' said Penny. 'It's going to be a damned sight more dangerous for us if he kills the boy. But how are you going to stop him? You don't like shooting, do you?'

'I do not,' said Morland. 'And so long as I'm here to prevent it, there'll be no shooting.'

'There's no other way,' said Penny.

'No,' said the Sultan, and borrowing matches from Kershawe, lighted a cigar. 'There is no other way.'

He had taken very little part in the discussion, but followed it with a grave attention—he had watched with frowning interest Penny miming the broken-necked boy—and now in a tone of voice that surprised the others, who had never heard him speak in sorrow, he said, 'I thought this sort of thing had stopped entirely. Even in our wildest parts.'

'I've never heard of a case for thirty years,' said Penny.

'It was my father who devised the law that put an end to it,' said the Sultan. 'That put an end to it for thirty years, perhaps. My father did a great deal to stamp out the worst kinds of sorcery; and fortunately he had a sense of humour.—Remarkable for a man in his position, wasn't it?—He realized that a sacrifice of this sort couldn't be put down by charging the sorcerer with murder, because the punishment for murder, a couple of years in prison, was too light to be a deterrent. So there was no reference, in the new law he made, to the killing of the victim, there was merely a penalty for restoring the victim to life. The penalty of death. And the practice, in consequence, fell into abeyance.'

Morland, a little angrily, said, 'But you don't really believe that a sorcerer could revive a man he had killed?'

'I believe, and very firmly believe, that sorcerers should be prevented from doing anything at all. No one who has lived in these mountains—no one who has lived with an open mind anywhere between the mountains of Assam and the northern deserts of Australia—can deny the existence of sorcery, and though I'm not prepared to define the scope and reach of the sorcerer's power, I take my stand against it. Quite dogmatically, and on very narrow ground. On English ground, Morland. I object to it because it's unfair, because it isn't playing the game. It's a detestable practice in all its manifestations, and if you have evidence that Samarai is proposing to sacrifice this boy you talk about, then I go so far as to say you ought to shoot him out of hand.'

Kershawe and Penny, little noises of approval grumbling in their throats, nodded their agreement; but Morland in a high-pitched voice declared, 'You're being extraordinarily inconsistent, sir! A few years ago, when I wanted to deport him, you gave him asylum; but now, when the only way to avoid trouble and save bloodshed is to refrain from any sort of violence, you tell me to go out and kill him!'

'Three years ago, when I gave him asylum,' said the Sultan, 'the situation was entirely different. Samarai, at that time, was committing no criminal offence. He was merely inventing a new religion, and I wanted to hear about it. I myself haven't the advantage of piety, but I'm sure there is nothing more important than religion, and anyone who shows a talent for it should be encouraged.—Give me a light, Kershawe. My cigar's gone out.—Samarai, unfortunately, had very little talent, and I found his creed meagre and unconvincing, his ritual vulgar. It is, of course, very difficult to invent a really good religion.'

'What's going to happen to him,' asked Penny, 'when his aeroplane doesn't come?'

'That's what we've got to prepare for!' exclaimed Morland. 'It isn't fighting them, it's feeding them that's going to be our problem. There'll be no real difficulty till all the excitement's died away and they know they've been deluded and misled. They won't admit it, to begin with. They'll put up with hunger, they'll deny their disappointment, they'll get lank and sullen, they'll be angry and melancholy before they give in. Their pride will be hurt, they'll be as tender as children who've been scolded and beaten. And we'll have to nurse them back to health. That's going to be our job and our trial, and that's all I'm worrying about.'

'If they've blood on their hands, if Samarai kills the boy, they won't take disappointment so quietly,' said Kershawe. 'If they get worked-up to that extent, hunger won't quell them.'

'Indeed,' said the Sultan, 'I think you will have to grasp the nettle, Morland.—But here is our charming Mrs. Pemberton coming to see us, and we mustn't say anything to frighten her. Only remember that in the long run there is nothing more dangerous than letting a law be broken with impunity.'

Mrs. Pemberton, a little breathless, climbed the steps and said, 'I hope you don't mind me coming, it's William's fault really. He went off without telling me why, he wouldn't even stay till he'd had his lunch, and I thought perhaps something was happening.'

'Something has happened,' said the Sultan. 'You have saved me from the tedium of a very solemn discussion. Now sit down and tell me where William's gone.'

'I was writing a letter,' she said, 'and I heard him outside talking to Oala. William spends nearly all his time with him. Oala comes to see him twice a day, because William gives him money—'

'I ought to have known it,' said Kershawe. 'I'll soon put a stop to that.'

'You mustn't incriminate Mrs. Pemberton,' said the Sultan. 'Now what was Oala saying?'

'I don't know,' she said. 'Even when he's talking English I can't understand him. But William seemed to be rather excited, so I went out and spoke to him, and he told me to have my lunch and go to sleep, because he mightn't be back before dark. That's all he would tell me, and then he went off with Oala. Over the hill towards that valley where the savages are.'

'Someone has started another wild rumour,' said Morland contemptuously, 'and he's gone to chase it.'

'You don't think he's running into danger?'

'No, of course not,' said the Sultan. 'I shall walk over there myself this afternoon.'

'I don't think you should, sir,' said Kershawe. 'I'm going, but I'm well known, and they won't pay much attention to me.

But they'd pay attention to you—they might get excited—and that would be a disadvantage to us. To Pemberton and me. They wouldn't tell us anything.'

'It's your district, of course.'

'I'll be grateful, sir, if you'll keep in the background.'

'I am going to make a determined effort to have a talk with Samarai,' said Morland. 'He has avoided me for the last few days—'

'And he'll avoid you today,' said Penny. 'He isn't going to talk to you any more, and the sooner you realize that the better.'

Mrs. Pemberton, looking from one to another with the tautly wide eyes of a lost child, said, 'I wish I'd gone back to Port Philip with Mr. Blakeley.'

'Surely you don't want to leave us?' said the Sultan. 'You're not as unhappy as that, are you?'

'I'm frightened,' she said.

'But of what? You're among friends, Mrs. Pemberton.'

'Of everything,' she said. 'Of the place itself, this horrid little shelf on the mountain that could slip down into the gorge at any moment, and the people with their murders and their witchcraft and their naked bodies. I never knew there were people so utterly savage—not in our world.'

'But are they so different?' asked the Sultan. 'They are, I admit, more ingenuous than Europeans or Americans, but are they really worse? They are very credulous, they are fond of dancing and making a noise, they are frequently unhappy and quite unable to discover why. They are easily amused—they have a remarkable fund of improper stories—and they dislike work, if work is prolonged. Sometimes the problems of life perplex them beyond endurance, and then they relieve their feelings in a little violence. But so do Europeans and Americans. No, my dear, there's not much difference between

113

the people of civilization and our simple highlanders, except the darker skins you see here; which they can't conceal because they have no clothes to cover them.'

'I'm not frightened of Europeans, or even Americans,' said Mrs. Pemberton, 'but I am frightened of these people. And I wish I were in Port Philip.'

'To me,' said the Sultan, 'Maipani has often seemed a haven of refuge. I have enjoyed the illusion of freedom here, and I know that I am perfectly safe.'

'Too right,' said Penny.

'Tom Penny agrees, and his experience of life has been rich and various. Isn't that so, Tom?'

'My word!' said Penny. 'I've been in tougher spots in Sydney and Melbourne than ever I've seen in the islands.'

'Isn't that reassuring? And to complete your comfort it's nearly time for lunch.—You realize, don't you, that I expect you all to dine with me tonight?'

'This is hardly the occasion for a dinner-party, sir.'

'It is my birthday, Morland.'

'So you told me.'

'And I don't intend to let the son of a village sorcerer interfere with the enjoyment I have promised myself: enjoyment, I hope, that we shall all share equally. You're not going to be unfriendly and refuse my invitation, are you?'

'It will be an honour,' said Morland stiffly.

'And you, Kershawe? Are you free, Tom?'

'Thank you, sir.'

'I'll be there,' said Penny. 'Too right!'

'At eight o'clock, then. Now come along, Mrs. Pemberton, and let's see what there is for lunch.'

The sky, now almost cloudless, was already drained of colour by the sun. The air was still, and the heat intense. The unpainted railing of the veranda was as hot as a dinner-plate, and Penny's bald head was beaded with sweat as if he had just come in out of the rain. The great hills that enclosed the valley had receded, as it seemed, into a glassy distance, and their rougher slopes looked like faded brown velvet. The prisoners who had been working in the gardens were now sleeping in the shuttered heat of the jail, and the landscape was untenanted but for the white-clad figures of the Sultan and Mrs. Pemberton walking slowly uphill to the Rest House. He walked easily, with a bold and upright carriage, and she with a pretty dependence leaned upon his arm.

'A dinner-party!' said Morland angrily. 'He tells me to take action against Samarai, and then settles down to enjoy a birthday feast!'

'It'll pass the time,' said Penny, 'and I want to meet his girl friend. Do you think she'll be in full evening-dress? Bare shoulders and a bit of a glimpse when she leans forward? My word!'

'Oh, be quiet, Penny. He's so damnably irresponsible.'

'I don't care so long as he doesn't come out and upset them this afternoon,' said Kershawe. 'They might be like sheep when a strange dog comes into the field; or they might mob him. I don't know.'

'Is lunch ready?' asked Morland.

'When you want it, sir.'

'Did Blakeley bring any mail?'

'Yes, there was a bag for you. I put it in your room.'

'Why didn't you tell me? There may be letters that should have been answered at once.'

'I'm sorry, sir, but you didn't ask for the mail. You went off with the Sultan.'

'And he,' said Morland bitterly, 'so fills the view when he comes that you can't think of anything else. Oh, why the devil did he come? And where are those letters?'

Ten

THE Rest House, designed by an architect in the Namuan Public Works Department, was a simple structure that could give accommodation and sparse comfort to eight people. It consisted of four bedrooms, with a bathroom between each pair, that enclosed a central hall which served as the dining-room. Like the other buildings in Maipani it stood on stilts above the ground, and was surrounded by a broad veranda. The doors that led into the hall, or dining-room, from the front and back verandas were merely wooden frames covered by mosquito-proof wire gauze; and strong springs shut them, after every one who went through, with a loud, disturbing bang. Behind the house was a smaller building of the same sort in which there was a large and well-found kitchen, and meagre quarters for half a dozen servants.

The Sultan and Mrs. Nottingham occupied the two rooms on the left of the entrance, and in the front room, in the late afternoon, Mrs. Nottingham and Mrs. Pemberton sat amidst a finery of silk and taffeta, of transparent stockings and pale chiffons, that adorned the bare appointments of the chamber with rich and delicate incongruity. It was furnished, according to government specification, with two single beds of black-enamelled iron, two wooden chairs, a varnished wardrobe and a chest of drawers on which stood a looking-glass in a mahogany frame, and a washstand carrying two large china basins and a jug; but on one of the beds lay three evening frocks, white and lilac and pale green, and within the open wardrobe hung the softness and colour of other garments. Scents and cosmetics stood on the chest of drawers, whose drawers were ill-fitting and would not open easily nor could be closed without anger, and the slowly turning ceiling-fan circulated the odours of feminine luxury.

The two ladies were lightly clad—Mrs. Nottingham's dressing-gown was white silk, Mrs. Pemberton's a chequered cotton—but though dressed for comfort their expression was serious, their minds were gravely engaged. Choice ranged from side to side, from taffeta to chiffon, and decision hovered in the balance.

'I think,' said Mrs. Nottingham, 'you had better take the white one. Try it on again.'

Obediently Mrs. Pemberton put off her dressing-gown, and holding up her slim arms entered the dress, which Mrs. Nottingham held open for her, as if it were a life-belt. It fell to her feet, and she clutched it to her bosom. 'But it drops right off me!' she cried.

'Hold it,' said Mrs. Nottingham, and regarded her with a judicious, measuring eye. 'We can sew a dart under each arm, and a couple at the waist, and it will fit very well and suit you too. You have pretty shoulders,' she added for encouragement.

'But it's too long.'

'I'll turn up the hem, that's not difficult.'

Mrs. Pemberton tilted the small looking-glass and stood away from it to find a partial image of her borrowed splendour. She twisted her body, she patted and pulled, and said with a deep respect in her voice, 'It's a lovely frock. You are being kind to me.'

'I'm so grateful to you for being here. A week in this God-forsaken place with nothing but male conversation to listen to would drive me mad. With you here I may just be able to endure it.'

'It never occurred to me that anyone would dress for dinner in Maipani.'

'It's the Sultan's birthday, you must remember that. And in any case, a man who likes to see his women well dressed deserves all the encouragement we can give him.'

'William knows nothing about clothes. He just thinks they're something I ought to economize on.'

'What wicked nonsense! Now take it off, and I'll go to work on it. I'm a good dressmaker, I've had to be.'

Mrs. Pemberton put on her dressing-gown again, and Mrs. Nottingham laid the white frock on the unoccupied bed. Mrs. Pemberton threaded a needle, and Mrs. Nottingham with a pair of small scissors unpicked a seam.

'I've suffered from poverty in my time,' she said, 'and I've suffered from thrift. And I know which I resented more. There are few things more infuriating than a wealthy man with a thrifty mind.'

'But William isn't wealthy.'

'You ought to look for someone who is. Have you threaded that needle?'

Mrs. Pemberton was shocked by the suggestion that marriage could be regarded as a stepping-stone to a better marriage; but not so deeply shocked that she could not laugh at it. She made some trifling remark to hide her embarrassment, another to show her amusement; and was interrupted by the older woman.

'Do stop calling me *Mrs. Nottingham*! My name is Elizabeth, and the sooner you get used to it the more comfortable we shall be. Has your husband come back yet?'

'No, not yet. But everyone has told me there's nothing to worry about, so I try not to look worried because I don't want to hear it again.'

'He'll be all right. He is, I imagine, the sort that escapes mishap by sheer insensitivity. There's a lot of men like that.'

'He's clever at his own work, and quite sensitive about people who aren't civilized. He pays far more attention to what these horrid cannibals tell him than to anything I say. He respects their opinions, but mine don't interest him at all.'

'What are his other weaknesses?'

'He can't bear to be wrong. He's very proud—if that's a weakness?'

'It gives you a point of attack. Try to undermine his confidence, to begin with. Let him think you're on the point of running off with someone. Then he'll treat you more seriously.'

'He wouldn't believe me. He wouldn't think it possible that I could prefer anyone else; or that anyone else would prefer me.'

'He would, if you went about it in the right way. It's remarkable how many people can be shaken if you threaten them with the loss of something—a house or a job, a woman or a reputation—even though they're already tired of it and wouldn't feel out of pocket if it vanished.'

'I really don't know much about men. I've only been married a year, and at the university they're all so wrapped-up in their work and their classes; they don't seem interested in anything else. And I've never been abroad till now. I don't know nearly as much as you. You've travelled a lot, haven't you?'

'Always in the wrong direction, unfortunately. If you once get east of Cairo it's difficult to stop, and almost impossible to return.'

'Didn't you want to travel?'

'No, indeed! If I'd had my own way I'd never have gone east of Menton or north of Oxford Street.'

'I thought—well, I thought perhaps you wanted to see the world.'

With a movement of her lovely head that looked like a gesture of acquiescence, Mrs. Nottingham bent down to bite a thread. But her teeth snapped sharply on the cotton and her voice grew a little harder, as if to assert her competence in larger affairs than dressmaking, and keep sympathy at a distance.

'I was driven from home by the vulgar calamity of our times,' she said. 'My father was killed in the first war, my husband in the second. The only difference between me and the draggled heroine of a Victorian melodrama was that I hadn't a baby, and I wasn't driven on to the streets. I was driven into the Ritz bar.'

Fascinated by this admission, and balanced uneasily between sympathy and horror, Mrs. Pemberton asked in breathless interest, 'Did you just sit there, and wait till someone spoke to you?'

'No, Emily. The Ritz doesn't encourage behaviour of that sort. But in war time, and just after, there are men—young, old, or middle-aged—who can afford to drink at the Ritz but haven't quite enough assurance to use it as if it were the village pub. And to that sort of man a woman who knows her way about is worth quite a lot.'

'But surely they want you to do more than show them round?'

'Some of them don't want much more. You might be surprised how little. Those inordinate demands that one dreaded are not, in fact, overwhelming. Not as a rule. In a year of marriage you must have discovered for yourself—'

'It isn't quite what I thought it would be.'

'At school, I remember, there was a volume of the *Arabian Nights*, in a French translation, that circulated quietly, and a lot of girls looked forward to life with a sort of enchanted apprehension. But by now, I imagine, they have learnt that the only excessive demands men make are on their patience. They like to be listened to, and they want to be constantly reassured of their importance. Give them confidence, and you'll keep them happy; but don't give them too much, or they'll start to neglect you and presently get up and leave you for something better.'

Emboldened by such talk, and by the sense of familiarity it engendered, Mrs. Pemberton drew a deep breath and asked, 'When did you become a Communist?'

'When I married Gino Tratteanu,' said Mrs. Nottingham. 'He asked me to, and I said yes. It made him happy, and cost me nothing.'

'But do you believe in Communism?'

'Not as he did. He was a good man who knew very little about people as they really are. I spent three years looking after him—I never knew anyone who had so small an instinct for self-preservation—and I enjoyed every day of it. He was very gentle, and curiously cheerful for a man who truly believed that life wasn't worth living.'

'But that isn't what Communists believe?'

'He was a Communist because he believed that Communism required an absolute negation of self, and according to him self-regard and self-assertion were the real cause of our general unhappiness. He was a Buddhist as well as a Communist, and often I couldn't follow his reasoning. But it would have been heartless to dispute it. He was the kindest man I've ever known.'

Out of her depth but unwilling to show it—eager to keep on friendly terms with a woman who knew so much of the world and its dark ideas, and yet had the simplicity and clever fingers to re-fashion an evening frock—Mrs. Pemberton tried to look wise, and said, 'Do you believe that everything we want to do is wrong?'

'No, indeed! I found it possible—possible within a decent conception of honesty—to say I was a Communist because I came to the conclusion that Communism was the only contemporary belief strong enough to create a new hierarchy. You can't have a civilized way of life without an established society, and that means a hierarchy. But there's nothing in the tattered remnants of what-used-to-be that's fit to build one. Only the Communist Party—especially in the Far East—has the seeds of a new aristocracy which, as soon as it becomes hereditary, will re-create a social scale and social values.'

Mrs. Pemberton had often listened to discussion of Communism in the university circles to which her husband had introduced her, and though she had seldom paid much attention to what was said, she felt sure that she had never heard such an argument for it as Mrs. Nottingham had discovered. Gravely she said, 'That's very interesting,' and waited for further explication.

But Mrs. Nottingham began to laugh, and her laughter, which was infrequent, had an unexpected quality. It expressed a charitable amusement, its note was gentle, it was almost maternal in character.

'It was by talking like this,' she said, 'that I shocked poor Leroy. You know about him, of course? Leroy Cooney. He was a dear creature, I was so fond of him, and he was infinitely helpful when I really needed help. He rescued me from the depths of Indo-China, where I was left, after Gino's death, feeling truly desperate. I'll never cease to be grateful to him, but oh, how he irritated me! And one day, when I lost my temper, I told him that what America needed was discipline, and only Communism was big enough to supply it. He got very angry, and still more angry when I said that Communism needed America just as badly as America needed Communism. Feminine influence, I said, with all the elegance of Fifth Avenue behind it, could sell dialectic materialism to the whole world—and what a world they could create between them! And then he went and denounced me to the police. A dear boy, but he'd no sense of humour.'

'Perhaps he lacked confidence,' said Mrs. Pemberton, 'like the men who didn't feel at home in the Ritz.'

'He was like a ship that carries too much sail. He was very good-looking, and full of energy and competence, but he hadn't enough ballast.'

'I wish I knew more about men,' said Mrs. Pemberton with a sigh.

'You will learn,' said Mrs. Nottingham.

'Is the Sultan the same as the others? Has he got any weaknesses?'

'The Sultan,' said Mrs. Nottingham 'is in a class by himself and nothing I've said applies to him. I think he has always been happily convinced that he knows what's right, and I don't suppose he's ever been afraid to do what's wrong. He doesn't approve of self-denial, and he doesn't practise self-delusion except on a rather grand scale. He has his principles, but not so many that they cause him inconvenience, and his conscience is a kind of large intestine: it eliminates from his memory anything that could occasion remorse. He's an aristocrat, but it might be straining the point to call him a gentleman. A hundred years ago he might have become a great man, but the circumstances of today, and a really extraordinary capacity for enjoying himself, have stopped all possibility of that . . . Now try this on again, and I think you'll find it fits very well.'

Mrs. Pemberton stood up and put off her dressing-gown. She held up her delicately rounded, girlish arms, and entered again the social life-belt of a white evening frock.

Eleven

WITH a glass of barley-water on a small table beside him, the Sultan sat on the front veranda reading, in a collected edition of Peacock, *Nightmare Abbey*. The last hour of daylight was richly coloured, and the mountains, now imminent and sharply focused, were enormous but seemed benign. The sky above them was a pellucid veil, the hue of pomegranates, and a distant grove of trees was dark as cucumbers. A vagrant breeze dispelled the heat of the day and fluttered the little plantations of sugar-cane, the vegetable gardens that shone in the level sun like green grapes with a morning bloom upon them. It fluttered the pages of *Nightmare Abbey*, and the Sultan, grateful for its coolness and Peacock's wit, sighed with pleasure.

His pleasure, however, was interrupted by a slow and heavy tread on creaking timbers, and with the irritated, sudden movement of a bull disturbed at pasture he turned to see Morland climbing the steps to the veranda. Morland, in a sweat-darkened, khaki shirt, looked tired and out of humour, and the Sultan subdued his annoyance to make a kindly pretence of welcome. In a dull voice Morland said 'Good evening, sir,' and sat heavily in an opposite chair.

'I'm a little tired,' he said, 'and I'm suspended between two difficulties.'

'You need a drink,' said the Sultan, 'and you'll get it quicker if I fetch it myself. The servants—all I've been able to muster —are busy preparing our dinner. But in addition to my other talents I am an admirable butler.'

He stood up, and ignoring Morland's gesture of dissent—his half-hearted protestation—went indoors and quickly returned with whisky and ice and soda-water.

'Drink that,' he said, 'and tell me how else I can help you.'

Morland, despite his temperate habit, drank his whisky and soda gratefully, and said, 'I must admit I was hoping for that, though in another way it makes it more difficult for me to do what I've got to do.'

'Take your difficulties in the order of their importance,' said the Sultan. 'What have you been doing this afternoon?'

'I went to look for Samarai, and I couldn't find him. I had a rather disturbing experience, and I want to tell you about it exactly as it happened. But I beg you, sir, not to overestimate its importance. It was disconcerting, for a few minutes, but I don't think it meant anything at all.'

'What happened?'

'I had Sergeant Kula with me, and we walked over to that valley where they're all congregated. I spoke to several people —I knew one or two of them—and asked where Samarai was. But they all put on that dumb-ox expression, that look of utter, blank incomprehension, and we couldn't get a word out of them. So we went on, to where a crowd had collected, and found them preparing for a feast.'

'Tonight?' asked the Sultan. 'Are they going to celebrate my birthday too?'

'I'm afraid that's not their intention; but it's an important occasion, whatever it is. There were a couple of hundred pigs, tied to stakes and all squealing like the fury of hell, and the women were gathering brushwood and digging pits. They were nearly all women there—women and boys—and when I tried to talk to them they got angry at once. They surrounded us, and began screaming and shouting. Sergeant Kula has been in the service as long as I have, and he was upset. It wasn't ordinary abuse we got, it was more like the raving of mad women. There was nothing we could do, except clear out; and for a little while I wasn't sure if we could do that. But we managed it, and made a wider circuit to go higher up the hill towards the air-strip they've been clearing. And that did us no good, for a horde of the younger ones, yelping like beagles, came running to cut us off. They didn't pay much attention to me, but if Sergeant Kula had been alone they'd have pulled him down like—well, like beagles pulling down a hare.'

'So very wisely you came home again,' said the Sultan.

'Yes, sir,' said Morland, and finished his drink. 'But I don't want to exaggerate what happened. It may have been nothing more than hysteria. They were all women there—or nearly all—and they were excited by the prospect of a feast and the killing of the pigs. It was very hot, very close and hot, and Sergeant Kula—well, he's a big, handsome fellow. It might well have been mass-hysteria.'

'Poor Sergeant Kula.'

'He was very glad to get away.'

'I'm sure he was. Help yourself to another drink, Morland.'

'No, thank you. I want to stress the fact that I don't attach much importance to what we saw, but I admit the possibility that it may show a turn for the worse in the general temper of the people, and that being so I thought it prudent to take steps to defend ourselves in case some of the men lose their heads. I'm not pretending that's likely to happen, but it may. And so—'

'What have you done?'

'We've got eight or ten thousand sandbags in store. Kershawe wants to bridge the river, and thinks he can make the abutments by filling sandbags with concrete. But in the meantime I propose to use them to fortify the Rest House. There's a gravel-pit behind the hospital that Kershawe opened to patch a soft spot in the air-strip, and I've had the sandbags taken there and I've put the prisoners to work, and most of the police to fill them. I've been shovelling gravel myself for the last hour or two, to set the pace. You know what their notion is of working fast, if they're left to themselves.'

'My dear Morland, that's an admirable project. I commend you most warmly.'

'You don't think I'm being an alarmist, do you? I'm only taking precautions.'

'And very wise ones.'

'I don't anticipate an attack—I think it most unlikely—but there are women here, and just in case those poor devils get excited—'

'You're doing precisely what should be done. When will you start to build our fortifications?'

'Not till after dinner. They'll bring the sandbags up on hand-barrows.'

'If we are to be attacked,' said the Sultan, 'the Rest House is certainly the best place in which to make a stand. We have a good field of fire in front and on both sides, and from the kitchen behind there's a fairly open view. You might, perhaps, use the barbed wire that came in the aeroplane this morning. You could set up a circumference of trip-wire about fifty or sixty yards away.'

'I'll see that's done, sir.'

Morland's fatigue had been medicined by the Sultan's whisky, and he had recaptured most of his usual confidence: it was in some degree a departmental confidence, built on precedent and habit, on the tradition of his service; but largely it was the product of self-satisfaction and pride in his own judgment. It was with great reluctance that he had decided to fortify the Rest House—that he had admitted it was advisable to fortify it—for the decision seemed to impugn his judgment, and might be construed as the effect of his having been frightened by a horde of women. But he had done what he thought should be done, and now, with the Sultan's approval to stiffen him, he began secretly to applaud himself for his strength of mind.

But then he contemplated what he must do next, and felt a recurrence of the uneasiness he always experienced when he had to oppose His Highness on a personal matter. He had little respect for the Sultan's privilege or position, but he had never completely escaped from a small, unwilling admission of the Sultan's innate authority.

The Sultan had been unperturbed by Morland's story. It had, indeed, amused him to think of his stern Adviser surrounded and defeated by a swarm of obscenely hallooing, naked women; and having quickly decided that the measures which Morland proposed for the defence of the Rest House were reasonable and sufficient, his attention had wandered a little. The evening breeze was erratic and now more strongly blowing: his nose caught a vapour from the kitchen, and for a moment he wondered, fretfully, if his cook was showing proper respect for the pheasants he had brought from the cold-storage chamber of the yacht. But then his eye perceived a changing pattern of light on the mountainside, the invasion of lilac, the descent of blue-purple, and when Morland introduced his second theme, his voice, now harshly self-conscious, broke an almost purely æsthetic mood.

'The other thing I have to tell you,' he said, 'is unpleasant for both of us. I've never had a more disagreeable job to do, but it's my duty and I can't avoid it.'

'Take another drink,' said the Sultan. 'Oh yes, I insist! I myself can endure the most staggering blows, but I've often noticed that those who administer them are very susceptible to the impact. So if you are going to be depressing you need a little cushion of alcohol—and there it is. Now tell me your bad news.'

'You're very kind, sir, and I know you won't blame me for what I have to say. The fact is that Blakeley brought in a bag of mail this morning, and I got a letter that's bound to offend you.'

'In the course of years,' said the Sultan, 'I have acquired a remarkable instinct for unpleasant letters. My fingers tingle as soon as I touch them, and I throw them into the waste-paper basket, unopened. Haven't you learnt to do that?'

'I'm not as gifted as you, and I've never had as much freedom. Here it is.'

With the strained and reluctant gesture of one who, with a fireside shovel, stoops to remove a cat's mess from the hearthrug, the Sultan reached for the letter that Morland offered, and Morland, stiffly apologetic, said, 'I should have brought it earlier, but I didn't see my mail till Blakeley had gone, and then I thought the first thing I had to do was to try and find Samarai. And when I came back—'

'You re-read the egregious missive? How I wish people in government offices would learn to write English! They're so pompous that they defeat their own purpose. You can't take them seriously, can you?'

'You can't ignore it, sir.'

'Listen to this,' said the Sultan, and read from the letter: ' "Consideration had already been given to the possibility that a plea might be entered to the effect that as Mrs. Nottingham on the occasion and at the time of the offence was resident, or was shortly to become resident, aboard His Highness the Sultan's yacht, she was not subject to the jurisdiction of the court, but enjoyed extra-territorial privilege of a diplomatic or like nature such as, from time to time, has been claimed by His

Highness the Sultan and his predecessors for persons whom they have admitted, without warrant and by custom unsubstantiated by Parliamentary enactment, to a prescriptive asylum not established by statute. The learned counsel, however, whose opinion on this matter has been solicited, are unanimous in declaring that to the best of their belief and knowledge this plea would have no substance in law . . ." Well, perhaps it wouldn't. But if the fellow was a gentleman— I mean your righteous and oh! so fatuous Governor—he'd have seen it was a damned good excuse for dropping the whole business.'

'There's no intention of doing that. Not now. It did appear, to begin with, that they were looking for a way out. I think H.E. was genuinely anxious not to offend you, sir. And what has happened since then, to make him change his mind, I don't know. Perhaps the Colonial Office has taken a more serious view of the case: when a Communist, or an alleged Communist is involved, it isn't always possible to foresee the official attitude. But they're out for a conviction now: that's obvious.'

'And they have sent you a warrant, have they?'

'Yes, sir.'

'What are you going to do with it?'

'Here, in Maipani, nothing at all.'

'Good for you, Morland.'

'But next Friday, when Blakeley comes back, I shall have to take Mrs. Nottingham to Port Philip in custody.'

'Will that give you any satisfaction?'

'No, sir, it will not.'

The volume of Peacock lay open on the table and the evening breeze, eddying from the wall of the bungalow, ruffled and turned its middle pages with a minute chatter, with a flittering bat's-wing sound. 'Do you read Peacock?' asked the Sultan, and closed the book with a decisive clap.

'I'm afraid not.'

'He's very good. He might amuse you. You smoke, don't you?'

'Thank you.'

Carefully the Sultan clipped a cigar and lighted it. He got up and walked slowly to the end of the veranda, and turning, met Mrs. Nottingham as she opened the mosquito-proof door from the hall. She was still wearing a dressing-gown.

'I'm sorry,' she said, and with a little protective gesture of the hands, with a movement of withdrawal, was about to go in again. 'I didn't know you had a visitor.'

'Don't go,' said the Sultan.

'But aren't you talking business? Or has the party begun?'

'You had better join us and hear the news. Mr. Morland has brought me a birthday present.'

'How very kind of you, Mr. Morland!'

'It isn't what I would have chosen myself, but it's not as bad as it seems; so you mustn't be alarmed by it.'

'What is it?'

'A warrant for your arrest,' said the Sultan.

With a sharp and unexpected noise—with a discordant gasp of fear—Mrs. Nottingham retreated to the door and stood against it in an oddly theatrical attitude, her hands pressed flatly to the clapboard wall of the house. Unprepared and unguarded, the sudden shock stamped her with an hieratic impression of dismay, but roused no comparable expostulation. Her complaint was feeble, a stammered protest: 'But you said —you said you could stop them doing that!'

The muscles of her face and neck lost their tone, she could not control the movement of her lips, and her body grew slack, a little ungainly. In a voice that was dry and diminished by fear she cried, 'You won't let him, will you?'

'No,' said the Sultan. 'You are perfectly safe, I shall look after you.' And taking her by the hands—taking her hands from their panic-hold on the wall—he led her, with almost the formality of a cotillon, to the chair from which Morland had risen.

She kissed his hands before he let her go, and with a movement that seemed both defensive and defiant pulled her dressing-gown more closely round her. 'I'm sorry,' she said, 'for making a fool of myself. There's only one thing I'm really frightened of, and that's what did frighten me.'

She breathed deeply, with determination in her lungs. With a visible effort—her knuckles and the ridge of her nose pale in the shadow—she forced, by a moral compulsion, the return of physical composure. She grew again into her normal aspect, she plumped herself out, and said, a little harshly, 'I beg your pardon, I've been extremely ill-mannered. Emotion should be kept indoors.'

'It was my fault,' said the Sultan. 'I blame myself, and apologize to you, for a very gross insensibility. I should have told you at once that the warrant is invalid.'

'No, sir!' said Morland, indignation releasing him from the embarrassment with which he had watched Mrs. Nottingham's distress. 'That sort of statement can't possibly do any good. Neither to you nor to Mrs. Nottingham. It's only raising false hope in her—'

'I am not so heartless as that.'

'It really isn't valid?' she asked. 'If you say so—'

'Mr. Morland himself will confirm what I have said, and you will have no difficulty in believing him.' He turned to Morland and said, 'The outer limits of my privilege are, I admit, a little clouded, and somewhat obscure. On more than one occasion my father had difficulty with the Administration; as I have had. But on no occasion has the Administration ever disputed our absolute right to protect the members of our own family.'

'I grant you that,' said Morland.

'You could not, for example, arrest my wife.'

In the growing darkness of the veranda—the sun was down —the shadows were roughly dislodged as Morland made an angry movement, his arms uplifted like an orator rebuking interruption, to protest against the invasion of an idea so wildly irrelevant. 'What's the point of saying that?' he demanded. 'There's no sense in it!'

Mrs. Nottingham, too, sat bolt upright in her chair, and with a relapse from her new-found composure—with a shrillness in her voice that she could not subdue—asked, 'Shouldn't I be consulted about this?'

The Sultan, standing behind her, put his hands on her shoulders and said, 'Be quiet, my dear.'

'If Mrs. Nottingham is your wife—oh, but it's absurd on the face of it. If that's the truth, why is she still known as Mrs. Nottingham?'

'She has a lot of relations,' said the Sultan, 'and so have I. And on the occasion of a wedding relations are often a great nuisance: before the wedding, and at the wedding, and after it. Privacy and concealment of the marriage contract have great advantages—especially for someone in my position.'

'You have a wife in Penang,' said Morland. 'Has Her Highness been advised of the new contract? Doesn't the mere fact of her existence spoil your story?'

'I have never set myself up as a pattern of my faith,' said the Sultan. 'I have never pretended to be a good Moslem, but I am a Moslem: by conviction in some degree, and by the habit of a lifetime. That being so, I am less restricted in this business of matrimony than you who are, at least by repute, a Christian. There's nothing to prevent me from having a wife in Penang and another in Namua.'

133

'Nevertheless,' said Morland, 'I want proof that she is your wife.'

'Under Mahomedan law a marriage isn't made by religious ceremony. It is contracted, quite simply, by offer and acceptance; and if you don't believe the contract has been made, we can easily repeat it.'

'No, no!' exclaimed Mrs. Nottingham. 'That isn't necessary. It can't be! Mr. Morland is bound to take your word for it.'

'I should like to put his mind at ease and settle this tiresome business once and for all. It is quite easy to repeat the declaration. All I have to say is, "I, Zafrullah bin Ismail bin Said—"'

Turning awkwardly in her chair—the Sultan still stood behind her, his hands on her shoulders—Mrs. Nottingham entreated him, 'Oh, please don't go on! This isn't the time, or the place, for that.'

'Under Mahomedan law,' said Morland—and turned his head, with a quick frown of attention, to listen to a sound of drums that the breeze carried over the slope of the hill. Every day there had been little explosions of drumming, a gust or a ripple or dull reiteration, from the valley where the pagans had congregated; but this was a sonorous concert of drums. It gathered volume and came over the hill in waves of sound. The last light of day had almost gone, the darkness of the sky was coming down to meet the darkness of the mountains, and the noise became a reverberant pulse that seemed to give night and day a living, organic unity.

For nearly a minute no one spoke, and then, impatient of the savage irrelevance of the din, and shrugging-off what was beyond his control, Morland returned stubbornly to his subject and said, 'Under Mahomedan law a declaration of marriage requires two witnesses to make it valid. In the absence of witnesses your statement would have no weight, and I couldn't accept it.'

'That's a deficiency I can easily make good,' said the Sultan, and pressing down a switch on the wall filled the veranda with a harsh and slightly flickering electric light. 'The kitchen is full of witnesses, and if you'll wait a moment—but no, you won't have to. My witnesses are here already.'

In the overflow of light two figures had appeared, walking slowly, and the Sultan, leaning over the veranda railing, welcomed them cheerfully. 'Come along, Kershawe. Hurry up, Pemberton. You never timed your arrival better.'

Twelve

THE Sultan's confidence waned, his geniality—or his assumption of geniality—ebbed and ran out when Kershawe and Pemberton climbed the steps and stood, a little dazzled, in the light. They gave no answer to his welcome, but stood for a moment, comfortless and blinking, in stained and draggled clothes, and in their drab look of weariness there was, it seemed, a quality of resentment, a latent hostility towards the comfort to which they had returned. Kershawe in a sullen posture leaned against the railing, and Pemberton, sitting down with clumsy relaxation, reached for the whisky and Morland's glass. 'Can I have some of this?' he asked.

'As much as you want. And you, Kershawe? I'll get another glass.'

'No, I'm all right.'

'What has happened?'

Pemberton gulped his whisky and said, 'He's done it. By God, he's done it.'

'Samarai? What has he done?'

'He's killed that boy.'

'Who told you so?' asked Morland harshly.

'We saw it,' said Kershawe.

'You would be the better of a drink,' said the Sultan.

'No, sir. I don't want one.'

'I must be told,' said Morland, 'exactly what occurred.'

'It's a story,' said Pemberton. 'Oh, God, it's a story. And I'm damned glad Kershawe was with me.'

136

'If that's barley-water,' said Kershawe, 'I'd like some of it. I'm as dry as a rock.'

Morland, nervous and humiliated, moved to and fro in fretful impatience, but Mrs. Nottingham sat within an appearance of composure that was only betrayed by the unruly haste of her breathing. The Sultan, as calm as a butler when the dinner-table breaks into argument, poured barley-water for Kershawe and said, 'I hope you don't mind drinking out of my glass? I could bring another, but we're so anxious to know what you saw.'

The transparent door, the mosquito-proof wire door of the Rest House was thrown open, and Mrs. Pemberton appeared. She had put on a linen frock, but her hair was untidy, the frock had a lop-sided look, and it was evident that she had dressed in a hurry. She ran towards her husband and cried, 'William! I'm so thankful you're back. I heard those drums, they're far louder than ever before, and I wondered what was happening. But now you're here—'

She stooped and kissed his forehead. He sat, with his elbows spread on the table, and made no response. She looked about her and saw discomfort, restraint, or hidden alarm on every face, and asked the reiterated question, 'What has happened?'

Morland, with a deliberate affectation of official calm, said, 'We've had a rather disconcerting account of a recent development in the situation, Mrs. Pemberton—'

But Pemberton interrupted him: 'Don't talk like a government commission! She's got to hear about it, and what she's got to know is that Samarai hanged that boy of his, and Kershawe and I saw him do it.'

With the sound of a child choking on a glass of milk, Mrs. Pemberton sucked in a deep gulp of terror and began to whimper. Her fear grew shrill, and rose to an hysteric note.

Mrs. Nottingham, in sudden movement, stood up and taking two steps towards her slapped her loudly on the face, forehand and back-hand, and said fiercely, 'Be quiet, you little fool! And now come and sit down.'

Pemberton uttered no protest, nor moved to protect her; but the Sultan said gently, 'Don't be too hard on her. She's distressed, of course—we are all distressed—but you mustn't take it too much to heart, Mrs. Pemberton. Violence is always unpleasant, but violence isn't necessarily catastrophic.'

Mrs. Pemberton sobbed, 'If William had only let me go—'

'Be quiet,' said Pemberton.

Morland, with a petulant anger, as if the frayed skin of his patience had broken at last, exclaimed, 'I insist on being told exactly what you saw!'

'That,' said the Sultan, and sat down comfortably beside Mrs. Pemberton, whose hand he took, 'is what we are all waiting to hear. Will you begin, Pemberton?'

'It was before lunch I went out,' said Pemberton, 'with Oala, the interpreter. I wanted to find Samarai, but no one would tell us where he'd gone. They weren't very friendly. They weren't exactly hostile, but they were excited and sometimes insolent. We couldn't do anything with them. And then, after a couple of hours or more, I met Kershawe.'

'I'd had much the same experience,' said Kershawe. 'I talked to a lot of people I knew: mild little men, as a rule, who wouldn't say *boo!* to a goose—they never said *boo!* to me, at any rate—but now they're riding sky-high. They were damned rude, some of them. And when I got in among a crowd of women I thought my ears would go up in flames.'

'I got in amongst the women,' said Morland. 'They were very offensive.'

'I'm not over-sensitive, after living in Maipani for a couple of years, but some of the things they said would make a stone idol blush. And they hustled me, too. I felt very uncomfortable. But I got away from them, and then I saw Pemberton with about a score of men round him. They were all dressed-up in wigs and necklets and plumes of their best feathers, and they made us go along with them. They weren't really unfriendly, but they wouldn't let us go.'

'You know where the tall trees are, beside the air-strip they've been clearing, beyond the valley. That's where they took us, and that's where Samarai was. Samarai and the boy beside him. There were only men there. About three hundred; or more perhaps.'

'It was very quiet, after the noise the women had been making. They stood round, waiting for Samarai to speak, and no one said anything. About half of them were dressed-up, a lot of them in full fig under a cascade of feathers, but others were naked and dirty as if they'd just come from working on the roads. You know what they are: there's a sort of unanimity in them when they get together, but no proper discipline. They never put on a really good show.'

'Samarai,' said Pemberton, 'was looking more like a bad picture of a ghost than a man. He'd covered his face and body with a plaster of clay—a grey smear of clay—and when he spoke it was like an old-fashioned actor playing the part of a ghost.'

'He'd a wreath of white flowers round his shoulders, it hung down to his midriff, and the boy beside him had a wreath of flowers on his head. They were standing on a platform they'd built, a few feet above the level of the ground, and there was a big tree behind them with a branch over their heads like the yard of a ship.'

'Samarai made a speech,' said Pemberton. 'A lot of it was just what he'd been saying before, about the cargo-plane that's coming, and all the riches in it. But for some reason that wasn't clear, the effect was different. The people round us were shuddering and shaking as they listened to him. They didn't pay any attention to us. They'd forgotten about us.'

'Then he took a rope,' said Kershawe, 'and threw one end over the branch above him, and made a noose at the other end, and put the noose over the boy's head. He knocked off the wreath of flowers the boy was wearing, and picked it up and put it on again. The boy stood without a movement, looking dazed and stupid. He must have been drugged.'

'Samarai told them why the boy had been chosen—this particular boy—as a sacrifice; but Oala couldn't understand what he said about that, or else I couldn't understand Oala. What he said clearly enough was that a human sacrifice was necessary to make sure the cargo-plane arrived safely, and after the boy had been killed he would come back to life and tell them what to do next.'

'Are you sure he said that?' asked Morland.

'I heard him,' said Kershawe, 'and so did everyone else. They got very excited when they heard that, and frightened too. You could almost hear them shivering, and you could smell the sudden stink of them. Then Samarai gave a shout, and two men who had hold of the loose end of the rope—I know who they are—heaved and hauled it up, and the boy hung in the air, dancing.'

'Samarai caught hold of his feet, and held them still. But the boy jerked and jumped on the rope for half a minute or more. It seemed—O God, I don't know how long it seemed.'

'When he was still, and his arms hung without any movement, they let him down and Samarai laid him on the platform where he stood. As soon as the boy had been hauled up and started kicking, the crowd gave tongue like a pack of hounds; but now they were quiet again, and Samarai let them have it.'

'I've never heard such a voice, and I never want to again.'

'He screamed at them, but it was a deep-down scream, it seemed to come out of his bowels—and he told them he was going to bring the boy back to life, but he couldn't do it unless every man there took an equal part of praise or blame, and lent his will to what was done. And they all got down on the ground, and beat their heads on the ground—we did too—and a sort of groan went up from them, and became a repeated thing, like the beating of a drum, and the pitch rose and got shriller and shriller.'

'Then Samarai lay down on the boy.'

'Everyone stood to see what was happening, and presently Samarai got up, and pulled the boy up with him.'

'The boy stood on the platform with his head hanging down on his shoulder—his right shoulder—and his neck was broken. There was no doubt of that.'

'It looked very like it,' said Kershawe.

'But when Samarai told him to walk, he walked.'

'And to tell you the truth, his expression wasn't much stupider than it had been before.'

'He walked,' said Pemberton. 'He came down from the platform, and the crowd divided for him, and he walked between them with Samarai's hand under his shoulder. Do you know what a spastic gait means? Well, that's the way he walked, with his head on his shoulder, and you could hear the breath of the people going in and out like the tide coming in on a beach.'

'They went back to their valley,' said Kershawe. 'We waited a little while, and followed them. But when we caught up with the rear-guard we decided it wasn't safe to go any further.'

'They seemed to have got drunk all of a sudden,' said Pemberton. 'They were like the roughest part of a Scotch football crowd whose team's just won the Cup Final. They were looking for trouble, they wanted to celebrate a victory.'

'So we took the first opportunity to get away,' said Kershawe, 'and came back here.'

In the valley, two or three miles away, the drums were still being beaten in concert, but more quietly now, and for a little while they were a sombre accompaniment to unquiet thoughts —thoughts spiring into fear, searching distractedly, or soberly calculating—thoughts that could find no immediate or useful expression until, in mild inquiry, the Sultan asked, 'Where are your constables, Morland?'

'There are four of them here, two on each side of us. The corporal and a constable are checking stores, and the rest are looking after the prisoners, who are filling sandbags. I've told Sergeant Kula that when we've got the sandbags in place he's to bring his bed on to the back veranda.'

'If we're going to take action,' said the Sultan, 'we'll have to concentrate our forces.'

'What action—what possible action—can we take?'

'Samarai is practising an abominable form of sorcery, the punishment for which is death.'

'But we haven't the strength to punish him.'

'If you make a law, you must enforce it.'

'Even at the risk of our lives?' asked Mrs. Nottingham.

During the recital by Kershawe and her husband, Mrs. Pemberton's fear had been kept under control by the firm pressure of the Sultan's hand, but now she gave it release and in a voice of sheer misery cried, 'If only you had let me go! You ought to have listened to me, William. I'm not brave like the rest of you, I can't bear it—and I'm so ashamed of myself.'

'You're making me ashamed too,' said Pemberton roughly.

'It would do you more credit,' said the Sultan, 'if you showed a little sympathy.'

Surprised by rebuke, Pemberton took it to heart and rising stiffly from his chair said with a candid astonishment, 'I'm very sorry! I didn't mean to hurt her feelings.—Come on, Emily, let's go in. I want to change my clothes, I'm feeling cold, I'm soaked in sweat; and you can help me.'

Obediently she followed him, and Kershawe, shivering in the evening breeze, said, 'I think I'll go too, sir.'

'In a moment,' said the Sultan. 'I want to know if there's anything you could do to keep our neighbours under observation.'

'My corporal could go over and join the party, sir. He's a good man, and out of uniform he looks just like the rest of them.'

'I don't think that's necessary,' said Morland. 'They won't do anything but dance themselves into a stupor tonight, if we leave them alone; but if they recognize Corporal Apu there may well be a tragedy. A tragedy we could do nothing to prevent.'

'He can dress-up and paint himself so that his own wife wouldn't recognize him,' said Kershawe.

'I don't like the idea of it,' said Morland.

'To me it seems a good and prudent suggestion,' said the Sultan, 'and at the risk of offending you, Morland, I should like Kershawe to make the necessary arrangements.'

'If it's your wish, sir—'

'It is. And before you go, Kershawe: you remember it's my birthday-dinner tonight, and you'll have to put on a black tie?'

'You can't have a dinner-party now,' said Morland.

'Why not?'

'After what we've heard?'

'This is the very time for a dinner-party: the perfect occasion for assuring ourselves that civilization is not only stronger than

143

savagery, but infinitely more agreeable.—Off you go, Kershawe.'

'In a situation like this,' said Morland, 'it's wantonly irresponsible to sit down and enjoy yourself.'

'I am not going to be deprived of my proper entertainment by a prancing, clay-besmeared, hysterical witch-doctor who's trying to revive an old-fashioned habit of beastliness—and I'm not alarmed by the ancestral drums of my own tribesmen. Will you try to get that into your head?'

'A few minutes ago you told me to go and arrest Samarai, and now you ask me to a party. I find it very hard to follow you, sir.'

'We have an abundance of time, Morland. It will accommodate both duty and pleasure.'

'I am going to leave you,' said Mrs. Nottingham, and stood up; but just beyond the range of the veranda lights—on the dim frontier of light—a shape of whiteness caught her attention, and as it advanced, and acquired definition, she said to the Sultan with a dry displeasure in her voice, 'Is this your friend Mr. Penny? He seems dressed for dinner and duty too.'

Tom Penny came up the steps, and with a genial declaration of his spirit, saluted. He wore black trousers, a black silk cummerbund, and a short white mess-jacket. Round his waist was a bandolier of ammunition, he had an army rifle slung on his shoulder, and jauntily on his head sat a steel helmet.

'My dear Tom!' said the Sultan. 'You look ready for anything.—My dear, let me present my faithful friend, Mr. Penny.'

Penny shook Mrs. Nottingham warmly by the hand, and explained, 'I heard the news about half an hour ago, and I thought to myself, well, we'll just have time for a nice slice of dinner, and then we'll get ready for a bit of a dust-up. So I brought along the old bundook.'

'What a charming ornament for a party,' said Mrs. Nottingham.

'I daresay it'll come in useful before we're finished,' said Penny cheerfully, and threw down his helmet and his bandolier, and set his rifle against the wall. 'When are we going out to pick up Samarai?' he asked Morland.

'You may be disappointed,' said Morland. 'My responsibility is larger than yours, and even at the price of your displeasure I mean to behave as I always have done. That is to say, reasonably and dispassionately.'

'There are times,' said the Sultan, 'when dispassion is not the height of virtue. There are times when it is better to be angry.'

'And there's nothing like a bit of action for keeping up the spirit,' said Penny.

'That's an argument worth more than the superficial critic would allow,' said the Sultan. 'What will you drink, Tom? A glass of sherry?'

'Well, if you haven't anything else. But I'd rather a drop of gin.'

'I'll go and get it,' said Mrs. Nottingham.

'The fact is, sir, that I'm a Liberal in politics, but Conservative in drinking. Beer before lunch, gin before dinner, and whisky before bed: that's what suits my constitution, and the policy I like to stick to.'

'If you'll excuse me, sir?' said Morland. 'There are several things I have to do.'

'Yes, of course. And remember we dine at eight.'

'You insist?'

'I do.'

'Very well, sir.'

Protest and indignation visible in the stiff and angular carriage of his thin body, he went down the steps, and Mrs. Nottingham returned to the veranda carrying a heavy tray that Penny, with a nimble politeness, took from her and set upon the table.

He looked admiringly at bottles and glasses, and said with some emotion in his voice, 'We go to all the trouble of being civilized, we shoulder our burdens and do our best, but what I've always said is there's no point in it if you don't get a bit of fun as well. And in my time, I must admit, I've had my share.'

'I too,' said the Sultan, 'have on occasion decorated the passing hour.'

'Too true!' said Penny. 'We've got our trials and tribulations—the worst thing ever happened to me was waking up beside a dead policeman—but we've got a taste for enjoyment too, and when I think of those howling savages out there, who can't suffer life without going half-mad to make themselves believe in it, well, I thank my stars for civilization. Lousy though it looks if you get too much of it.'

Mrs. Nottingham gave him a claret-glass half-full of gin, to which he added a little water, and bowing politely said, 'Here's luck, sir and madam, and many happy returns of the day!'

Thirteen

Less by three days than its full circumference, the moon rose over the mountain-tops into a grapeskin sky that already was lighted by a huge concourse of stars, and dimmed the brightness of the cooking-fires on which the pagans were grilling odorous slices and richly dropping gobbets of pork. The evening breeze was still blowing, and the whole sky was cloudless. The drummers, squatting on their haunches, would beat for a long time a steady pedestrian rhythm, and the dancers, dully balancing, stamped their obedient feet on strips of ground that their reiterated tread had worn bare and dusty.

The dancers were all men in this beginning phase. They stood opposite each other in ranks of eight or ten or twenty—there was no regular and ordered pattern in their dancing, it obeyed only the changing time and fervour of the drums—and when the drummers beat more urgently the women would come in behind the men, and dancing more wildly than they, chant above the voice of the drums their brutal endearments or incitement to battle. Each rank of men then turned about, and men and women danced to a tumultuous rhythm an obscene and violent parody of the sexual act, to which the moon gave inhuman dimensions by throwing on the pallid ground enormous, elongated shadows of leaping breasts and arms beseeching, legs demanding and heads nid-nodding in fictitious agonies of desire. The women finally repelled their urgent men, who turned against their ritual foes and tried to thrust them, breast to breast, from their established ground.

Gradually the pace and fervour of the drums diminished,

and the women with a casual and slouching gait retired from the dancing ground. For a little while the men turned and pranced in solitary fancy, and then grew tired of play. Men and women, chattering easily, went to the cooking-fires and were given hot strips and clumsy pieces of half-roasted, half-raw pig that they gnawed and swallowed with an almost declamatory greed. Appetite had a rhythm, a quickening, which recreated something of the excitement of the dance.

A few dancers still obeyed the drums, now beating a dull traveller's pace, and maintained the sequence of the festival. But the majority wandered here and there between the fires, taking now a stringy rib and now, by favour, a sizzling hot kidney, to show the community of the fires, the unity of the feast; for hostile tribes and half-tribes and disparate families had all been reconciled, and the slaughtered pigs were a sacrifice before they became regalement. The odour of burnt meat was the incense of a common faith, and the fat running down lean chins or reflecting firelight from the plump cheeks of a strutting young man who had danced in the forefront of the dance was a holy unguent.

The drums again began to beat more loudly, more urgently, and wiping their greasy hands on naked thighs the dancers went forward to revive in their barbaric measure their ritual frenzy. Above the valley where they danced the stench commingled of wood-smoke and gross humanity, the moon exaggerated their postures in the caricature of leaping shadows; but within their narrow minds there beat a faith, responsive to the drums, that blessed their dark shoulders and their pointed dugs, their trumpery ornaments and greasy flesh, with a rapt and fearful joy.

At the Sultan's dinner-party there was no such unanimity, no exuberance, and little enjoyment. His table was handsomely furnished from the refrigerators of *White Heather*, there was an abundance of champagne, and the silver shone like starlight. The Sultan himself, when he first sat down, was in a jovial mood, eager to be amused and attentive to his guests. But his guests lacked the enviable gift of their savage neighbours to be wholehearted and spend all their faculties on immediate occupation; to live within the bright moonlight of the present. His guests could enjoy neither the geniality of their host nor his caviare, neither his pheasants nor his Bollinger, because they were thinking also of the dancers on the hill and conjecturing the dawn. Only Tom Penny and the Sultan himself were untroubled by surmise, and the mere robustitude of Penny's mind gave new alarm to Mrs. Pemberton.

Mrs. Pemberton, despite the advantage of her borrowed frock and her assurance that she looked very well in it, had been in poor spirits before dinner. The Sultan had paid her a gratifying compliment, and Kershawe by the astonished and scarcely deviating attention of his eyes had plainly shown his admiration; but still she was depressed.

The Sultan made her drink two glasses of sherry and told her, 'Fear is very like hunger. It means your mind is short of calories: that's all there is to it.'

'But what can I do about it?'

'You're going to sit next to me at dinner, and I'll put some confidence on your plate.'

'I think sherry is a help too.'

She was more cheerful when they sat down, but still wanted to discuss her feelings. 'When the drums all started together, just as it got dark,' she said, 'I thought it was the end of everything. I thought it was all the dreadfulness of life bursting its shell and coming out to destroy us.'

Penny, who sat between her husband and Morland, on the Sultan's left, leaned forward and said with solemn disapproval,

'And that's the awful consequence of being ignorant, if you don't mind my saying so. The drumming, when it first began, was more like a bloody great shout of joy—and I beg your pardon for the word I used.'

'It was meant to frighten us, I suppose.'

'You're right off the target, Mrs. Pemberton. They weren't giving us a thought, I promise you. At that moment there was nothing in their heads but roast pork, and the drums were just an accompaniment to killing the pigs.'

'Do they make a ceremony of it?' asked Mrs. Nottingham from the end of the table.

'They do their best, and they always enjoy a bit of noise. My word! So they lay into the pig with a nice supple bit of bamboo, and when he's screaming his head off, and the drums are going hell-for-leather, and everyone's shouting like mad, an old man slips the knife in and there's your dinner waiting to be cooked.'

'They must be the cruellest people in the world,' said Mrs. Pemberton faintly.

'That I won't accept!' said the Sultan. 'In comparison with civilization—though civilization is what I prefer—they are innocent and harmless creatures. What you don't understand is that a pig means much more to them than to you or me. A pig is great wealth, and killing it is a serious matter. So serious that the pig itself has to be convinced of the importance of the occasion.'

'Does that excuse brutality?' asked Mrs. Nottingham.

'Of course it does!' said Pemberton. 'Because it isn't callous brutality, it's passionate brutality. If you want to see callous brutality, go to an up-to-date slaughterhouse where they kill for so-much a week. But here the butcher's a priest, and killing's an act of faith.'

'It's a bit of fun for them too: don't forget that,' said Penny.

'And I don't grudge them their fun. God knows they don't get much of it.'

'I can't understand you!' exclaimed Mrs. Pemberton. 'I can't understand you at all. Now you seem to be defending these people, but a little while ago you were quite ready to shoot them.'

'I've got a sense of proportion, that's why. Or put it another way, I can see both sides of the question.'

'With a rifle to keep your balance,' said Mrs. Nottingham.

'That's right,' said Penny complacently.

'I accepted an invitation to dine with you in Maipani,' said Mrs. Nottingham to the Sultan, 'but I wasn't asked to share a battle with you.'

'Would you object to a battle?'

'Very strongly. I'm a pacifist by nature as well as conviction.'

At Mrs. Nottingham's right hand Morland maintained an expression of cold indifference to the conversation. He had added nothing to it, and carefully refrained from taking an interest in it. He had come to the dinner-table under compulsion, and in the childishness of wounded dignity was determined to show his resentment. The Sultan, aware of his silence and observing his expression, experienced a similar emotion. His caviare, his champagne and his pheasants deserved a better reception than the vinegar juices of that pinched and self-righteous stomach. Nowhere, indeed, were his fowls and his wine finding the welcome to which they were entitled. Mrs. Nottingham had retreated into cold disapproval at the sight of Tom Penny's rifle and the bold slant of his helmet, and her disapproval now chilled the table; and Tom Penny, though as convivial as anyone could wish, did not really appreciate what he was drinking. Mrs. Pemberton was trying to enjoy the party, and the champagne was abetting her good intention; but her spirit was still tremulous. Her husband had said nothing, except for an occasional rather surly interjection, and it was clear that his mind was intent on the savage business of the afternoon. Kershawe, as silent as Pemberton, was over-awed by his neighbours: he sat on Mrs. Nottingham's left, and on his other side was Mrs. Pemberton. Their white shoulders and the movement of their bare arms caused him exquisite dis-comfort, for in Maipani he had grown used to the innocence of total nakedness, but here was an artful and allusive nudity, not generalized by the uniform of the sun but powdered and scented for a particular attention. As children at a circus, enthralled and frightened by acrobats on the high trapeze, will shut their eyes against a moment of peril, so Kershawe from time to time kept his eyes on his plate; and never thought of conversation.

It was a miserable party, the Sultan decided, and on a splenetic impulse addressed himself to Morland.

'Are you paying attention?' he demanded. 'Did you hear what Elizabeth said? Her admission that she's a pacifist? Now you ought to be taking note of things like that. She's a sub-versive influence, isn't she? Did I ever tell you what she said about her visit to the Teachers' Training College at Fair-weather?'

'I think not, sir.'

The Sultan looked round the table to summon attention, and said, 'You know it was discovered, a few days after she'd been there, that one of the students had Communist pamphlets in his possession? What the authorities call Communist "literature". And naturally she was suspected of having given them to him. So I asked her if it was true, and she said no. It wasn't necessary, she said. "No one," she said, "needs to under-mine the power of England, because England's policy is to destroy itself." Now what do you say to that, Morland?'

'It's a large assertion, but I don't see much substance in it.'

'On the day she visited the college the senior class was writing an essay on a sentence from a speech by Edmund Burke: a sentence, I think, from his speech on the necessity of conciliation with America: "Freedom and not servitude is the cure of anarchy."—And now do you see any substance in her charge?'

'No, sir, I don't. The statement seems to me quite consistent with our colonial policy.'

'I really don't want to discuss my private opinions,' said Mrs. Nottingham, 'for the simple reason that they are private. That's to say, I don't try to impose them on anyone else. But in a place like New Brabant—a rich colony that you're trying to develop, and a very primitive colony—it does seem odd that one of the first ideas you ram into the heads of the people you're educating is the necessity of freedom. The very idea, you see, that's going to kick you out of New Brabant as soon as it becomes general.'

'Our colonial policy,' said Morland, 'is based on a recognition of human rights.'

'And your colonies begin to crumble as soon as the policy has been published and misunderstood,' said the Sultan. 'I wish I had the patience of a scholar and the formative skill of a good writer! What a comedy I could write about the British Empire. I didn't know, till Elizabeth told me, that Burke had been made a cornerstone of education in New Brabant, but university students in India all had to study him. It was one of the sternest commandments of the British raj that every young Indian who had learnt to read must read Burke. And when they read about the "refreshing airs of liberty", and assertions that "the people are the masters", and those who are crushed by law "have no hopes but from power"—why, of course they were persuaded that their first duty was to sack their teachers and turn their masters out. Burke was a most persuasive man—but you know him better than I do, perhaps?'

'I think I read some of his speeches at school,' said Morland, 'but I don't remember much about them.'

'What do you read? Neither Peacock nor Burke—well, what?'

'I haven't much time for reading; not for pleasure, at any rate. In my position I have to try and be practical.'

'If that's your aim,' said Mrs. Nottingham, 'you should take a few lessons from the Communists. They don't give children schoolbooks that teach them to overthrow Communism. They teach them to believe in Communism.'

'Now you see her in her true colours,' said the Sultan. 'She's a dangerous woman, Morland. She'll be converting you if you don't take care.'

'I think I know my own mind too well for that.'

'I wish I did,' said Mrs. Pemberton sadly. 'I've got a mind like a sieve. It lets everything go through except straws and rubbish.'

'You've got a bad memory? Is that what you mean?' asked Penny. 'Well, you ought to be thankful, like I am. If I remembered all I've done and seen I'd never get to sleep at night.'

'I think Emily and I will leave you to your brandy,' said Mrs. Nottingham. 'I suppose it's safe to sit outside?'

'It won't be very comfortable,' said Morland. 'I'm going to start sandbagging the veranda as soon as I'm allowed to leave here.'

'In a quarter of an hour, shall we say?' The Sultan's voice was bland, but there was malice in his smile. 'And don't desert us, Elizabeth. You would take away all the decoration from our party. And I think, too, that now we have dined and are comfortable, we should face the facts of our situation and accept the burden of what may be a somewhat unpleasant duty.'

He poured a little brandy into a glass and gave it to Mrs. Pemberton; and Morland, suspicious and resentful, said, 'I've done all that's immediately necessary, I think. I've made preparation to safeguard the Rest House and defend it if necessary—'

'You've made a good beginning, Morland. A very good beginning. A strong base is our first requirement, and with a strong base to fall back on we can act with confidence.'

'We can await events with confidence.'

'We have to do more than that.'

'I intend to do nothing more.'

' "Where you find a notable injury, spare not to give course to the torrents of your wrath."—Do you know who said that?'

'No, I don't. Someone in a book, I suppose.'

'It was the advice of an English king whom the English never appreciated because he spoke with a Scotch accent. But he knew something about the art of being a king, and in a book he wrote for his son he advised him: "Study to know well your own craft, which is to rule your people", and "where you find a notable injury, spare not to give course to the torrents of your wrath".'

'In our present circumstances we can't afford a display of anger.'

'We have suffered a notable injury, and we can't afford to ignore it. My father made a law against the revolting form of sorcery that Samarai is practising. The law has been broken, and for that my father decreed the penalty of death.'

Pemberton, expelled from the isolation of his own thoughts, exclaimed, 'But you can't kill Samarai!'

'Of course we can't. We haven't the strength to arrest him.'

'The law doesn't require him to be arrested. The law requires him to be killed.'

Pemberton, with passion in his voice, declared, 'Then that law's got to be ignored! Samarai's life must be protected.'

'You're very warm about it,' said the Sultan.

'Yes, I am,' said Pemberton. 'I'm in a responsible position here. I'm a trained anthropologist and I've got a chance to investigate something of first-rate scientific importance. Something that never has been investigated. Something you can't accept as a fact, and hasn't been explained as a trick. But I'm going to find out!'

Impatient of such levity, and annoyed by the interference of a tourist, Kershawe said scornfully, 'You're talking as if the whole thing had been arranged for your benefit.'

'It's a great stroke of luck that I happen to be here,' said Pemberton, 'and I can't agree to any course of action that's going to spoil my opportunity or interfere with my observation.'

'You've heard what the Sultan said. You know there's a law against sorcery—'

'Law's only a convention,' said Pemberton. 'Anthropology is science.'

'Science for the sake of science?' asked Kershawe.

'All knowledge is valuable.'

'Even if we don't know what to do with it?' asked the Sultan. 'Isn't the pursuit of knowledge for its own sake merely a form of dissipation?'

'Perhaps you don't realize, sir, exactly what is at stake,' said Pemberton. 'There's nothing known about this form of sorcery except a fairly wide belief in its existence—'

'If it hadn't existed,' said the Sultan, 'my father would hardly have taken the trouble to abolish it.'

'Then you must realize the importance of the next few days!'

said Pemberton. 'Nothing—nothing at all—should be done to interfere with Samarai, and I've got to have absolute freedom to observe his behaviour.'

'You may not agree with Pemberton's point of view,' said Morland with a smooth pretence of impartiality, 'but I don't think you can disregard what he says. He's got an opportunity which isn't likely to recur, and he's a trained observer—'

'What does he do with his observations?' asked Kershawe. 'Put them in a book like a schoolboy sticking in foreign stamps?'

'That's the crude and vulgar abuse of an illiterate mind!' said Pemberton.

'Now, now!' said the Sultan. 'Let us keep our temper. My father used to say, "Better lose a fortune than your manners", and though that may be going too far—'

'You put a high price on manners,' said Mrs. Nottingham, 'but I see more value in common sense. I'm on Mr. Morland's side, and Mr. Pemberton's, when they say this isn't the time to indulge in "torrents of wrath".'

The Sultan regarded her with, as it appeared, an affectionate concern, and asked, 'Have you ever ridden a bicycle?'

'Not lately, thank heaven. I did when I was a girl.'

'Then you know what happens when you stop pedalling. You fall off. And the same thing happens to a ruler who stops ruling. You think it would be dangerous to take action, to go ahead and do what the law commands us to do. But I say it's far more dangerous to stop and do nothing.'

Morland closed his eyes and pressed his fingers to his temples, as if to impose patience; but the Sultan did not wait for his objection, and in a slightly louder voice continued: 'Before making a definite plan we should wait, I think, for a report from—what's the name of your corporal?'

'Corporal Apu, sir.'

'For a report from Corporal Apu, who has gone over the hill to see what's happening. When he comes back he may have information that will help us to determine a course of action. I have told you that in my opinion action must be taken, and now you'll have an opportunity to adjust your minds to that necessity. In the meantime, Morland, you may want to get on with your sandbagging?'

'I do, sir. And also I want to say—'

'I know you do. But let us have no more discussion till we've heard Corporal Apu. And as we'll have to take turns of watch-keeping tonight, perhaps you would all like to go and change your clothes. Thank you for coming to my party.'

'Come on,' said Penny, and with Kershawe went quickly away. Morland followed, after a little hesitation, and they heard him shouting for Sergeant Kula. Pemberton, still rebellious, made no movement, and the Sultan with an easy geniality said to him, 'Will you find my steward, Mr. Pemberton, and tell him to clear everything away except the coffee and the brandy? And then, when you've changed, come back and have another glass.'

Pemberton got up clumsily and did not reply. But he went to the back veranda and called for the steward, and then, closing the door loudly behind him, disappeared into his bedroom. As if the slam of the door had started a chain of echoes, a sandbag fell with a thud on the front veranda, then another and another, ten or a dozen of them. There was a chattering of high, round voices, the quick fall of naked feet on a wooden floor, sharp words of command. There was a movement of busy men all round the house, and again and again the thudding drop of the sandbags. The prisoners from the jail carried them up on handbarrows, and two constables built them into a wall behind the veranda railings.

The Sultan went out to watch them, and looked down at the

air-strip, blanched by the moon and slanting to the deep gorge that divided the soaring, star-high mountains. A cluster of stars seemed to balance on the crest of the opposite hill, and the air still throbbed with the beating of drums in the more populous valley. A light breeze blew, and the air was almost cool.

He spoke to the constables who were building the sandbags, and went in again. Mrs. Nottingham, sitting under an indifferent light, was idly reading a six-months-old copy of the *Tatler* she had found in a pile of soiled and weary magazines, and Mrs. Pemberton, her hands folded in her lap, sat looking at nothing in a corner of a hard brown sofa. The Sultan turned to the door again, and called for Sergeant Kula.

The Sergeant came in and saluted with a lavish movement of his thick brown arm. He was a strongly built man with cheerful, Polynesian features. His open-necked tunic, of dark green with yellow piping, reached from his shoulders to within a handsbreadth of his knees, and was confined by a broad leather belt from which a bayonet hung in its scabbard. His feet and legs were bare, and his densely growing, closely curling hair was cut to a median crest. The Sultan spoke to him in his own language.

'Kara hakam lei so do?'

'Kara hakam manka hai.'

'Ruku!'

He sat down beside Mrs. Pemberton and said, 'Doesn't he give you confidence? Don't you feel you can rely on him to look after you?'

'Yes,' she said doubtfully, 'I'm sure I can.'

The Sultan spoke again to Sergeant Kula. 'Yui ben-so, mantil ay?'

'Tora hunda chui leh.'

'Ruku hai. Ruku!'

The Sergeant saluted, turned about with a smack of his bare heel on the floor, and returned to the veranda.

'They are working very well,' said the Sultan. 'They are working together, and with alacrity. I wish there had been as much amiability and co-operation at my dinner-party.'

'I thought you and your friend Penny enjoyed yourselves,' said Mrs. Nottingham.

'Nobody proposed my health. Nobody made a speech and said what a fine fellow I am, and what a good man I might have been. It was very disappointing.'

Gently he lifted Mrs. Pemberton's nearer hand, and stroked her fingers. 'I feel inclined,' he said, 'to make the speech myself. I could say such a lot in my favour. I might really become a very good prince if I had the opportunity. You saw tonight how I kept my temper as well as my point of view, and that is very important if you are going to be the successful chairman of an executive committee; which is what a ruling prince should be. And how satisfying a job it might be! It would be an absorbing job if there was always a crisis. But in ordinary times, when nothing much was happening, but you had to listen intelligently to discussions on public health, and the proper appropriation for the schools, and the new waterworks —well, then I might grow a little bored and play truant. There are so many other things to do, and sometimes, I admit, I see more profit in a pretty woman's fingers than in the most sagacious discussion of the best-informed committee that ever sat.'

Mrs. Pemberton looked at him shyly, and looked away again; and Mrs. Nottingham, noisily turning the pages of her magazine, said sharply, 'Fingers don't argue, of course. If they can't acquiesce, they take themselves away.'

'You're under-rating them, my dear Elizabeth. Fingers are much more eloquent than that. They transmit the most delicate shades of meaning and emotion. They can be reluctant, or merely pretend to be reluctant, and let you know they are pretending. They can be simple and friendly, or as clever as a pianist, as clever as a diplomat in the old days of diplomacy. They can touch your heart with tenderness, or bargain like a Jew. They can say Yes, today; or Yes, tomorrow; or Yes, when it suits me. But you can't understand them, of course, unless you have learnt how to finger-read—and then you can understand them all.'

'A universal language without the burden of literature,' said Mrs. Nottingham. 'As you describe it, it sounds enchanting.'

'And because it has no literature,' said the Sultan, 'there are no professors to expound it, and therefore it never becomes boring.'

'I don't know how it is,' said Mrs. Pemberton, 'but you make me feel confident in a way William never does.'

'Scientists do very well in their proper place,' said the Sultan, 'but in a country like Namua old-fashioned methods are more reliable.'

Fourteen

THE moon was nearing its apogee, and under a clear, almost vertical light that cast little shadow, the landing-ground which the savages had cleared for the arrival of their miraculous aeroplane looked like a hillside which had been lashed by the tail of a passing storm. The stumps of the felled timber, of the two or three hundred spindly trees that had been cut, shone white on the rough slant of the ground, and the little craters from which boulders had been dug were like potholes that a river's overflow had scoured. The clearance suggested the havoc of nature rather than a purposive and deliberate work of man.

To the east of it, in the upper part of the glen that sheltered the tribal cooking-fires, grew a clump of stouter and more richly nurtured trees, and here, perhaps half a mile from the nearest dancers, about a dozen elders—none was young, and one or two were shrivelled with age—squatted on their haunches and in silence watched Samarai and the boy.

Samarai sat on the trunk of a fallen tree, his knees widespread, and the boy like a ventriloquist's dummy perched on his left thigh. The face and body of the boy were daubed, in the same fashion as Samarai, with a whiteish clay, and in the full light of the moon, against the dark background of the spinney, the pallor of their rude adornment had the hard stare of dry bones. The face of the boy, drooping to his shoulder, was the lolling, witless countenance of an imbecile—an imbecile on the point of death—but Samarai's expression, despite

162

the roundels of clay on his cheeks and the bar of white on his forehead, was tense and luminous with intelligence.

He was of different stock from the others. His native village was in the foothills where for long the indigenous strain had been adulterated by foreign addition. Samarai was darker than his companions, but his features were more finely shaped: his nose had a bridge, his high forehead was aggressive, his eyes were large and brilliant. When he was preaching his new religion on the coast and in the lowlands he had had great success with women, whose common excuse was that they had only done what his eyes commanded them. His body was lithe and muscular, but very thin. He carried himself with an ostentatious pride, and when he addressed a crowd he used his hands to make supple expressive gestures that seemed to give life and wings to what he said.

Now, as he held the boy in his left arm, his right hand rubbed without ceasing the child's belly and chest, sometimes with a smooth circular movement, sometimes deeply kneading. Quietly, in a slow monotonous voice, he put a question and repeated it ten or a dozen times. Then, his eyes shining in the moonlight, he waited for an answer, and after a long time — after a silence of two or three minutes — the boy replied. It was no more than a hoarse murmur from his sagging lips, but the elders, squatting on the ground, grunted with approval.

They listened, and watched the performance, with an absorbed but not a continuous interest. One of them would suddenly become more intent on scratching, another on picking his teeth. They were incapable of quiet and prolonged attention. They fidgeted and were restless, and one got up and walked away, but only a few yards, to stoop to the ground and make water. But always their interest revived, and whenever the boy spoke they were hushed and still, and then would mutter approval or more loudly give assent. Sometimes their response was a murmur of acquiescence, sometimes it grew shrill.

The elders were all dressed for ceremonial occasion. They wore short kilts of blue or red cloth, and necklets of crude bone ornaments, or shells, or birds' bright feathers. Some wore ponderous wigs, and others a headdress of tall red plumes. But much of their finery was soiled or broken and they wore it carelessly, without apparent pride in it. It had a ritual value, but its appearance was less important. All carried weapons, or had weapons on the ground beside them.

Samarai put another question to the boy, and patiently repeated it, as though softly driving in a nail. Hoarsely the boy muttered his reply: a simple affirmative. The performance had been going on for nearly two hours, and Samarai at last was satisfied. Now he spoke, not to the boy but to the elders, and presently, with a chorus of agreement, they rose and came towards him.

The oldest of them, a little shrivelled man, put his arm round the boy to support him; but Samarai kept the boy's right hand in his. They stood up, and went downhill towards the dancers. The boy walked with a curious, spasmodic movement, now lifting his knees high, now dragging or jerking his feet, as though he had no proper control of his legs.

When the nearest of the dancers saw their approach they disregarded the drummers and ran to meet them. As though this had everywhere broken the rhythm of the dance, the other sets faltered in their steps, and the drums, in a stammering diminuendo, fell silent. For a moment or two, as if lost, the pagans looked about them in vacant bewilderment. But then, seeing movement further up the hill, they followed in its wake. They crowded round Samarai and the boy, pressing close upon them. They shouldered each other like cattle, all hot and greasy, but unaware of discomfort as they jostled and breathed each other's rank odours. The elders drove them back, and made a little space. Samarai set the boy on a rock, and a man stood behind, his hands in the boy's armpits to support him.

Samarai began to speak, and in a little while his audience broke into a shuddering, ecstatic cry. . . .

The Sultan, Mrs. Nottingham, and the Pembertons had played bridge till after midnight. Pemberton, who was a good average player and had held good hands, recovered his equanimity, and his wife, with laudable self-discipline, did her best to exclude all thought of their wild neighbours and keep her attention on the cards. The Sultan had played a dashing game, and Mrs. Nottingham had tried without much success to hold him within her own respect for security and the conventions. The Sultan, losing heavily, had consoled himself by taking an occasional game with calculated audacity; and Mrs. Nottingham, shuffling with carelessly expert fingers, seemed to imply that she had learnt her bridge in better company than this.

It was one o'clock when the ladies went to bed, and the Sultan told them, as they said good night, 'Now remember, there is nothing to be afraid of, and you can go to sleep with an easy mind. There'll be no sudden attack, no call to arms in the middle of the night. Whatever happens, there'll be ample warning, for these people don't take action without a great deal of preparation and the proper ceremony; and we're going to keep an eye on them. You can rely on us to be vigilant, and you can trust them to be conventional. It's only civilized people who dare to break immemorial rules.'

He and Pemberton went on to the front veranda and found themselves behind a sandbag wall four feet high. A narrow entrance had been left at the top of the steps, protected by an overlapping rampart between it and the door, and on either side of the gap were loop-holes for kneeling riflemen. The wall was continuous on both sides of the Rest House, and the constables and the prisoners were now working on the veranda of the other house: the kitchen and servants' quarters. Morland, with laudable energy, was building the sides of a loop-hole, and on the hillside seventy yards away Kershawe with two constables was pegging a circumference of trip-wire. Penny, in a quiet corner, lay sound asleep and snoring in a deck-chair.

The Sultan and Pemberton went indoors again, and the Sultan said, 'I'm going to follow Penny's example and sleep for a couple of hours, but I think we can afford a nightcap first. A little whisky with a lot of soda-water does much to mollify the rigours of undressing.'

Pemberton took his glass and said, 'There was a remark you made earlier this evening that interested me a lot. About this business of sorcery. You said if it hadn't existed your father wouldn't have made a law against it. Well, if it did exist, how much do you know about it?'

'Tom Penny claims to have seen it being practised.'

'That was thirty years ago when he first came here. He was only a boy. And memory plays funny tricks in thirty years.'

'I have never seen it myself,' said the Sultan, 'but when I was a boy I often heard about it, and belief in it was general. Whether it exsisted or not, the belief was dangerous—perhaps belief was always a major partner in the practice—and I'm determined to prevent a recurrence of belief.'

'I want to examine the belief,' said Pemberton. 'I want to find out exactly what the element of fact in it is. There is an element of fact, for I saw the boy being hanged, and when they took him down it looked as if he was dead. But a little while later he got up and walked. Well, how do they do it?'

'This is where our interests divide,' said the Sultan. 'I'm content to say they mustn't do it, but you—'

'I'm on the other side,' said Pemberton, 'and when you were talking that way at dinner-time I naturally lost my temper—and I apologize for being rude to you. But don't you see what a challenge it is? We ought to know these things! We've got to know. And here's an opportunity to find out.'

'I suppose,' said the Sultan, 'that in the deepest parts of my mind I believe in sorcery. And that is why I am against it.'

'I don't,' said Pemberton. 'I can't believe in it. But if it's true—my God, what a book I'll write about it!'

'Will you dedicate it to me?'

'I will,' said Pemberton seriously. 'I promise you that, if you'll help me.'

They heard footsteps on the veranda, the flimsy door was pulled open, and Kershawe and Morland came in. Kershawe, a little excited, said, 'They're moving over here. They're going to occupy the air-strip.'

Resolutely denying the anxiety he felt, Morland said, 'That is the gist of Corporal Apu's report. He's just come in.'

'Have they started?' asked the Sultan.

'No,' said Kershawe. 'They were just sitting about, talking, when Corporal Apu left them.'

'They can sit for hours and talk. They say the same things over and over again. Do you think they'll move before daylight?'

'It'll be unusual if they do,' said Kershawe, 'but I've sent two constables up the hill, to that big rock that looks like the gable-end of a house, to keep watch. They look right down into the other valley from there.'

'Sit down, and tell me the whole story.'

'I want to emphasize the fact that there's nothing in Corporal Apu's report to suggest they're planning an attack,' said

Morland. 'They're coming to take possession of the air-strip: that's all we know, and we must be on guard against jumping to conclusions.'

'We haven't far to jump,' said Kershawe.

'I want to know what Corporal Apu saw,' said the Sultan patiently.

'They were all dancing when he got there, and he joined a party and danced with them. But after a while—I don't know how long—the drummers gave up, and the whole crowd moved uphill to meet Samarai. Samarai and the boy. And Samarai made a speech. He said they must all do what the boy told them, for his spirit had gone down to the place of the dead, and learnt the wisdom of the dead, which was greater than their own. He said that he and the elders had been waiting a long time for the boy's spirit to come back and speak to them, and at last they had heard it. And it told them their own landing-ground was no good, and if they wanted their aeroplane to come safely in, they must go and take possession of the air-strip here.

'Well, that made them very excited, and according to Corporal Apu a lot of them were frightened at first. But Samarai went on talking, and told them again they must obey the boy, whatever he said. The boy was standing on a rock beside him, and Samarai put one hand on the boy's belly and the other behind his back, and laid his chin against the boy's chest and looked up at him, and asked him to speak in his own voice. And presently the boy said yes, they must come here, and the aeroplane would land on the strip the foreigners had made. But his voice was very faint, and not everybody heard him.'

'I wonder,' said the Sultan, 'if it is only ventriloquism?'

'We saw him walking,' said Pemberton. 'If he can walk, I daresay he can speak. '

'Did the boy say when they were to move? Or did Samarai tell them?'

'No, I asked about that, but there was no mention of time. After the boy had spoken Samarai and the elders took him away, and the others just sat down and began telling each other what they'd seen and what they'd heard: all talking at once and saying the same things. You've seen them behave like that, haven't you, sir? At the pitch of excitement for a little while, and a few minutes later they're gossiping and scratching.'

'If the boy has been made to speak,' said the Sultan, 'and the wisdom of the dead has told them to come here, it means they're coming quite soon. You don't play on the emotions of a crowd to make the crowd do something next week.'

'Then he's changed his plans,' said Pemberton. 'According to the story I heard, the boy was going to come to life again after three days. Well, if that was the intention, that was altered. Then Tom Penny heard there was to be an interval of three days between the resurrection, so to speak, and the coming of the aeroplane. But now, if you're right, that programme's been changed too.'

'I wasn't much impressed by the talk of "three days",' said the Sultan. 'I thought, when I heard of it, that probably it only meant "presently", or "fairly soon". But I agree with you that he may have modified his plans and decided to hurry things on. Perhaps they're running short of food.'

'You talk about his plans,' said Morland, 'but where's the evidence that he ever had a plan? The whole situation—the nonsensical supposition, the absurdity of his promises—they exclude all possibility of a plan. You can't make plans to the scale of a miracle.'

'What do you expect him to do, then?'

'Precisely what I have expected from the beginning. They'll

sit here as long as their patience lasts, and they have anything to eat; and when they've given up hope, and are getting really hungry, they'll go back to their villages with their tails between their legs.'

'And Samarai?'

'He'll be the first to go. And he won't advertise his departure.'

'I don't like the idea of them camping-out beside my storesheds,' said Kershawe. 'I can't see how to protect them and keep a proper defence here too.'

'Doesn't that give you a hint of Samarai's intention?' asked the Sultan. 'Do you still think he's an idle visionary, trapped in his own hysterical imaginings? Well, you're wrong, Morland. He's a practical man, and his heavenly aeroplane is even solider than he is. His heavenly aeroplane has already landed. What have you got in your store-sheds, Kershawe?'

'They're full, sir. We flew in extra supplies about three months ago, before our budget was cut, when we were going to establish a new district headquarters to the south, and use Maipani as a base.'

'There's the aeroplane, Morland; or its cargo, at any rate. It needn't come gracefully out of the clouds and roar to a standstill in sight of everyone. It's here already, and it only has to be identified to fulfil Samarai's promise and satisfy his followers. The boy will have to speak again. He'll have to say the aeroplane arrived unseen and discharged its cargo without the help of man. And there it is, ready for their use and pleasure. But before they can take it, of course, they'll have to dispose of us. That must be part of the plan.'

'There's not a scrap of evidence for what you're saying! It's supposition only, a fantasy built on pure imagination.' Morland, his anger almost beyond control, stood and railed at the Sultan like a schoolmaster at an unruly boy who had torn his patience to shreds, and fretted too his confidence. 'You're almost as great a trial to me as Samarai himself!'

The Sultan said to Pemberton, 'You heard Samarai promising someone guns or rifles.'

'I did,' said Pemberton.

'Firearms aren't usually regarded as a heavenly export, but there are twelve constables here who carry rifles.'

'And I've twelve in store,' said Kershawe, 'and 2000 rounds of ammunition.'

'I think that's conclusive. All Samarai has to do to redeem his promise, and create his reputation as a miracle-worker, is to get rid of us and take possession of everything that's here. That's his intention—it always has been his intention—and I don't see how you can dodge or deny it any longer.'

'You've been telling us,' said Morland, 'that Samarai is an intelligent man. Not a visionary, but a practical man. A man who has concocted a definite plan. And then you say his plan is armed rebellion. But if he has the smallest fragment of intelligence he knows the consequence of that: sooner or later he would be caught and hanged. And when you tell me that he's setting out on a course of action which, as he knows, will inevitably lead him to the gallows—well, I simply don't believe you.'

'Intelligence has its limits, and perception doesn't go all the way,' said the Sultan.

'We're on the Dutch border,' said Kershawe, 'and Dutch territory has been practically unadministered for the last three or four years, because of trouble with the Indonesians. If Samarai took his people across the frontier—'

'That's juvenile romanticism,' said Morland contemptuously.

'It would create a problem,' said the Sultan. 'I wonder how you would deal with it? But if he succeeds in doing that, you won't have to deal with it, of course. You won't be here.'

There was a little interval of silence, and then Morland said, 'I haven't time for speculation, I'm afraid. I've got to deal with the situation as it is. If Samarai's people are coming here, we can't stop them, and we'll have to evacuate the jail and the married quarters.'

'The women and children are here already, in the servants' rooms,' said Kershawe. 'There are only seven of them.'

'That leaves the prisoners,' said Morland, 'and the best thing to do with them is to send them up the hill to where you've been felling timber. You've got a hut there where they can sleep.'

'I built it as a shelter against rain,' said Kershawe. 'It's poor accommodation for twenty-three men.'

'They can put up with it,' said Morland. 'It won't be for very long. But we'll have to send two constables to look after them, which is a pity. And rations are going to be a nuisance.'

'They've three days' rations in the jail,' said Kershawe. 'They can carry their own.'

'That should do them,' said Morland. 'Well, sir, I'll have to go and make some arrangements. Would you like to come along, Pemberton?'

'Do you think he is rescuing Pemberton from my bad influence?' asked the Sultan when they had gone. 'Oh, God, how I wish I could persuade him to be sensible! But he's got so much veneration for his own judgment that he can't imagine anything happening to disprove it. And he won't see reason, because reason doesn't acknowledge his jurisdiction.'

'Sixteen years in the service, and never heard a shot fired in anger: that's on his mind too,' said Kershawe. 'He never tires of telling you that.'

'He's a man of very high principle,' said the Sultan irritably, 'but at the moment he's a great nuisance and a source of danger. There's no point now in saying he should have arrested Samarai as soon as this business started—I'm not sure I'd have done that myself; I don't like interfering with people till I have to—but it's certainly fair to say he should have acted as soon as he heard the first rumour of this damned sorcerer's jobbery. It's not too late even now. If you took half a dozen constables and went straight in, I think you could pick him up without much trouble.'

'I think so too.'

'And if he resisted, you'd be fully justified in shooting him. You'd be justified in shooting him whether he resisted or not. The law's quite clear about that. And if Samarai was eliminated, there'd be no trouble from the rest of them.'

'I'm quite willing to try, sir.'

'You couldn't without open defiance of your superior officer, and I'm not going to let you ruin your career.'

Kershawe, with youthful vanity, said his career meant very little to him, but the Sultan, telling him not to be a fool, said impatiently, 'In any case you couldn't defy him. Not effectively. He would order the constables to stay where they are, and they wouldn't know which of you to follow.'

'If he did that, wouldn't you be justified in putting him under arrest?' asked Kershawe hopefully.

'I might have done it at your age; but not now. I'm rather anxious, at present, not to offend him. Not to offend him, that is, more deeply than I have done.'

Kershawe said, 'If I had your approval—if you would stand by me afterwards—I think I could do something on my own, without bringing the police into it. Except Corporal Apu, perhaps.'

'What are you proposing?'

'Corporal Apu found it easy enough to mix with them. He

was standing within a couple of yards of Samarai at one time. And what he did, I can do.'

'Have you done it before?'

'We've been out together three or four times. And nobody recognized us. I usually wear nothing but a pair of shorts, so I'm nearly as dark as they are. And I've got one of their wigs.'

The Sultan stood up and went to the table, and poured a whisky and soda. He offered the bottle to Kershawe, who refused it. 'You couldn't tell Morland,' he said. 'That's obvious. But eventually you would have to explain why, without consulting him, you undertook a mission—a personal mission—of which you knew he would disapprove. And what would your explanation be?'

'That I'm District Officer here, and it's my duty to take all proper measures for the security and welfare of Maipani. But I'd like you to back me up when I say so.'

The Sultan regarded him with a grave intensity, but when he spoke his voice was brisk and unemotional, a good chairman's voice. 'Let us consider the risks,' he said. 'The avoidable and the unavoidable risks. Let us estimate, if we can, the feasibility of the adventure.'

Fifteen

WITHOUT apparent need for secrecy—with no tactical reason for it—but obeying a primitive impulse to conceal their movements, the pagans took a difficult route to the air-strip, and reached it unobserved. They went down the glen where they had congregated, and along a very narrow, and in many places a dangerous track, that ran some two hundred feet below the edge of the great ravine. Throughout their march they were in utter darkness in the ravine, but they moved quickly and silently, in single file, and came up and on to the air-strip still under cover of the dark; for by now the moon had gone beyond the rampart of the tall, further mountains, and the lingering stars shone small and dim—or so they seemed to those who had watched all night from the Rest House, and were tired of watching, and a little cold and tetchy in the chill silence of the last hour of the night.

One of the constables was the first to see movement in the darkness. He gave the alarm softly and without surprise, as though what he had been waiting for all the time was a thickened obscurity, a more solid-seeming shadow cushioning the ground and moving on it, that would presently be recognized as a closely packed horde of men and women advancing very slowly and as quietly as sleep-walkers.

He gave the alarm, and with a little rush and flurry of movement, with the occasional thud of a rifle-butt on the resounding floor of the veranda, the small garrison of the Rest House stood to their posts. The native constables were unperturbed. They had acquired, by drill and discipline, by some measure of general education and much practice on the rifle-range, a genial contempt for their fellow-countrymen, whose ignorance they despised and whose weapons they derided. Sergeant Kula walked round the outpost-line—which consisted of two constables in front of the Rest House and two behind it—as calmly confident as an inspector of the Metropolitan Police making his last review of traffic control before an international football match.

But in the bungalow Morland, though he controlled his nervousness, could not quite conceal it. Some hours earlier he had lost both temper and dignity—dignity foundering in a gale of anger—when he discovered the absence of Kershawe and Corporal Apu, and the Sultan told him that Kershawe, using the normal discretion of a District Officer, had gone to make closer observation of any menace to their safety that Samarai or his followers might utter or intend. Morland immediately accused the Sultan of encouraging Kershawe to defy him; and the Sultan admitted that he had, indeed, approved of Kershawe's proposal. Morland promptly declared, with a fevered lack of discretion, his intention to ruin and dislodge both of them—dissolute prince and insubordinate officer—from their privilege and position. He would over-ride the Governor, if necessary, and state his case directly to the Colonial Office. . . .

Morland had betrayed himself. He had uncovered the stratum of fear that underlay his ponderous insistence on the necessity, in any circumstances, of a patient mind and a pacific policy. He had revealed his hatred of those who, lacking his fear and less sensitive than he to the iniquity of taking life, were prepared to be brutal when brutality was logically—or, on the lesser scale, empirically—required. His language grew more offensive than his imputations, and the Sultan, with a discretion that he did not always use, chose not to listen. With a remote and abstracted air he looked for, and found, his volume of the collected novels of Thomas Peacock, and a box of cigars, and retired to his own room.

Now, reviving his anger, Morland perceived in the absence of Kershawe and his corporal an irremediable weakness in the defence of the bungalow. They had fifteen all told, counting the Sultan's cook and steward, but he insisted that Kershawe's defection had left gaps they could not fill. He still did not anticipate attack—this he repeated in a high-pitched voice—but if they were attacked, their flanks would be insufficiently protected.

The dark mass of the slowly advancing savages, now a little more obvious, halted four or five hundred yards away, and Tom Penny, aiming his rifle, said, 'Christ! What a target!'

Morland immediately said, 'Put down that rifle, Penny, or I'll have you under arrest.'

'What do you want me to do?' asked Penny rudely. 'Take out cups of tea to them?'

Somewhere in the crowd drummers began to beat a strongly marked rhythm, and the mass of people, opening and dispersing on level ground, grew less opaque.

In the bungalow there were now no lights but candles burning behind cardboard shades: Mrs. Nottingham, nervous of the arrows that a well-lit target might attract, had suggested this, and Morland had approved of the precaution. She and Mrs. Pemberton, coming from their rooms at the same moment, alarmed by the drums, met in the dark hall where the yellowish flames of two candles floated, detached and ineffectual and almost irrelevant, in the general obscurity; and Mrs. Pemberton asked in a small, dried-up voice, 'Do you know where the brandy is?'

'I've come to look for it,' said Mrs. Nottingham, and pulled a half-drawn cork from a bottle on the sideboard. She sniffed, and said, 'Can you find any glasses?' She poured, with a splash, reckless measures into two tumblers, and Mrs. Pemberton, after a nervous sip, drank more boldly and said, 'I suppose this is how people feel in a sinking ship when they've been told to put on their life-belts.'

'Don't exaggerate, Emily. We're not cold, and we're not drenched with spray.'

'But I felt, when I got up, as if the floor was sinking under me.'

'Your knees, you mean. It's only for the sake of my knees I'm drinking. My brain's perfectly clear and fairly calm. We really shouldn't be frightened. I'm sure of that, though my knees aren't. We're in no more danger than people caught in a street row, a continental students' riot.'

'People get hurt in a riot.'

'Not if they keep their heads and behave reasonably.'

'I don't know if I'm really frightened or not, but I feel awfully miserable, and I think I want to be sick.'

'Brandy will cure that. Drink it up.'

Morland came in and asked loudly, 'Is Pemberton here?'

'No,' said Mrs. Pemberton. 'I haven't seen him—oh, for an hour at least.'

'I can't think where he's gone.'

He went out again, and Mrs. Pemberton said defiantly, 'I'm not going to feel worried about William! He brought me here, and he's enjoyed himself. He doesn't deserve any sympathy, whatever happens to him.'

Morland went round the veranda to the servants' quarters in the other bungalow, and found Oala, the police interpreter, and the native dresser from the hospital sitting in gloomy silence with a couple of houseboys and four or five women, wives of married constables, in a small, close-smelling, candle-lit room. They looked up as he opened the door, raising their

178

heads in slow inquiry as if fearful of ill-tidings, and in their glittering eyeballs the candle-flame found dancing pin-points of reflexion, like the reflexion of a star in a sluggish stream in the jungle.

Oala was a smallish, lightly built man with a clever-seeming head and the quick, ingratiating manner of one who, bred in a mixed community, had learnt from childhood to adapt himself to circumstances and protect himself against injustice. As soon as Morland asked if anyone had seen Pemberton he scrambled to his feet and protested shrilly that he was wholly and entirely blameless. That master, he said, had wanted him to go down to the office, down to the store-sheds, but he had refused to have anything to do with so foolish a proposal. He had refused point-blank, because it was against orders to leave the Rest House, and might also be extremely dangerous 'to life and limb'. Oala clasped his hands and shook his head in virtuous negation of the wicked suggestion.

But why, asked Morland, had Pemberton wanted to go down to the office?

Because of his great interest in the people, Oala explained. Always he wanted to walk among them, and hear what they were saying, and watch everything they did. Whether they were dancing, or cooking, or only talking together, he must always be close to them.

'Why didn't you come and tell me, at once, when he asked you to do this?' Morland demanded.

Oala put on a pitiable expression and said he had been frightened to come between one master and another, and Morland, without waiting for him to finish, shut the door with a bang, and hurrying to the front veranda told the Sultan and Tom Penny, in a voice of exhausted indignation, what had happened.

'It's always the white man who makes trouble,' he exclaimed.

'Any white man's a bigger nuisance than five hundred natives. If Pemberton interferes with them, at this stage, they'll put their spears into him—and who can blame them?'

Tom Penny sucked his teeth and with genuine sympathy said, 'It's a fair cow!'

'I don't see what you can do about it,' said the Sultan. 'If he gets cut up, you won't be held responsible.'

'Nevertheless,' said Morland, 'I am responsible. I gave him permission to come to Maipani, and so long as he's here I've got an obligation to look after him. Oh, damn the man, I'll have to go and bring him in.'

'Don't be a fool, Morland.'

'If he's kept close to the office, or one of the store-sheds, they probably haven't noticed him yet, and I can go down behind the gardens. I think it'll be fairly safe that way.'

'You're taking a big risk, and it may be quite unnecessary. He's probably safe enough, so long as he keeps his head down.'

'You know Pemberton. That's just what he won't do.'

'But if anything happens to you—'

Morland's lips were twitching nervously, but with a bitter humour he said, 'You needn't be afraid. I've a reputation for caution that's much too valuable to throw away.'

'I'll go and have a look, if you're really fretting about him,' said Penny.

'No, it's my job. You stay where you are.'

'Then you'd better have my revolver,' said the Sultan.

'I shan't need it. I'll take this stick.'

He took a hill-walker's long stick that someone had propped against the wall, and running down the steps turned left towards the gardens.

'Well, who'd have thought it?' said Penny.

'Poor fellow!' said the Sultan. 'Poor devil! What a damnable great burden a sense of duty is. He was trembling all over, poor chap. And as for being cautious, my God, he's gone off without a word to the outposts. You'll have to warn them, Penny, or they'll shoot him on his way back.'

'Too true,' said Penny, 'and I'd better have a word with the rear rank too. Hasn't it struck you that all this corroboree might be just a performance to keep us interested, while the real attack comes in from behind?'

'It's possible. But I expect Kershawe is somewhere out in front of us—that's where the main body certainly is—so we've got to keep our eyes to the front.'

The darkness was thinning and slowly dissolving before the approach of dawn. The mountains, hard and solid and black, were discernible against the now irresolute obscurity of the sky, and on the fringes of the savage crowd single figures could be distinguished. The drums were loud and insistent, but as yet there was no excitement in their rhythm—only a promise, a threat of excitement—and in the middle of the crowd, where dancing had begun, there was a turbulence that became more manifest, and acquired form, as the circumference drew back to give the dancers room.

Penny said, 'I'll go round and have a word with them at the back.'

'And make sure the constables in front know their orders. Let them know about Morland, and remind them of what I told them. Two blasts on the whistle means five rounds deliberate fire—and cocks only.'

'I'll tell them, sir. Don't you worry, there's plenty of time.'

'Too much, if not too little,' said the Sultan in a draught of morning melancholy; but Tom Penny did not hear him, and a few minutes after he had gone Mrs. Pemberton came out, inconspicuous in the shadow—she had changed into a brown linen dress—and stood for a moment, hesitant before she asked, 'Have you found William yet?'

The Sultan, leaning on the parapet, looked round and said, 'Not yet, but he'll turn up all right. Come and see what Penny calls "the corroboree". Not that you can see much at present, but it's getting lighter every minute.'

She stood beside him, her elbows on the sandbags, and said, 'I suppose William's down there, watching them. Mr. Morland said he was missing, but I told Elizabeth I wasn't going to worry about him any more.'

Her face, in that light—or absence of light—was colourless as a drypoint, and her anger, or the dusk, gave her features a hardness that emphasized their good line and showed, as daylight had not, the firm and comely structure of her prettiness. The Sultan looked at her with a new admiration, and decided to say nothing of Morland's errand.

'William,' she continued, 'is a Doctor of Philosophy, and this is how he behaves. Without a thought for anyone but himself. And two days ago, when I was copying some notes for him, he called me a fool—me a fool!—because I spelt fertility rites like right or wrong: you know.'

'In a way,' said the Sultan, 'he deserves our admiration. He's a good example of the single-minded scientist.'

'Then single-minded scientists oughtn't to get married.'

'I'm afraid marriage was made for the middle classes, Emily, and those who don't belong to the middle classes—whether by circumstance or temperament—are usually not much good at it.'

'But I belong to the middle classes! And I could be very good at it—very good indeed—if only he would give me some encouragement.'

'Now don't get excited. Please don't. You've been very good so far, and very brave. Would you like a little brandy?'

'I've had some brandy.'

'Well, have some more.'

'I've had some more. I suppose that's why I'm brave.'

'Dutch courage is better than none: that's certainly true.'

'Are you never frightened?'

'Good heavens, yes! If I stop to consider possibilities I can be frightened of almost anything: of thunder-storms, and crossing Piccadilly Circus, and going blind, and choking on fish-bones, and dying. If we really thought about death we could all paralyse ourselves with fear. But we don't. I don't, at any rate, and I don't suppose you do.'

'I never have done till now. But now I can't help it. Do you think Mr. Kershawe has been killed?'

'No, I'm sure he hasn't. We'll see something of him before long, I expect. Don't worry about him, but if you're getting nervous again, try deep breathing. Breathe deeply and slowly.'

'Does that help?'

'It's one of the most useful of the physical aids to courage. The best of all, of course, is toothache; but you seldom get toothache when you really want it. With a raging toothache no one can be afraid, because there's nothing worse. I have never been a brave man, but I once behaved with the utmost gallantry, merely because I had a gumboil.'

'What did you do?'

'I was in the Army at the time, in one of our wars, and the attack we were making was held up by a machine-gun about two hundred yards away. I was lying in a very wet hole in the ground, suffering indescribable agony from my gumboil, and when I could endure it no longer I seized a rifle and bayonet from a private soldier who was lying beside me, and leapt from my hole with an ear-splitting yell. The impetus of the pain was so great that I covered the ground like a jet-propelled kangaroo, and it was with intense relief that I assaulted the wretched men who had been firing the machine-gun. I hit one of them so hard, with the butt of my rifle, that

I burst my gumboil, and when my company followed up they found me sitting on the ground, spitting blood and crying my heart out. In pure gratitude.'

'You're making that up. You're trying to help me, aren't you? By taking my mind off things.'

'Every word of it is true: I promise you! Why, good heavens, they gave me a medal for it. A Military Cross.'

'My brother got a Military Cross.'

'For toothache?'

'No, for blowing up a bridge.'

'That must be a most satisfying thing to do. But you're not breathing deeply.'

'I'm trying to.'

'Do you know where your diaphragm is?'

'Here.'

'No, a little higher.'

They had turned about, they had their backs to the parapet now, ignoring deliberately the sombre din of the drums and the sullen fervour of the prancing savages on the air-strip. The Sultan put his left arm round Emily's acquiescent shoulders, and gently laying his right hand on her midriff, showed her how to breathe and be calm.

'Breathe in, and out,' he said. 'In, and out.'

Tom Penny came round the corner, and whistled in admiration of the tender scene. 'It's nice work when you can get it,' he said.

'In—out, in—out,' repeated the Sultan. 'That's the rhythm, now try to keep it up.' And turning to Penny explained, 'For an attack of nerves, my dear Tom, I always recommend a simple breathing exercise. I've found it useful more than once. But you, of course, don't know what nerves are.'

'Don't I indeed!' said Penny. 'I've had my bad times like everyone else. My word!'

'Are you frightened now, Mr. Penny?'

'Well, I'm not exactly shaking in my shoes, but I won't deny that I'll be glad when this bit of fuss and bother's all over.'

'Have you ever been really frightened?' she asked.

Penny took off his steel helmet to scratch his head, replaced it, and said thoughtfully. 'I got engaged to be married once—only once—and my young lady took me to see her father and mother. I was shaking in my shoes that day! So before I met her I had a few beers, see? Just to keep my pecker up. And when I got there I didn't behave too good, and the old man said, "My daughter's been brought up as a lady, and she isn't going to marry no roustabout like you." And threw me out on my ear. And the next thing I knew I was hanging on to a lamppost, singing "Jerusalem the Golden", I was so pleased and thankful.'

'You're just like the Sultan,' said Mrs. Pemberton indignantly. 'You're making up stories to amuse me, as if I were a child.'

'I'll take my oath it's true! Every syllable.'

'You needn't bother. I'm not going to embarrass you, I promise that.'

'In—out, in—out,' murmured the Sultan.

'I wouldn't say no to a nice cup of tea,' said Penny, 'if someone was to bring it out to me. Do you think you could do anything about that, Mrs. Pemberton?'

'I'd love to make tea for you,' she exclaimed. 'And for you too?' she asked the Sultan.

'Yes indeed. Tea for two, and brandy for yourself, if you feel like it.'

'Thank you,' she said gravely. 'Perhaps I will.'

They watched her go in, and Penny asked, 'Got her under control?'

'I think she'll be all right. She's a delightful creature, I'm very fond of her. And what a pleasure it is to be kind to a young, good-looking girl.'

'Not for me, not if they're white,' said Penny. 'I got cured of them years ago. I transferred my interest to brown ones, and I've stuck to them ever since. They're less trouble and give more satisfaction.'

'You should be open-minded, it's a great mistake to specialize.'

'Some like variety, some like what they're used to: that's human nature, always at cross-purposes. — No sign of Morland yet?'

'No, not yet.'

'They're warming up, aren't they?'

The crowd had divided into unequal parts. On the right, on the east side of the air-strip, were two or three hundred men in loose array, stamping or shuffling in time to the drums, in front of whom half a dozen dancers leapt high and shook their spears, gestured and pirouetted, each apparently in lonely abandon to his emotions, for there was no uniformity in their steps. On the other side, applauding the dancers and now surging towards them, now retreating, was a much larger throng, many of whom were women. At the far end, sitting together, the drummers with arms as frantic as the dancers beat upon their tabors. It was now light enough to see them clearly, but the light did not yet show the colour of their barbaric ornaments. It was a picture in monochrome, and the to-and-fro movement of the larger crowd had raised a thin powdering of dust. There were no clouds above the mountains, and the promise of the sky was a clear morning.

'Between four and five hundred yards,' said the Sultan, and pressed up the slide on the backsight of his rifle. 'I've known him for years, Tom, and never till this morning have I ever wanted to see poor Morland. But I wish to God he'd show up now.'

Mrs. Nottingham came out and asked, 'Is it true that Pemberton's still missing?'

'He's not the only one,' said Penny, and turned his head to listen to a thin, wailing voice that came from the servants' quarters, and before it reached its despairing height was joined by another, as shrilly mournful. 'It's that bitch Tata,' he said. 'Constable Pehu's wife. She's been giving trouble already, and if she really starts howling she'll set all the others off.'

'Shall I go and speak to her?' asked Mrs. Nottingham.

'No,' said Penny, 'she'd pay no attention to you, you'd be too gentle. I know how to deal with her. God, there she goes again.'

He hurried off as another wail rose and shivered into loneliness and terror, and a second voice picked up the note and howled in unison. But presently the din stopped, as abruptly as if a knife had cut it; and Mrs. Nottingham asked, 'What did he mean by saying Pemberton wasn't the only one?'

The Sultan told her of the recklessness that a sense of duty had demanded, so improbably, from Morland; and she leaned on the parapet and looked at the savage crowd beneath, stamping and advancing in a haze of dust, as if searching for him in the tangle of their arms.

She watched them intently, silent and absorbed for several minutes. Then she said, 'We haven't much to be proud of, have we?'

'Don't you see the germs of poetry and the ballet? Their minds are in a turmoil of creation.'

'I see nothing but dirt and horror.'

She watched them moodily, silent again until a sharp-edged thought woke in her brain; and suddenly she asked, 'Did you encourage Morland to go?'

'Indeed I didn't.'

'Did you try to prevent him?'

'Yes, after a fashion. I told him not to be a fool, and I said he wasn't responsible for Pemberton's folly. I couldn't do much more. He would never agree with me, whatever I said.'

'I thought, for a moment, you might have been glad to see him go—and realize he mightn't come back.'

'That,' said the Sultan, 'is a remark in extraordinarily bad taste.'

'It would save you a lot of trouble if he didn't return.'

'It would be a great grief to me if he didn't return.'

'You don't like him, and he doesn't like you.'

'But I don't want him to be killed. I would miss him. I would miss him dreadfully.'

'If we're all alive next week,' she said, 'if we're alive next Friday when the aeroplane comes in, will he still say he's going to arrest me and send me back to Fairweather?'

'There's not much doubt of that. A small police action, such as this that we're involved in, isn't going to make our good Morland forsake the path of duty.'

'But you promised—'

'And if it comforts you to hear it again, I'll repeat my promise. Whatever Morland threatens, you will not go to Fairweather except by your own desire. Now does that satisfy you?'

'It sounds ridiculous, but I wish you didn't feel so confident,' she said. 'You were too confident in the beginning, and over-confidence misled you then. When we first met, I mean. It misled me too, of course. You were so sure that you were deeply attracted to me, but the fact is you were only attracted because I was in trouble, and it pleased you to help me.'

'That, my dear Elizabeth, is a wild and silly distortion of what happened, and why it happened. When I asked you to come for a voyage with me, I wasn't moved by charity, I was moved by a simple desire for you and your company. It was you I wanted, not your misfortunes.'

'You found me crying one day, and you thought I would always be soft and clinging. And if I had been, we might have got on very well together. I do keep you amused, when we're not quarrelling.'

'You understate your case. You've taught me to add respect to my affection.'

'Respect!' she said scornfully. 'Yes, and that makes us really incompatible. As soon as you saw that I wasn't prepared to be always subservient, you knew I wasn't what you wanted. Respect was the last thing I should have taught you. Because it was subservience you were looking for.'

'Now let us be fair and dispassionate,' said the Sultan. 'Oh, damn those drums, I wish they'd be quiet! But let us be as calm as we can, in the circumstances, and tell me if subservience isn't what you also were hoping for? On your own admission you have usually had men whom you could dominate—'

'And all your women have been clinging vines.'

'So in spite of affection—or because of respect—we can't live happily together for the shocking reason that we resemble each other too closely. Is that it?'

'Well, now you see the trouble we're going to have when Morland comes back and your police action, as you call it, is happily concluded. If it can be concluded.'

Now the sky above the mountains was bright with the ascending radiance of the sun, and on the pale ground of the air-strip—pale green and worn patches of yellow soil—the dancers and their attendant crowd were decked in gaudy colours that gave them, from a distance, a savage splendour. Feathers of golden-brown and peacock-blue fluttered about prancing knees, and plumes of parrot-green and parrot-scarlet jigged on heads among heads monstrously enlarged by cere-monial wigs. There was no glint of steel, for all their spears and axe-heads were dull with rust and dirt, but the rude war-paint of the men—ochre stripes or red, or blotches of white clay—distracted the eye. It so broke and dissipated the brown mass of humanity that sometimes the number of leaping bodies seemed to double itself, sometimes strangely to diminish. Only the women were still naked and unadorned. The men wore loin-cloths or short kilts of faded red or blue, as well as their plumes and necklets; they were dressed for great occasion and to impress their enemies. The clamour of the drums was now accompanied by a hoarse and rhythmic shouting.

'I've got everything ready, as far as I can,' said Mrs. Not-tingham. 'There was a lot of stuff in the medicine-chest: bandages and dressings, antiseptics and morphia, thank good-ness. And there's plenty of hot water.'

'You're a fine woman, Elizabeth. You've got splendid nerves.'

'And they're all ringing like fire-alarms.'

'One's bound to feel apprehensive. But the constables are very good. You can rely on them.'

'For God's sake don't tell me we're in no danger. That's what I've been telling Emily, but I don't believe it. And if I did, I'd have nothing to think about except next Friday, and Morland coming to arrest me, and you telling Morland "You can't arrest my wife!" Can't you understand that I don't want to be your wife, and nothing will induce me to marry you?'

'Not even to save yourself from prison, or from being deported? Deported to Rumania?'

Before she could reply—before she could repair the sudden fracture of her composure and set words in their order—there came a shout from below the bungalow, on the right-hand side, and Penny, waving an excited arm, cried, 'There's half a dozen of them down in that banana-patch. Can you see anything from there?'

The Sultan went quickly to the corner of the veranda, where a constable stood on guard; but neither could see any movement under the enormous ragged leaves that made a green harbour beside Kershawe's old bungalow. Penny came on to the veranda, a little breathless, and said, 'I was just scouting round when I saw the bastards running. Then I lost sight of them. There may be more than half a dozen.'

'That's the way Morland would come.'

'I went down to see if there was any sign of him. But it looks like he's been unlucky.'

'My poor old Morland. He wasn't the sort to bring off a last-minute rescue.'

'He ought to have let Pemberton stew in his own juice.'

'We'll have her on our hands now, I suppose. But don't say anything to her yet, Elizabeth.'

'I certainly shan't,' said Mrs. Nottingham bitterly. 'If an explanation's wanted, you're the one to make it. You can prove to her that the whole situation's still perfectly normal.'

'We still control it, I assure you of that.'

'And we won't have any argument now,' said Penny. 'We're on our own now, sir.'

'And I think the curtain's about to go up.'

The smaller division—the long, wavering double rank of shuffling, stamping warriors—was wheeling clumsily to face the Rest House, and the larger throng was pressing back against the buildings—the office and the store-sheds and the hospital—to give them room. There was much confusion in the movement, it was slow and ragged, but the intention was obvious.

'You'd better go inside, Elizabeth. And please don't be

fanciful. Don't exaggerate what's happening just because you hear some rifle fire.'

'I shan't be worrying about next Friday, that's one thing to be thankful for,' she said; and went indoors.

The lines of painted, decorated warriors advanced with a slow, fantastic, and wavering movement. They had spread out, and covered a front of about two hundred yards. Here and there a man stopped, as if suddenly remembering what he had to do, and stooped and strung his long bow, or fumbled for an arrow. Others, waving their spears, broke the line to dance a whirling, eccentric dance of some private frenzy. They were under command, though it was impossible to see who commanded them; for some three hundred yards from the bungalow the advance was halted, and though no man stood still, they came no nearer. The drums now sounded far away, for the drummers, squatting on the ground, had remained where they were, and some of the larger crowd of women and uncommitted men had come forward in front of them, and muted their sound.

There were four constables lying out behind breast-works fifty yards from the bungalow, and one at each corner of the front veranda. The Sultan and Penny knelt at the loop-holes on either side of the steps.

'They haven't made up their minds yet, Tom.'

'Do you think it's all a bluff? I wish I could see what's going on behind us.'

'I think Samarai's bound to be somewhere in the crowd, and if he's there Kershawe's not far away.'

'Unless he's been scuppered too.'

'For God's sake don't say that!'

Then, suddenly, the drumming stopped and the shouting and screaming wavered and diminished into a sibilant murmuration, a grunting restlessness. The quiet—the croaking, chattering, half-quiet—lasted a few seconds only, and was sharply broken by two shots fired in quick succession. 'It's him!' cried the Sultan, and blew a whistle.

Penny was the first to fire, but the constable at the right-hand corner was only a moment behind him. The Sultan was taking a deliberate aim when the front door of the bungalow was clumsily opened and Mrs. Pemberton came on to the veranda carrying a tray on which were a brown earthenware teapot, two large blue and white cups, and a rack of toast. The Sultan fired, and there was a ripple of shots from the constables in front. She winced at the hard, ear-thudding reports, but did not falter. She blinked in a glare of light—for now the sun was a molten inch above the eastern mountains—but she was not disconcerted. 'I've brought your tea,' she said.

Her cheeks were flushed with exertion and the two or three glasses of brandy she had drunk. She was solemnly intent on doing what she had been asked to do, and when no one paid attention to her she set the tray on the small table that stood beside the door, and to the echoing accompaniment of the fusillade poured carefully two cups of tea. She added milk and sugar, and was about to carry a cup to the Sultan when a rattle of fire and a concert of screams from the rearward bungalow disturbed her calm. But she remembered her duty, her promise to be brave, and with only a tinkle of the spoon in the saucer to betray a revival of emotion, she put the cup on the sandbag wall and said again, 'I've brought your tea.'

But the Sultan, still ignoring her, rose to his feet and shouted with the whole power of his voice, 'Cease fire!' Then, turning to Penny, cried, 'It's all over here, Tom. Get round to the back and see what's happening there.'

'I'll do that, sir.'

'You little fool,' said the Sultan.

'They're all running away!' she exclaimed.

'Yes, look at them. Take a good look, for I don't suppose you'll ever see that again. That's panic.'

As if a sudden storm, a whirling devastating wind, had broken on the valley and now carried them before it like the refuse of autumn leaves in a wood, the savages had scattered and fled, but in their flight were still uncertain of direction. A hundred, two hundred, running pell-mell, would pause and stop, caught in some eddy of doubt, and turn to run the other way. They ran in flocks, and darkened the ground like the shadow of racing clouds. Then, as though the gale that afflicted their minds had steadied and found a settled course, the greater number of them took to the western hillside and disappeared in the direction of the glen where they had lain before; but some headed the other way and trampled through Kershawe's gardens, while a few ran desperately uphill behind the Rest House. They left behind them a litter of weapons, and five or six bodies asprawl and still on the grass.

Penny came back and reported that the attack on the rear had been driven off, but one of the constables was badly wounded; and Mrs. Nottingham was looking after him.

'There were about eighty of them, so Sergeant Kula says, and they were a determined lot of bastards. They got within range before they were spotted. The sandbags there are stuck so full of arrows they look like a porcupine. And all the women started screaming, of course, and went on screaming till I caught that bitch Tata a smack across the face that shook the ham out of her teeth.'

'Go and help Elizabeth,' said the Sultan to Mrs. Pemberton. 'You're quite safe now, and you've nothing more to worry about. Tom Penny and I are going down to look for Kershawe.'

'But I'm coming with you,' she said. 'There's William—look, there!—and Mr. Morland with him.'

Sixteen

MORLAND had been unable to find Pemberton till it grew light, when he saw him lying on the thatched roof of one of the store-sheds. They had argued for some time with increasing warmth, Pemberton protesting that he had a damned good view and wasn't going to leave it. Morland stood on the blind side of the shed, but Pemberton, sitting up, showed head and shoulders above the ridge. A man and three women came round the corner and discovered them.

'The man threatened me with his spear,' said Morland, 'but I jabbed at him with my stick, and they ran away.'

Pemberton, with a belated acknowledgment of danger, slid down the roof and they tried to return to the Rest House through the gardens. But they were seen and pursued, and took refuge in Kershawe's old bungalow. The door hung loose on its hinges. They forced it, unobserved, and buttressed it from the inside with a discarded, broken-legged sofa. When someone tried to open the door, the buttress held. A man pressed his face against a window and stared in, but apparently saw nothing, and went away. They heard voices outside, but the savages made no further attempt to break in, and they had stayed quietly in the house till they heard firing.

'Then it was my turn to be sensible,' said Pemberton. 'He wanted to run out and try to stop it, but I said no. I stood in front of the sofa and went on saying no, till we heard peace and quietness again.'

'I am most grateful to you,' said the Sultan. 'If Morland's

recklessness had led him into danger, we might have had a loss beyond repair.'

'I want to know,' said Morland, 'who gave the order to fire.'

'I did,' said the Sultan.

'On what grounds?'

'We can go into that later. Pemberton, I think your wife is looking tired. You should take her back to the Rest House.'

'Yes, I'll be glad to. I could do with a cup of tea now.'

'She is expert at providing tea. Off you go, Mrs. Pemberton, and I'll come too as soon as we've found Kershawe.'

'Where do you expect to find him?' asked Morland.

'He can't be far away,' said the Sultan, and watched for a moment the two retreating figures. Mrs. Pemberton, her late displeasure with her husband apparently forgotten, was holding his hand and talking earnestly to him.

'O God, look at that—and that!'

Morland pointed to two bodies that lay nearby in the wild attitude of their death, and said with great bitterness, 'In all the years of my service I have never seen such a sight before. There's the ultimate confession of failure! You've got a lot to answer for, sir.'

'You might have had more,' said the Sultan.

Penny, who had gone ahead, stood some fifty yards from the office, and signalled them to join him. But Morland paid no attention. Morland, his fingers trembling and tears in his eyes, was very deeply moved, but he himself could not have said whether sorrow for his children or anger with the Sultan was his true emotion. 'How many?' he demanded.

'I saw five drop in front of us, and there are more, I'm afraid, at the back of the house.'

A body that lay on the further side of the air-strip began to move, and rose loosely to its hands and knees. 'God damn you for this!' cried Morland, and hurried towards the wounded man

Should one be damned for self-preservation? thought the Sultan. Should I be damned for preserving Morland and Tom Penny and Elizabeth, and that dear child Emily? Well, perhaps. Perhaps it depends on one's motive. And I wonder what my motive really was. . . .

'Here they are,' said Penny. 'Both of them.' And he pointed to two bodies that lay, face down, with gaping, ruddy holes in their backs.

'Samarai?'

'And the boy.'

They were startled by a hoarse, unhappy voice that shouted, 'Tom Penny! Tom! I'm Kershawe.'

They looked round, and in the open door of the office saw what appeared to be a painted savage, kilted and be-feathered.

'My Christ,' said Penny, 'is that him?'

'Don't shoot, I'm Kershawe!'

'It's him, all right.'

'Of course it is,' said the Sultan, and walked towards him. 'What's the matter with you, Kershawe?'

'Do you recognize me, sir?'

'I know who you are, but I doubt if your mother could recognize you, looking like that.'

'I'm sorry, sir, I fell into a panic after it was all over. After we'd done it. I wasn't frightened of them—well, not much—but then I thought we might be shot by our own people. And Corporal Apu got the same idea. He's in the back room and he won't come out.'

Kershawe, looking inane behind his warlike paint, began to cry, and said, 'I'll be all right in a minute, sir, but it was a bloody awful thing to do, and we'd had a difficult time with them, it was a bit of a strain all through, and then we got frightened, for no reason, I suppose, but just reaction, don't you think? But I'll be all right. I'm all right now, as a matter of fact. I'll just have a word with Corporal Apu and let him know we've got nothing to worry about, and then I'll tell you what happened.'

He went into the inner room, and the Sultan said, 'Will you stay here, Tom, and take charge? Don't let anyone touch Samarai and the boy. I'm going with Kershawe to his own bungalow; I want to give him a drink before Morland sees him. He's had as much as he can carry.'

'He's had more than I could carry, going round with that mob half the night. I wouldn't have done it for all the oil in Te Aku.'

'The corporal had better stay here in the meantime, and I'll send a constable to get him some proper clothes.'

'I'll help him to clean up. He'll feel better when he's looking respectable.'

Kershawe came out of the other room, the paint on his cheeks smudged with tears, but his carriage erect and his voice firm again. 'I feel a bloody fool, sir,' he said, 'but I'm thankful it was you and not Morland who found me. We were sitting in here shivering like a couple of small boys who thought they'd seen a ghost, and with just as little reason. But that's over, and if you want to hear exactly what we did—'

'I want to hear nothing till you've had a bath and a drink. We're going to your bungalow now, and I think we should go the back way, and keep out of sight.'

The Sultan was full of an exhilarating sense of well-being. Kershawe was safe, whom he had sent on a hard and perilous mission; and the calculated risk had been justified, his judgment vindicated. Kershawe was safe, and Samarai's revolt had been put down at little cost. Elizabeth and Tom Penny and the Pembertons were all safe, Morland was safe, and the Sultan had discovered, with a renewed delight, that he was truly glad of Morland's survival: though Morland had already damned him and was clearly going to be intolerant in opinion and obdurate in error, he was happier to see Morland living than Morland dead. A battle, thought the Sultan, is only the preliminary to peace, and peace has always presented more problems than war. But peace had rewards as well as difficulties. The mountains rose soaring in grandeur to a blue pellucid sky, and in their narrow valley they lay, sun-warmed, on the lap of the mountains. After a long, tormented night it was bliss to be alive in the bright space of morning, and the air they breathed was euphory.

Briskly, in Kershawe's bungalow, the Sultan—his pleasure now paternal—turned on the bath and spread a towel on a chair. Blandly he patted Kershawe's shoulder, told him he had done well, and bade him wait for his return.

He strode to the Rest House and found Morland as busy as himself, seemingly as immune to weariness, but less genial. He had sent the hospital orderly to look after the wounded man on the fringe of the air-strip, and now, with the constables on parade before him, he was harshly instructing Sergeant Kula to search the whole neighbourhood for wounded stragglers, and to bring in the prisoners who had spent the night in the timber-camp and set them to grave-digging. He paid no attention to the Sultan who, after listening for a little while, went up the steps and found Pemberton eating a hearty breakfast.

'Emily's gone to bed,' said Pemberton with his mouth full, 'and I think Mrs. Nottingham has too.'

'Then let us not disturb them,' said the Sultan, and tip-toed to the sideboard. He knelt to open a cupboard, and took from it a bottle of champagne. 'We have found Samarai and the boy,' he said. 'Or, to be more accurate, we have found their bodies.'

Pemberton, his breakfast forgotten, jumped up and followed him, demanding to know where. The Sultan went down the steps, and with an apology for his intrusion on the parade told Morland that the bodies of Samarai and the boy lay fifty yards from the district office, and Penny was in charge. 'I think you should inspect them before the constables begin collecting casualties.'

He refused to answer questions, but said, 'I'll come and see you presently.' He went back to Kershawe's bungalow, and found him already washed and shaved, in clean khaki shirt and shorts, and brushing his hair.

'Glasses,' he said. 'I want a couple of glasses, it doesn't matter what sort. I'm going to give you a morning draught.'

'Will beer glasses do?'

'Admirably.'

The cork hit the ceiling and the Sultan poured champagne. 'I've never been so glad to see anyone,' he said, 'as I was to see you in your revolting war-paint. And now I want to hear all you did.'

'It was easy enough to begin with,' said Kershawe. 'We dressed-up and went over to that other valley, and no one paid any particular attention to us. Half of them were asleep when we got there, and the others sitting about talking. We couldn't find Samarai. Then they started the march here, and that was difficult. They started almost as if they were automatic. No one shouted orders at them, it was just as if they all got the same idea at the same time. Not exactly at the same time, they weren't in any hurry about it, but after a lot of talk they drifted into some sort of formation and set off down to the ravine. There's a path along the cliff, under the edge, and that's the way we came. And that was hell. It was black as a boot in the ravine, and the path's only a scratch on the cliff. Sometimes not that. Sometimes it crosses an old fall of rock with vines and creepers growing in amongst it, and sometimes loose scree. But they never halted, they kept going—we were in single file, of course—and I held on to Corporal Apu, who was in front of me, and wished I was a goat. By God, I was frightened! And dripping like a sponge. I had to fall out and have a rest after we got up to the air-strip, and that was a stroke of luck, for that's when we found Samarai.

'He was right at the end of the procession, with some of the old men. They were lagging a bit. But there was one big fellow with them, who was carrying the boy on his shoulders. —I want to get hold of him, I can use a man like that.—Well, from then on we kept as close as we could to Samarai, and I daresay you saw the dancing and preparation for attack as well as we did. But you couldn't see Samarai because all the people in the bigger crowd were pushing to get near him. They all wanted to touch the boy. They touched him on the head and the genitals, and then they'd move on and tell their friends what they'd done.

'Samarai had the boy beside him, holding his left arm just under the shoulder, as if he were supporting him. And he kept saying to the people as they came up to him, "Kill the foreigners and the aeroplane will come. The aeroplane can't land till you have killed the foreigners." And the boy, with his head on his shoulder and gaping like an idiot, would say just the one word, with a gasp as if he was using his last breath to say it: "Muru!"—That means kill, sir.'

'Yes, I know.'

'I wanted to get plenty of evidence, so I waited till we'd both heard them saying that—oh, four or five times, at any rate—but then we got pushed away, and because it was daylight by then, and we didn't want to make ourselves conspicuous, we had to wait till the flow of the crowd naturally took us close to them again. By that time we'd all fallen back towards the office, so it seemed a good opportunity. It would give us a chance to take advantage of confusion and look for cover. We got right behind them just in that moment of silence when the drums stopped. And I took out my revolver—it was in a holster under my kilt—and shot Samarai between the shoulders.

'But then, sir, there was a bad mistake. I'd told Corporal Apu to shoot at once if I missed, but either because he'd misunderstood me, or because he got excited, he pulled his revolver and shot the boy. And then we heard rifle-fire and knew we were fairly safe.

'I think we'd have been safe enough even if you hadn't opened fire, because the moment Samarai fell there was panic. They all seemed to feel it at the same time, just as in their own valley they'd all known when it was time to march. You've seen big flocks of starlings in England, haven't you, sir? You know how they all move together, thousands of them wheeling and turning as if there was only one brain among them; or breaking up as if there'd been an explosion in the middle of the flock. Well, that's how they scattered.

'There was a sort of cry of anguish when I shot him. It wasn't like voices, it was like fiddle-strings. Perhaps they didn't think he could be killed; and then they saw him dead. And they let out this wail of anguish, those who were near him, and the rest of them, as if they were a flock of starlings, all seemed to hear it at the same time, and the whole crowd broke and ran. They might have stopped to think again, after a minute or two, but by that time you were shooting from the Rest House, so they hadn't a chance. And then, when it was all over, Corporal Apu and I fell into a panic ourselves, and you know the sort of fool I looked when you found us.'

The Sultan poured more champagne into Kershawe's glass, and a little into his own. 'You deserve the utmost credit for what you have done,' he said, 'and I'll do my best to see you get it. If the attack had developed as it was intended, we might have had to kill a very large number before we broke it up. We might have suffered casualties on our own side. But you prevented all that. You've shown the greatest fortitude and remarkable enterprise.—No, don't interrupt me. Drink your champagne, that'll do you far more good.—But we have to admit that Morland won't be very willing, at first, to see the situation as we do; and I want you to keep out of his way till I have stated our case. Have you anything to eat in your house? Can you make yourself some breakfast?'

'I'm going to eat my biggest breakfast for years. I'm as hungry as a pack of wolves.'

'That's the spirit,' said the Sultan. 'And now, with your permission, I'll drink a little more of your very good champagne, and go and tackle Mr. Morland.'

He drank, and stood up; and in a manner both princely and paternal said, 'You'll receive praise in plenty, Kershawe, but keep the first place in your memory for my simple expression of gratitude.' Then, squaring his shoulders, and with a renewed sense of euphory, he went to his argument with Morland.

The bodies of Samarai and the boy were now concealed by grey blankets, and on the office veranda Penny stood remote and glum in a corner, while Pemberton and Morland sat side by side on wooden chairs in vociferous debate. Pemberton, earnestly excited, immediately hailed the Sultan as a probable supporter.

'Come here, sir, and listen to this,' he cried. 'Come and tell me I'm right and Morland's wrong. He says the boy was murdered this morning, and I say that's impossible because he was dead already. I've examined him.'

'And what did you find?'

'His neck's broken. There's a definite fracture in the region of the sixth cervical vertebra. And that means that when Samarai hanged him he was well and truly hanged, and when they let him down again, life as we know it—*as we know it, sir!*—was extinct.'

'So you admit your belief in sorcery?'

'For a man of science,' said Pemberton solemnly, 'it's an admission of the utmost gravity. It's a revolutionary admission, and it's going to rouse violent disagreement among my colleagues. But I'm prepared to state on oath that I saw this boy hanged, that subsequently I examined the body and found evidence that his neck had been broken by hanging, and in the interim I and other reputable witnesses saw him walking and heard him talk. And if that amounts to a statement of my belief in sorcery, I accept the implication.'

'I want to know who shot the boy,' said Morland.

'That's immaterial! You can decide that any time. What I'm telling the Sultan is important.—You see the significance of it, don't you, sir? This is going to take the scientific world by storm. I don't want to exaggerate my own position as an anthropologist, but when I issue a statement in which I describe what's happened, and declare that I myself am satisfied that it can only be attributed to what is commonly known as sorcery—well, that's going to be recognized as something more than science. That's news!'

'Yes, indeed. Yes, I appreciate that,' said the Sultan. 'You're about to become a famous man, Mr. Pemberton.'

'In a modest way I think that's true.'

'I want to know,' said Morland, 'who killed the boy. I gather it was Kershawe who murdered Samarai—'

'I never said that!' exclaimed Penny.

'You said enough to let me infer it. But the boy's death I know nothing about. Did Kershawe shoot him too?'

'I'll tell you the whole story from the beginning,' said the Sultan, 'if you'll promise not to interrupt me till I've finished.'

'Go on.'

The Sultan came on to the veranda, and refusing Penny's offer to find him a chair—Pemberton made a belated movement, but was waved down again—he sat on the low wooden railing and with engaging frankness, only slightly marred now and then by an exhibition of condescension, of patience with a slower mind, he related all that had happened since his parley with Kershawe on the previous evening.

Morland lay sprawling on his chair, his eyes closed, and now that he was relaxed the lines of weariness showed deeply on his sunken cheeks. His clothes were crumpled and untidy, his morning beard grew dark and thick. Pemberton, leaning forward in his eagerness, looked even more soiled and creased, but his unshaven face caught the light and brightly reflected it from bristles of ruddy gold. The Sultan felt his own chin, and was grateful for a scanty and slow-growing beard; he looked down at his coat and trousers and was pleased to see that his appearance was still respectable.

'Have you finished?' asked Morland.

'I've told you everything that needs be told.'

'Then I have three observations to make on your story. In the first place, you and Kershawe deliberately planned agressive action in open defiance of my known wishes and my stated policy; and in furtherance of your plan you gave the constables, without my knowledge, orders to open fire on your command.'

'I agree. And our reason was that we could no longer rely on you to give us adequate protection.'

'In the second place, at your instigation Kershawe shot Samarai in cold blood: an act of murder.'

'Samarai was inciting his people to attack and kill us. And his life was already forfeit under my father's law against the sorcery he was practising.'

'Your first statement will have to be proved, and as to your second, that law has never been invoked during my service, and I doubt if it was ever formally enacted.'

'You'll find it in the old statute book.'

'We'll look into that later.—In the third place, Corporal Apu, under Kershawe's command, shot and killed the boy.'

'No, he didn't,' said Pemberton.

'Will you please be quiet? This has nothing to do with you. —I say Corporal Apu, whether or not he misunderstood Kershawe's order, shot the boy, and that was another act of murder for which Kershawe was responsible.'

'I was equally responsible,' said the Sultan.

'I am glad you admit it. And the last of my observations is that you opened fire without my orders—'

'You, at that time, were hiding in Kershawe's old bungalow.'

'I'm not sure that is relevant. You opened fire, in accordance with a prepared plan, on people who were certainly demonstrating in a hostile fashion, but whose intention to attack has not been proved, and who, I believe, had no serious purpose of attacking. On the face of it, it's utterly improbable. Would you, in command of perhaps three hundred men, armed only with spears and bows, order a frontal attack on a position defended by modern weapons?'

'I might, if I were careless of my men's lives, and if I had planned a simultaneous attack from the rear, which was to go in on my signal.'

'What was the signal?'

'The stopping of the drums. It was by sheer good fortune that Kershawe was able, at that very moment, to shoot Samarai, for we had arranged, as I told you, that he wouldn't try till I could give him some protection. Then, when I opened fire immediately I heard his shot, the constables under Sergeant Kula were alert for attack from the rear and had no hesitation in firing as soon as it began.'

Morland rose from his chair, and in a voice rough with anger said, 'Every word you utter stamps your guilt more clearly. You've made it perfectly evident that from the beginning you deliberately planned assassination and aggression, and I tell you, sir, that you and Kershawe both stand in grave danger of the charge of murder. I'm going to see Kershawe now, and unless he can find some extraordinary means of exculpating himself, I may well have to put him under open arrest.'

'You could hardly arrest him without arresting me too. It would be gross discrimination.'

'I am well aware of that.'

'Then I should like to be present at your conversation with him.'

'Certainly. Will you come now?'

They went down from the veranda and walked together, but with some distance between them, towards Kershawe's bungalow; and Penny in his corner said, 'Poor bastard! He used to say, "Sixteen years without a shot fired in anger," and he made it sound like a testimonial from a grateful people. And he's fond of his bloody savages in his own way: you've got to grant him that. But he won't ever be able to say "seventeen years", and he's taking it to heart too much. That's why he's making a fool of himself.'

'He's making a big mistake,' said Pemberton, 'if he thinks you can murder a boy who's been dead for thirty-six hours.'

Seventeen

A PAIR of constables were carrying a small, shrivelled old man on a primitive litter consisting only of two fallen branches, roughly trimmed, on which he sat sideways and nursed a swollen knee. The constables were in a jocular high humour, and when they saw Morland and the Sultan walking towards Kershawe's bungalow they set down their burden and one of them ran across the air-strip, halted abruptly, and flung up his hand in impressive salute. His military bearing, however, was discounted by the merriment in his luminous brown eyes and the gleaming white teeth disclosed by uncontrollable laughter.

He began at once to talk, with tumbling speed, in his own language, and the burden of his discourse was that the old man they were carrying was a village sorcerer called Ruateki— a man of great power and repute, and very evil—whom they had found lying in a hole with a twisted knee, no more than a mile away. And now, brought down by misfortune and un-manned by pain, Ruateki was complaining like a child that his father had disappointed him. They had called Samarai their father, said the constable, and the old man, the sorcerer who had frightened and deceived so many, was whimpering because he had hurt his knee and Samarai had deceived him. Samarai had said that all they had to do was to kill the foreigners, and that was easy enough, and then they would be rich and happy for the rest of their lives, and he would be a great king reigning over them and protecting them. And what made the old man angrier than anything else was that Samarai had let himself be killed. Samarai had made fools of them, and then most shamefully deserted them.

The humour of Ruateki's discomfiture so overcame the constable that he had to turn aside, with averted head and hands upon his face, to conceal his giggling; but Morland, speaking sharply, brought him to attention again. To Morland there was nothing humorous in the recital. He looked, indeed, like a man who, in well-mapped and open country, begins to think he has lost his way.

He spoke to the constable in the man's own language, and with manifest reluctance—with, as it seemed, disliking for the taste of his words—asked him, 'Is this a tale you have invented for amusement, or is it true that Ruateki told you it was in their minds to kill the foreigners?'

It was true, and wholly true, said the constable; and repeated the old man's words.

Morland went a little way apart from them, and walked slowly to and fro. Then, for a moment, he stood with his head bent and his hands clasped at the level of his chest, in the attitude of a soldier bowed above reversed arms. He returned, and with no apparent emotion told the constable to take Ruateki to the district office, and then find Oala the interpreter. To the Sultan he said, 'I have decided to hear this man before I see Kershawe.'

The Sultan made no comment, but now, walking back to the office, walked closely with Morland, side by side, as if to show sympathy for his prospective, his possible return to the companionship of reasonable men. But fifty yards from the office, where the bodies of Samarai and the boy still lay under their blankets, Morland stopped beside the insignificant grey mounds, with their petty hillocks and meagre shallows, and kneeling down lifted the cover from Samarai's head, and turned it sideways as if seeking in his last expression a reflexion of the truth. But already there were ants in the rim of his upturned eye, and with an exclamation of disgust Morland put back the blanket and brushed from his hands the sensation of mortality. He did not join the others, but walked up and down in the full stare of the sun.

The constables carried Ruateki on to the veranda, and set him down on the floor. He was a pitiable yet ludicrous figure, his small body still decorated with the remnants of his tattered finery, his malevolent, wrinkled face absurdly daubed with clay. He chattered in a tongue they could not understand, his eyes like chocolate-drops in discoloured whites, and pointing to his swollen knee, his parched mouth, made fluttering gestures that demanded comfort. Penny went into the office and brought him a mug of lime juice and water, and a piece of chewing tobacco. He drank with noisy exclamations of delight, and mumbling his tobacco nodded his head in simple contentment while a thin dark stream ran down his chin. Pemberton, leaning against the rail, studied him intently; the Sultan regarded him with benign amusement.

Oala came hurrying to the office, breathless but buoyant with importance, and Morland, wrapt in the isolation of his predicament, climbed the steps and pulling a chair into position sat down facing Ruateki. The interrogation began, and to formal questions the old man gave wandering but sufficient answers. Then Morland asked him to say exactly what Samarai had promised when he first spoke of the heavenly aeroplane and the riches it would bring; and the old man, growing incoherent with rage, began to abuse Samarai in language so vehement and picturesque, so lurid with obscenity, that the two constables, who knew his language and listened avidly below the veranda, broke into loud and happy laughter, and were angrily dismissed.

Abandoning his attempt to trace the history of the rising,

Morland told Oala to ask why the boy had been sacrificed; and the old man, with a fine parade of aversion—he seemed to deprecate the unnecessary introduction of an unpleasant subject—answered that there had to be a sacrifice, and the boy, after all, was a stranger without relations in the country. He came from somewhere over the western hills.

'Ask him the purpose of the sacrifice,' said Morland.

Ruateki looked at him with ingenuous astonishment, incredulous of such ignorance, and said that good people like the people of Maipani, and of all the other nearby valleys, would never gather up their weapons to murder the foreigners who lived among them, and had paid them so much money and treated them so well, unless they were told to do so by the voice of the dead; which was a voice that none dared disobey.

'Ask him,' said Morland, 'if he ever heard Samarai or the boy telling them to kill the foreigners.'

The old man grew angry again, and answered contemptuously that Samarai had said that many, many times.

'When was the first time?'

The old man saw his danger, and said that after the boy had been hanged, and the dead had spoken, Samarai told them they must shed blood before they could enjoy their wealth. This very morning, he said, Samarai had declared again and again that the aeroplane could not come in to land until they had killed the men in the big house. And now, he added, and spat tobacco-juice through the railing, I am here all alone because I believed Samarai and he made a fool of me. There is no aeroplane, there is no Samarai, there are no people except me, and I am very old. And you are thinking, What a fool that old man is.

Morland with a weary gesture rubbed his eyes, and looked for the constables; but they had gone. He told Oala to give his compliments to Mr. Kershawe, and ask him to come to the district office; and a moment or two later, in a flat, uninterested voice, said to the Sultan, 'I have never before been completely humiliated.'

Tom Penny, at the other end of the veranda, whispered to Pemberton, 'He believes this old monkey Ruateki, but he wouldn't have believed Kershawe. And that's typical of Morland, and others like him. Well, you're a scientist: why don't you investigate Morland?'

Kershawe arrived, conspicuously smart and clean in comparison with the others, and said, 'Good morning, sir.'

Morland said, 'I'm not going to ask you, at present, for a full account of what happened. I want only to know what Samarai was saying to those about him when, as I understand it, you were beside him in the crowd here.'

Kershawe repeated what he had told the Sultan, and Morland said, 'Thank you, that will do.' Now manifestly tired, and giving way to his tiredness, he said to Penny, 'Will you try and find the hospital orderly, and see that he looks after this man? I want him kept here.' And to Kershawe and the Sultan: 'If you will come with me, there is something I have to say to you.'

They walked slowly from the office, and presently Morland said, 'You have known my mistakes for some time. I have just found them out. It has been a great shock to me, with my experience of the country, to discover that I could be so far wrong in my judgment of a man and a situation; but I am not going to make excuses. All I want to do is to say that I am profoundly sorry for maintaining, too stubbornly, opinions that were unwarranted, and for expressing them in a way you may have found offensive. If you did so, I apologize.'

The Sultan, who was feeling sleepy, and had indeed been dozing throughout Morland's examination of old Ruateki, replied with a vague benevolence that meant little more than a disinclination to pursue the argument, 'That's handsomely said. Very handsome indeed. We all make mistakes from time to time, but it isn't everyone who owns up to them. Let's say no more about it. It's a good thing you didn't arrest us, isn't it?'

'A very fortunate omission,' said Morland drily.

His humiliation, however, was not yet complete. Outside Kershawe's bungalow Sergeant Kula was waiting, and even his ingrained discipline could hardly confine the rage and grief that filled his mind; and Kershawe, when he knew the cause of it, was almost as distraught.

The two constables who, the night before, had been sent up the hill to the great rock that looked like the gable-end of a house, to keep watch from there on Samarai and his dancing followers, had been found dead and mutilated. They had not been caught sleeping—one had an arrow through his throat— but they had apparently been surprised and given no time to use their rifles. 'We have never been allowed to shoot first,' said Sergeant Kula. 'We have never been taught to open fire.' But the constables, before they were overwhelmed and murdered, had fought fiercely and with brave endurance: there was abundant evidence of that. And after their death their rifles and ammunition had been taken.

'And now,' said the sergeant, finding in his own tongue and his burning anger the rhetoric that tragedy demanded, 'we of the Constabulary say there must be a punishment for this. These men were our brothers and our comrades. Our hearts are sore for the loss of our brothers, and our pride is hurt for the loss of comrades. We must take a swift and terrible vengeance, or our love will be laughed at, our pride will become a mockery, and their ghosts will torment us to the end of our days. We must wash away our tears in the blood of our enemies, and for our two brothers take twenty, forty lives from among those who slew them.'

'No,' said Morland, 'you will take no lives.'

Kershawe looked at him morosely, the Sultan with a quick respect. They had seen on his face the sudden pain of a man, already wounded, whom another bullet hits, and they both knew him well enough to realize the depth of his hurt. He was struck by a grief nearly as simple as Sergeant Kula's, for he had known the murdered constables, they were his own people, almost his own creation; and his pride recoiled in the anguish of knowing that he, by the obduracy of his judgment, was responsible for the crisis in which they had died. He was unaccustomed to such a bitter responsibility, for he had never commanded troops in battle, and his repugnance to violence had hitherto enabled his police to live in the security that he demanded for the wildest tribesmen. But Morland, though flinching from the double blow, made no retreat from principle. He listened to Sergeant Kula as though patiently accepting a due punishment, and then, with a conviction that almost visibly energized his lean and weary body, he said, 'No!'

He allowed himself, for a moment, to be sympathetic. 'I know how strongly you feel,' he said, 'because I feel as you do. But we, in our position, mustn't give way to our feelings. You speak about your pride, but what is the foundation of your pride? Isn't it the performance of your duty in all imaginable circumstances?

He spoke with a fervour that out-matched the sergeant's emotion. His fervour had reason at the core, and like a hot wind it shrivelled and dried up the sergeant's protests. 'There will be no reprisal,' he said, 'because reprisals are brutal and we do not behave like brutes; and because it is foolish to punish many who are innocent for the faults of a few who are guilty. We shall search and find out the guilty, and punish them in accordance with law. But we shall do nothing against the law, nothing in anger. . . .'

All he said was compact of grave good sense and high principle; but perhaps he said too much. He went on too long, and the Sultan, who had listened at first with lively admiration —for he thought it remarkable that Morland should rise so strongly from defeat, and in spite of weariness defend his ideals with so much vigour—found his homily less agreeable when he began to suspect that Morland was enjoying it. The Sultan could appreciate virtue, but the sight of a man taking pleasure in his virtue was not engaging; and as the dissertation became more ponderous he grew sleepy again, and decided he must either go to bed or drink a large dry martini. He nodded to Kershawe, and unobtrusively walked away towards the Rest House.

But Morland, as though revived by moral exercise, seemed to throw off fatigue, and having rebuked Sergeant Kula, told him to see that graves were dug by sundown, and preparation made for the burial of the dead of both sides. To Kershawe he said, 'The constables must receive military honours. You will have to find a firing party this afternoon, and see that they know their drill. Get everyone on parade, inspect clothing, and make sure that they turn out smartly. And I want you to write a full report of this incident, because I have a great deal to do on larger aspects of the situation. I'm going to have a bath now, and then I must begin my own dispatch. I shall have to cover, of course, the whole history of the rising and its suppression. I shan't come to lunch, but I'd like to have coffee and some sandwiches sent in to me.'

Morland ran briskly up the steps of the bungalow, and Kershawe went unhappily with Sergeant Kula to see the dead constables.

Eighteen

THE two constables were buried at sundown, and the last salute echoed and re-echoed in a rapid *diminuendo* among the mountains. Mrs. Pemberton and Sergeant Kula wept openly, and Morland, addressing the parade at some length, repeated most of his morning homily.

The parade was dismissed, and the Sultan and his party went to the Rest House, where the Sultan shook cocktails. The layer of gloom which had overcast their sense of deliverance was gradually dispelled, as if they realized they had done all they could for the dead by burying them with dignity—the ceremony had been well conducted—and now, with relatively easy minds, they might enjoy the relaxation to which they were entitled.

Mrs. Nottingham and Tom Penny had spent much of the afternoon helping the hospital orderly to dress the wounds of a dozen minor casualties who had been brought in, and Mrs. Nottingham, having found an occupation, admitted that she felt almost at home in Maipani, and was looking forward to a week of peace and calm before the aeroplane returned.

'Another week!' said Mrs. Pemberton, and looked with foreboding at an enormity of emptiness and a barrier of violet hills now receding into darkness under a last flourish of dusky orange light. 'Another week.'

She had slept till mid-afternoon and wakened a little dizzy and uncertain of the time; but then, remembering the events of the early morning, grew suddenly light-hearted to think she had heard rifle-fire and not failed in terror at the sound of it.

In memory, indeed, that hard reverberating din seemed exhilarating. 'But I was,' she admitted, 'a little drunk,' and got up to look for the water jug. 'Nevertheless,' she told herself, 'I was extraordinarily brave,' and dressing hurriedly went out to talk of her experience to anyone who would listen. She heard instead a tale of two murdered constables, and her husband insisted on describing in detail the anatomical discovery which had converted him to a belief in sorcery. Mrs. Pemberton felt that another week in Maipani might test her new-found bravery too severely.

Pemberton himself was less exuberant than he had been. His confidence in the importance of his discovery had been slightly undermined by a doubt as to whether the boy had in fact met his death by hanging. Was a broken neck absolute proof that death had occurred? He went to see Morland, who was writing his report and resented the intrusion, and asked that the body should be buried apart from the others, so that as soon as a pathologist could be flown in it might be exhumed and subjected to proper examination.

Morland lost his temper and declared with a passionate vexation that he had no time to waste on tomfoolery; but Pemberton, indifferent to rebuke and quite unmoved by petulance, described again the momentous addition to human knowledge that lay at stake, and vehemently declared that all might be lost if there was no examination of the boy's lungs. There, in the cavity of his chest, was the final and conclusive evidence of life or death, and he, in the name of the scientific world, demanded that the cavity be explored.

He sat down, stubbornly prepared to wait for Morland's surrender; and presently Morland gave in. Pemberton, dourly satisfied, went off and persuaded Sergeant Kula to dig a grave in light, dry soil that might preserve mortal tissues against decay; and meeting Oala, took him to the hospital, where for two hours he questioned old Ruateki about the current practice of sorcerers, of whom Ruateki virtuously denied all knowledge. At cocktail-time the Sultan was suitably interested in these activities, but Mrs. Nottingham refused to be entertained either by magic or pathology.

But the banishment of anxiety prompted geniality, if not accord, and the little company on the veranda that was still walled by sandbags became a party. Morland, conscientiously at work, had said he would prefer to dine alone, and in his absence the Sultan displayed something of the festive spirit that, in his youth, had made so many of his parties memorable. He hated parsimony, he said. He would rather feast on Saturday and fast all week than eat on every dull succeeding day a rationed teaspoonful of caviare and drink like a tame householder a medicinal glass of wine. The wine he had brought would not last the week, except in medicinal doses that could only tease and disappoint a proper thirst, so he invited them to drink generously for one night and let the remaining days look after themselves.

'Kershawe is a modest man,' he said, 'and tells no one when his birthday falls. It may well be today. Let us assume it is, and celebrate it. More cheerfully, I suggest, than you honoured my untimely anniversary. He deserves it, I promise you. Because if it hadn't been for Kershawe we might now be drinking, not for celebration, but for consolation.'

It was nine o'clock when they sat down to dine, it was a quarter to eleven when they rose; and the Sultan said to Kershawe, 'Let us take a walk in the moonlight.'

But an adverse thought occurred to him, and for a moment he stood and pondered it. Perhaps it was a mistake to leave the comfort of the bungalow for an unfurnished hillside? Soon, however, he devised a lenitive for the exercise he had proposed, and reminding Kershawe that their morning draught of champagne had tasted very well in beer glasses, he opened another bottle and filled two tumblers.

'Take that,' he said, giving one to Kershawe, 'and sip it as you go. As a diluent after brandy I recommend it.'

With a caution that enhanced his natural dignity he went down the steps, and together they walked slowly towards the air-strip, in the dry brilliance of the moon, over ground blanched by its light. The Sultan was in a mood of bland and benevolent regality. The mountains were his, and the silvered valley was his footstool.

'Is your father living?' he asked Kershawe.

'Yes, sir.'

'You must give me his address. I shall write and tell him what you have done for us. And your mother: is she alive?'

'Yes, sir.'

'I bought a lot of silk when I was in Bali a couple of weeks ago. It's very good silk. I shall send it to her and say you won it in a game of chance. Women are fond of silk.—How long have you been in the service?'

'About six and a half years.'

'And you were in the army before that?'

'Yes, sir.'

'Are you satisfied with your position here? And your prospects?'

By inclination and habit Kershawe was a temperate young man, and reticent. In departmental controversy, in argument on behalf of his district, he could be, if not fluent, forthright and determined; about his own interests, however, his own beliefs and aspirations, he had never cared to say much, and his lonely duty in Maipani had stiffened a natural reserve. But now, as the result of having drunk a good deal—perhaps half as much as the Sultan or Tom Penny had drunk—he felt strongly disposed to lay bare, in the candour of the moon, his innermost and dearest thoughts; and only hesitated because he had not handsome and compelling enough words to shape them as they deserved.

He began by saying, with naked insufficiency, that he liked the country and its savage people. He drank a little champagne, and saw moonlight diamonding the glass, and the bubbles breaking. 'But if only there was someone with imagination!' he cried. 'Someone who could see possibilities, and had the guts to bring them home!'

'What possibilities do you see?'

'We could double your territory in a year. There's a natural harbour forty miles to the west, a deep-water harbour, undeveloped; and good grazing in half a dozen valleys all about 3000 feet above sea-level. There's better timber than we have here, and in the south there's copper and manganese and sulphur. We could take all that country without any trouble.'

'But my dear Kershawe, you're living in the wrong century. It might have been possible a hundred years ago; but not today.'

'Other people are still doing it. We pretend it's politically impossible and morally unforgivable to take new territory by conquest, but what does that really mean? It only means we're too tired, or too frightened. It is possible! It's happening in other places, though it's often disguised, of course. And we could give you a new frontier eighty or ninety miles to the west so easily that we'd be administering the whole country before anyone knew what to complain about. And when they started to complain we could tell them to come and take a plebiscite, and the tribes would vote for you. There'd be no difficulty about that, and the votes wouldn't cost you much.'

The Sultan, himself a little dazzled by the moonlight, asked, 'Are you seriously suggesting that I should engage in war with my neighbours the Dutch? And do you really think the Dutch would pay no attention until I had advanced eighty miles into their territory?'

'It wouldn't be a war, sir, because there wouldn't be any opposition. The Dutch have lost interest in the country. They don't want to assert themselves, they don't want to develop it and draw attention to it—in case the Indonesians claim it. I've been over the frontier three times, and it's all tribal territory like this, but practically unadministered; and the people aren't unfriendly.'

'And how,' asked the Sultan, 'are you going to finance the expedition, and the development of my new domain? Won't it be a strain on Mr. Morland's budget?'

'It won't come out of the budget, sir, and we'll have to get rid of Morland. You're not compelled by treaty or statute to have an Adviser, and if you took over the government yourself you could finance your own policy out of Te Aku. You could pledge the oil revenue, if necessary.'

'You've gone as far as that, have you? In imagination you've already pledged my revenue, and launched me on the career of a pinchbeck Raffles with yourself as my *éminence grise*? You have a more remarkable character and a more interesting mind than I had suspected, my dear Kershawe.'

'Stamford Raffles made his own decisions, sir. He saw his opportunities and brought them home without waiting for anyone's approval. He saw Malaya and brought it home. Well, you've never asked for public favour either, and last night it was you who took the responsibility and told me to go out and get Samarai. You took command of the police, you gave them their orders. I don't think you'd be a pinchbeck Raffles.'

The Sultan drank the last of his champagne, and looked at the moon through the bottom of his glass. 'I have,' he said slowly, 'a mind of my own, and the faculty of *making it up*, as they say. I'm not unduly afraid of public voices, whether they speak out of the inflated bladders of officialdom or the vulgar prejudice of the newspapers. I have—you're quite right, Kershawe—a sort of natural title to responsibility; and I'm on my own ground, I feel, when I make a bold decision. All that's true enough, and yet . . .'

They had walked down the air-strip to the edge of the ravine, and turned back, and were now not far from the Rest House. The Sultan held up his glass to the moon, and saw in its sparkling emptiness a reproach to his princely state, an invitation to his princely spirit. 'Be a good fellow,' he said, 'and run up and fetch another bottle, will you? We must discuss your topic more closely, and with a generous mind.'

In a little while, with glasses refilled and the bottle hanging like a bludgeon from Kershawe's left hand, they trod the white ground again, with measured pace and frequent pause to sip and reflect and find new matter for debate; and presently, as their thoughts rose faster and filled larger concepts, their conversation gained in vivacity what it lost in coherence. There seemed no gross objection now to enlarging a principality, no difficulty either, and Kershawe said it would be foolish to demarcate the new frontier too soon, for tactical, economic, or political factors might require a further extension of their domain before they stopped to consolidate. The Dutch would welcome them, he thought, and see them as allies against the unruliness of Indonesian ambition.

The Sultan remembered how often in his ebullient youth he had been checked and rebuked by cold authority—how sorely his native spirit had been frustrated by stony circumstance—and foresaw in his expansion the vindication of his empty titles, and revenge on all that had belittled him. But prudence did not wholly desert him, and from time to time he

222

would say, 'I am committed to nothing. Remember that, Kershawe. I am engaged in nothing but the examination—the calm and objective examination—of your very interesting proposition. With glacial calm and pellucid objectivity: that's my present mood, and my intention. Are you sure about those minerals in the south?'

'I've seen the geological reports, and they're quite conclusive. And the tribes are more amenable than ours. Give me a dozen instructors and in twelve months I'll form a new constabulary out of their own people.'

Swaying slightly, with a visionary's rapt expression on his militant, hard face, Kershawe stood on the edge of the ravine and flung the empty bottle over his shoulder. 'I hate a damned cold caution and the cowardice in virtue,' he cried. 'I hate the impotence of waiting for public approval. We didn't always live like the gelded trustees of an international orphanage. Let's show we can do what the Victorians did!'

'By prescription,' said the Sultan, 'I am the Faithful Ally of Her late Imperial Majesty.'

'You'll do it, then?'

'You tempt me, Kershawe. You tempt what remains of my youth. And perhaps my arm is still long enough to reach—how far do you say? A hundred miles?'

They walked back to the Rest House, no longer talking but each in his moonlit dream; and at the foot of the steps the Sultan said, 'I've drunk too much, and yet, if one were always sober, what fields of the imagination would never be ploughed and sown! Good night, Kershawe. We've the better part of a week before us, and we'll think about your plan, and talk it over.'

His expectation, however, was unrealized. The morning again broke clearly over the mountains, and at nine o'clock the aeroplane from Port Philip, that was not due till Friday, came swiftly into the valley, and Blakeley landed with casual dexterity.

He was welcomed with astonishment and delight, as though he had raised a long-drawn siege; and he explained that a sky full of impenetrable cloud had prevented him from making his chartered flight to an eastern district, so taking aboard the batteries he had failed to deliver two days before, he had come to Maipani to ease his conscience and relieve their isolation.

The arrival of the aeroplane had a profound effect on all but one of the visitors to Maipani. It brought civilization—the small but secure civilization of Port Philip—within an hour's distance, and the loneliness of the mountains became intolerable to them. They discovered the most urgent reasons, of one sort or another, for returning to civilization; they realized their imperative need of it. Only Pemberton wished to remain, for Pemberton had his own views and interests, and the contemporary scene was to him a shallower pool than the minds of primitive people.

The others, by common consent, made hurried preparation for their departure, and within three-quarters of an hour of landing Blakeley took off again with a full complement of passengers: Mrs. Nottingham and Mrs. Pemberton, Morland and the Sultan, and the Sultan's cook and steward. The Sultan's luggage, however, weighed much less than before, and the load was not excessive.

Tom Penny and Kershawe stood together and watched the aeroplane leap and wheel away from the narrow landing-ground, and climb on a long slant out of the valley; and Penny, with sourness in his voice and contempt in his expression, made no effort to conceal his displeasure. It was the eagerness of the visitors' departure that had offended him. 'We drank all his drink last night, that's why he's in such a hurry to get back,' he said. 'You couldn't expect His Bloody Highness to face life without champagne, could you?'

But Kershawe felt a deeper hurt. Kershawe had betrayed a dream and lost a leader.

Nineteen

BLAKELEY landed on the airfield, three miles from Port Philip, an hour after leaving Maipani. The Sultan and his party disembarked on a concrete runway, shimmering with the lowland heat, and walked in the ponderous blaze of the sun to a shed as hot as an oven where no one expected them and no arrangement had been made for their transport to the town. The Sultan and Morland were both annoyed by the lack of respectful attention, to which they were almost equally accustomed, and while a slow-witted clerk was telephoning, through a sleepy exchange, for motor cars, Morland led the Sultan aside and in too brusque a manner inquired, 'Where are you sleeping tonight, sir?'

'In *White Heather*. Where else?'

'And Mrs. Nottingham?'

'Do you think I'm going to leave her here?'

'I thought you might be going to the Palace, which would be more convenient in the circumstances. If you intend to sleep in the yacht I shall have to put a police guard aboard.'

'What the devil for?'

'You know perfectly well, sir, that I have to keep some control over Mrs. Nottingham's movements until arrangements can be made for her return to Fairweather.'

'She isn't going to Fairweather.'

'My instructions are quite definite—'

'Now look here, Morland. We've had all this argument before, and you must realize that I'm not going to hand Mrs. Nottingham over to you and the processes of what you regard

226

as law. But I realize the difficulty you're in, and I've made plans that will suit your convenience as well as ours. I've offered to look after Mrs. Pemberton while her husband's anthropologizing in the mountains, and take her to Singapore, where he's going in a fortnight's time, or so. We'll sail to-night, and by tomorrow morning Mrs. Nottingham will be far beyond your jurisdiction, and you'll have no further trouble with her.'

'No, sir, that's impossible. I had decided to ignore, if I could, my orders to arrest her—'

'I should think so! In the last day or two you must have had your fill of trying to arrest the wrong people.'

'In Maipani, I admit, my judgment was at fault; and I apologized for the mistake I made. But if you think one solitary lapse of judgment—my only blunder in sixteen years of service—is going to hinder me in my duty now or next year, then you've very grossly misunderstood my character.'

'And you've grossly misunderstood your authority if you think you can arrest my wife.'

'I don't. But I remember, very distinctly, when you made that claim before; and Mrs. Nottingham showed a curious reluctance to take advantage of the immunity you offered her.'

'We had reasons, I told you, for not publishing our marriage.'

'And I have reason for thinking it never took place.'

'Then, by God, you'll see it take place again! We'll go to the Secretariat now, as soon as the cars arrive, and you'll be a witness to the marriage you don't believe in.'

'I should have to take advice before agreeing that a declaration of marriage, at this stage, would confer the privilege you expect.'

'Take my advice, Morland. Don't waste your time with lawyers, be content with what I tell you, and believe that this is going to be the reiteration of a marriage that has already been declared. A reiteration to satisfy you, and you alone. Because if you don't believe that, and stop making a damned nuisance of yourself, I'll see to it that everyone from the Governor down to the bar-boy at the Yacht Club knows exactly what went on in Maipani. I'll tell them that you were on the point of arresting Kershawe and myself because we saved the situation in spite of gross negligence on your part; and I'll make it perfectly clear that we were forced to take action by what I shall describe as your cowardly passivity.'

Indifferent to the pelting sun, they had been walking on a strip of brown, cracked turf beside the waiting-room, and for a moment they halted and faced each other, the Sultan's wrath held in a tenuous restraint that threatened to burst and let it spill at any moment; Morland as angry, but wary now and the better able to deny his anger.

They walked on, and Morland said, 'If you're determined to be malicious you could, I suppose, misrepresent what I said and did.'

'There'll be no need for misrepresentation, but you can certainly depend on malice, if you drive me to it.'

'That would do no one any good.'

'None at all.'

'It would be a great pity to start a controversy of that sort. I'm not thinking of myself, I'm thinking of the Administration, when I say it might cause irreparable harm if you created an open breach between us.'

'I have no wish to.'

'Well, that makes things a little easier. I thought, for a moment—'

'Damnation take it, will you stop hedging? Will you or will you not agree that a declaration of marriage gives Elizabeth Nottingham the protection I want for her?'

228

They turned and faced the sun again, before Morland answered. Then grudgingly he said, 'It will have to be made in proper form, and before witnesses.'

'I'm prepared for that.'

'And will you, on your part, undertake to say nothing, and write nothing, that's likely to discredit me?'

'Your reputation will be safe as soon as Elizabeth is ... Here are the cars coming now. Will you take Mrs. Pemberton?'

Mrs. Nottingham and Mrs. Pemberton were fanning themselves in the hot shade of a narrow veranda. They said goodbye to Blakeley, and the Sultan's cook and steward lay down to sleep beside the luggage till a truck should come for them.

Delayed by the necessity of argument, the Sultan and Mrs. Nottingham did not reach the Secretariat until fifteen minutes after the others' arrival; and Mrs. Pemberton was shocked by the appearance of the older woman. Her habitual calm—the severe composure of her usual expression—had become a caricature of equanimity, as if a plastic surgeon had lately refashioned her face with tissues that were still foreign to the emotions of his patient; but her heavy-lidded eyes were swollen and a little pink. The Sultan also was unwontedly grave. His movement seemed ponderous, his manner betrayed a deliberate and studied resolution. In his voice there was the heavy courtesy of an ultimatum.

They went through the outer office into Morland's room, and Morland called in a couple of native clerks. He sat down behind his table, and like a notary made cautious disposition of foolscap and blotting-paper, tried his pen and consulted the calendar. 'You know the customary form of declaration?' he asked. 'Then will you and Mrs. Nottingham stand in front of me.'

The Sultan, with Mrs. Nottingham close beside him—his arm in hers, her hand clasped firmly in his—said in a loud voice, 'I, Zafrullah bin Ismail bin Said, Sultan of Namua, Lord of the Island Sea—'

'One moment, please. I have to put your declaration in writing, and you are going too fast for me.'

Slowly, phrase by phrase, the Sultan affirmed his freedom and intention to marry, deposed that a fair and acceptable settlement had been agreed to, and formally offered marriage. Mrs. Nottingham, who had to be prompted, replied with equal formality in a drily breaking voice, and Morland, careful and unhurried—he asked Mrs. Nottingham to spell her former husband's name—wrote down their words, revised his punctuation, and slowly blotted the page.

'And now,' he said, 'I want your signatures. And the witnesses will sign here.'

Morland folded the paper and put it in a long envelope; and suddenly the Sultan shed his load of gravity. 'I feel as if I'd made my will and appointed Morland as sole trustee,' he exclaimed. 'But I'll outlive you, Morland! You won't get a chance to milk the estate.—Elizabeth, my dear, I hope you'll soon feel as happy as I do, and never regret this dull, superfluous ceremony.'

He embraced her, and kissed her heartily on the lips; but she made no response. Mrs. Pemberton, who had been sitting at the far end of the room, quiet and inconspicuous but seriously observant of all that passed, came shyly forward to offer the felicitations that she thought would be expected of her, and the Sultan said boisterously, 'But you should congratulate Mr. Morland before us! At great inconvenience to ourselves we've made an honest man of Morland—and I hope he's grateful.'

'I am,' said Morland. 'I should have found the other ceremony—the alternative to this—a very unpleasant task. I'm thankful to be spared it.'

'Then you'll propose our health this afternoon,' said the Sultan. 'I don't often get married, thank God, and I don't propose to let the occasion pass without some distinction. We must have a reception, and give Port Philip the pleasure of meeting Her Highness.'

'Oh no!' exclaimed Her Highness, most unhappily.

'But yes! A wedding's no wedding without a reception, and we can't waste time chattering here. We must make arrangements, and let Port Philip know what's afoot before Port Philip goes to sleep for the afternoon.—They'll need time to look out their best frocks, won't they, Emily?—What's the name of that fellow who's secretary of the Yacht Club?'

'Firbank.'

'I'll get Mr. Firbank to send out invitations—he can use his list of members—and I'll bring my own people from the Palace. What time do you suggest? Half-past four? Then we'll have to hurry. Come along, my dear.'

Morland went out with them, and stood under the hard stare of the sun until the car had gone. He shrugged his shoulders and returned to his office, walking slowly on a well-kempt path between walls of dark green, shining foliage sprinkled with scarlet blooms; and at the entrance to the veranda paused, and grimly frowned. The yellow trumpet of a flower growing on the lush vine that garlanded the roof had brushed his head. He shouted for his chief clerk, and demanded to know where the gardeners were.

'It is Sunday today, sir. They are not working.'

'Then see the head gardener first thing tomorrow morning, and tell him to chop down this vine. Tell him to take it out root and branch, I don't want to see a leaf remaining. I will not live in a jungle as if I were a fruit-bat or a cockatoo. Do you understand that?'

'Yes, sir, I understand.'

A little better pleased with himself, Morland went in and sat down to re-consider the marriage document. It exculpated him, he thought, though it might not wholly satisfy the Governor, or the Colonial Office. But H.E. would receive by the same post the dispatch he had written in Maipani—that he had not finished till two o'clock this morning—and H.E. would have no complaint with it. Morland opened his brief-case, and read again his report of Samarai's rebellion and its suppression. He had nothing to be ashamed of, that was perfectly evident, and he had not denied Kershawe the credit that was due him. He had stressed his own caution, in the interests of humanity and a traditional policy, and omitted to mention his opposition to Kershawe and the Sultan when they demanded action: that was no longer relevant, he had decided, and a long account of their discussions would only obscure the narrative. The narrative, as it stood, was clear and informa-tive. It was, too, written with a nice attention to picturesque detail. It could hardly fail to please and impress a Governor who boasted of his regard for literature.

Morland separated the carbon copies from the original leaves, and put them in another envelope . A few of his col-leagues, he thought, might like to read what he had written.

Twenty

ABOARD *White Heather* luncheon was not served till half-past two, and even then Her Highness was still manifestly nervous and unhappy. Mrs. Pemberton believed her state of mind to be the natural consequence—to a sensitive woman—of getting married; even though the ceremony, for some reason she could not wholly understand, was said to be only a repetition of previous rites. Mrs. Pemberton had been neither surprised nor offended by having to wait for her luncheon, and she would have been sorely astonished to learn that she was, in some degree, responsible for the *crise de nerfs* that kept her hostess in her cabin.

As soon as they went aboard the Sultan had become deeply and happily involved in preparation for the reception. His cook and his steward had already arrived, and they were well used to the sudden apperance of guests and the recurring necessity of immediate entertainment. So was the captain. But for his wedding reception the Sultan was unwilling to leave arrangements in their hands, and insisted on discussing every-thing from the awnings that must be spread, to anchovies and their proper disposition; and it was not until he felt sure that all his wishes were thoroughly apprehended that he went to inquire if his wife was equally prepared for the party.

He found her in her cabin, lying on her bed with her face to the wall. He sat down beside her, and gently tried to console her. He used reasonable and kindly arguments to dislodge her from her misery. And presently she sat up and said, 'You're very good to me, and everything you say is true. In a day or two I'll be able to believe it. But now I feel humiliated as I've never been before, and I have no sensation of anything else. Humiliation is the only thing I understand.'

She had put on a dressing-gown and cleaned the *maquillage* from her face. Her general pallor was accentuated by her lack of eyebrows, and her cheeks glistened slightly with a cosmetic oil. She was, thought the Sultan, like a very beautiful but almost inhuman mask of grief; and he could not understand her grief.

'Is it really so humiliating to be my wife?' he asked.

'Yes,' she said. 'To be your wife, and forced to accept your conditions—'

'A leisurely voyage, in good weather, to Singapore? In a yacht as well-found as *White Heather*?'

'With Emily aboard.'

'But you like the girl, don't you?'

She got up and lit a cigarette, and smoked quickly and without enjoyment. 'I suppose a lot of women who've led my sort of life come to this in the end,' she said, 'but I must admit that I hadn't expected it to happen quite so soon.'

'Do you find hospitality such a burden? She won't give you any trouble.'

'Wouldn't any woman find it intolerable—oh, beyond the furthest edge of tolerance—to become your wife on a Sunday morning, and see the prospect of being your bawd on Sunday night?'

'My dear Elizabeth, your imagination's running away with you.'

'You mean you'll put it off till Monday?'

'That would be much too precipitate. Even if I intended what you suppose I intend, I wouldn't look for a conclusion as quickly as that. And, as it happens, my feeling for Emily— I admit, quite freely, that I'm very fond of her—but my feeling has little or no relation to our sexual difference. I like her youth, her innocence amuses me—'

'Innocence and youth can take any man to a ship's cabin.'

'Not at my age, Elizabeth. At my age one can find enjoyment of different sorts, and keep them separate. I have learnt that pleasure doesn't always require love, and love doesn't always mean pleasure.'

She put out her cigarette and said, 'Everybody's bound to realize there was something odd about our marriage, and when they see Emily on board they'll assume it was just an arrangement for your benefit: to make it easier for you to seduce her.'

'You don't appreciate Port Philip and the Philippians. They're more intelligent than you think, and they've all got the nose of a pointer for political rumours, domestic irregularities, and departmental scandals. They know one from the other, and they much prefer departmental scandals: they don't chase a hare when there's a cock-grouse in the heather. It won't take them long to discover that Morland received certain definite orders from the Governor, and failed to carry them out. It won't take them much longer to guess the reason for his failure, and what they'll be telling each other, before the night's out, is that I, with a pair of queens in my hand, bluffed poor old Morland when he held a winning straight. And they'll be right. I did bluff him. He could have arrested you as soon as we arrived, but I raised the bid, I threw the fiction of a marriage on the table, and Morland hesitated and lost the game.'

'I'm not so sure. He forced you to make truth of the fiction.'

'But I got what I wanted. He may think he's scored—he probably does, he's good at turning things to his own advantage—but all he's done is to save his skin. I swept the table.

I've got security for you, and that's what I was playing for.'

'Don't tell me how kind you've been. Not yet. I can't bear it. I want above all things to say "Thank you", but I can't. Not yet. You've been unbelievably good to me, and God knows I'm aware of it. But I've never been in a position of utter dependency before, and I hate it! I can't feel as grateful as I ought. No one can be honestly grateful who isn't on equal terms.'

'But you are.'

'Not till I'm free.'

'It was to give you freedom that I married you. If I hadn't, you'd have gone to prison, or Rumania.'

'And to save myself from prison I've become a bawd. That's hardly freedom, and it certainly isn't equality.'

'I haven't given you a wedding present yet, but I know what I'm going to give you. And that will make a great difference.'

'I don't want anything to remind me of being married.'

'This will only remind you of it indirectly, or remotely.'

The Sultan rose and looked through a port-hole at a pale blue sea freckled with the glint of the sun, and palm-trees on the shore. 'It's notorious,' he said, 'that distance may improve a view, though sometimes that discredits the observer rather than the scene. In a year or two you may think more kindly of Namua, when you see it through the perspective of my wedding present.'

'What is it?'

'Mahomedan law doesn't approve of divorce. We dislike and deprecate divorce. But there are, none the less, several ways in which a contract of marriage can be terminated.'

'On what grounds?'

'Mahomedan law, in some respects, is more charitable than

English. There is no need to state the grounds. If you wish me to, I can annul the marriage by a simple declaration.'

'Immediately? Can you do it now?'

'It would be wiser, I think, to wait until we're in Singapore. To wait, perhaps, for a few months. Before we separate I shall have to make suitable arrangements for your comfort.'

Scornfully she exclaimed, 'Like a faithful ally of Queen Victoria!'

'She had no experience of divorce, had she?'

'None. But her subjects had a great respect for "suitable arrangements". Her subjects were notorious for two qualities. They had a habit of getting their own way, and a remarkable talent for putting the gloss of virtue on it.'

'The Victorians knew what they wanted, and didn't pretend they were at the mercy of events. They realized that events usually have a human origin, and if you have some control over yourself, and sufficient character to exert a little influence on your neighbours, you can probably decide what the event will be. That's how they got their own way.'

'And you believe, I suppose, that the world benefited accordingly.'

'Yes, much of it did.'

'As I have done?—Oh, I have, I know that. But I'm like the world, I'm not grateful. You'll have to wait till I get my wedding present.'

'I'm sorry you look forward to it so eagerly. I don't! I'm very fond of you.'

'It's easy for you. You saved me from prison, so I'm a walking testimonial to your benevolence. But all I've done for you was to dress your boils.'

'It was a carbuncle. And you dressed it very skilfully.'

'It isn't the sort of memory you cherish for the rest of your life.'

237

'I can remember more pleasant services too.'

'Yes.'

'And now that you have the promise of freedom—'

'You won't have to complain for the next couple of weeks. I'll earn my keep, and be kind to Emily.'

'Thank you, Elizabeth.'

He kissed her lightly, and with a fond despair she cried, 'Have patience with me, and I'll be grateful some day!'

Twenty-one

THE long white hull of the yacht was reflected with delicate and whimsical inaccuracy in the shimmering blue water of her anchorage. In the grace of the real hull there was power and solidity, the weight and purpose to divide high contrary waves and bear the strain of tall canvas filled with a Pacific gale. But the reflexion, rippling and relaxing in the slight movement of the sea, so manifestly insubstantial, was a dainty mockery of strength, a sunlit parody of high purpose. It was, however, the reflexion that took the interest of the ladies coming out to the Sultan's party, and exacted their admiration. 'How pretty,' they said. 'Look at the colours!'

And now, when the party was in full swing, a parody of another sort, rowdy and exuberant, was being presented on the fore-deck of the yacht, where the band of the Namuan Constabulary was playing for the third time the Wedding March from *Lohengrin*. Their first rendering had been a solemn performance, but the music had excited their simple hearts, and now they were playing with such dash and celerity that a bride, to keep in step, would have to march at the light infantry pace to which the Constabulary drilled.

Their speed and the militancy of their style, however, were not inappropriate to an occasion which had been arranged in haste and ordered with some asperity. There was indeed no evidence of haste in the parade of hospitality, no sign of remaining asperity in the temper of the host and his new-made wife; but to those who cared to listen, the music did suggest that the wedding had been no ordinary affair.

With the prospect of a divorce as soon as she should seriously ask for it, Her Highness had grown almost reconciled to her state, and to her guests she presented an appearance of calm and gracious dignity. She and her costume were both admired, and many people found it easier to recognize her beauty and acknowledge the distinction of her clothes when they heard her addressed as *Your Highness*. The party assembled in the main saloon, and in the dining saloon which opened off it there was a buffet of such magnificence that even the most sceptical were persuaded of the bona fides of Mrs. Nottingham's newly acquired title. The Sultan's guests from the Palace—obscure relations and old retainers of grave demeanour—wore jewels and robes of richly coloured silk that made the party frocks of the European ladies look like suitable dresses for a picnic; but the picnickers had a larger capacity for enjoyment than their more stately neighbours, and presently there was noise enough in the saloon to dispute the loyal music of the Namuan Constabulary. With open ports and electric fans the rooms were agreeably cool, and for some time no one followed Mrs. Marly's example when, beckoning to Mrs. Pemberton, she led her out and on to the after-deck, where the air was still oppressively hot under the awnings.

A steward followed them, obedient to Mrs. Marly's monitory finger, whom she told to bring whisky and soda. 'I don't fancy swilling champagne all afternoon,' she protested. 'That sour stuff does you no good, unless you like belching.'

She had stopped to light a cigar as she left the saloon, and Mrs. Pemberton saw with anxiety that a short veil which hung from the brim of Mrs. Marly's hat was in danger of fire. Mrs. Marly thanked her for the warning, and tossed the veil into safety.

'Hats are a nuisance,' she said, 'but you've got to wear them at a wedding, like black at a funeral. I don't see why you shouldn't smoke as well, though. Now tell me all about this business.'

'It was wonderfully exciting! I wouldn't have missed it for anything. I was terrified to begin with, but when they started shooting I almost enjoyed it.'

'Yes, people always do, when it's over. But that isn't what I asked you. I want to know why he's married her. It doesn't make sense to me, but Jim Morland won't tell me what's behind it all. He shut up like a clam when I asked him.'

'I don't think there's anything mysterious about it.'

'Oh, nonsense. There's no mystery about her decision, of course. Any woman would marry him. I did my best twenty-five years ago, though I'd a husband already, and he raised hell when he knew what was going on.'

'You wanted to marry him?' asked Mrs. Pemberton with ingenuous surprise.

'I didn't always look like this, my dear. I've had my fun, and I'm glad of it. And now I like a good cigar and I want to know what's going on. Well, why has he married her?'

'I suppose he's in love with her.'

'He married none of the others. No, there's a better reason than that. Did she take any interest in young Kershawe when she was in Maipani?'

'No, none at all.'

'I thought it might be jealousy. The Sultan's getting to an age when men do extraordinary things for jealousy of a younger man. But if she wasn't interested in Kershawe, that's out. For Jim Morland wouldn't take any notice of her, he's too sensible.'

'She doesn't like Mr. Morland,' said Mrs. Pemberton, showing with a tinge of pride what she had learnt in her new surroundings. 'And he doesn't get on very well with the Sultan either.'

'That's absolute rubbish,' said Mrs. Marly indignantly. 'The Sultan has the highest opinion of him! He told me himself that Jim did very well at Maipani. He said, "Morland behaved exactly as you'd expect him to do". And by what I've heard from Jim himself—I've read part of his report, as a matter of fact—it was his knowledge and understanding of the natives that saved your bacon.'

'Oh no, it wasn't,' said Mrs. Pemberton. 'It was the Sultan and Mr. Kershawe who took control.'

'I daresay they did well enough. Jim gives a lot of praise to Kershawe. But Jim was the senior political officer there, and he'll get the credit. And he deserves it, as the Sultan admitted. "Morland did all you could expect of him": that's what he said.'

'When the Sultan makes a joke, it's to amuse himself, not other people,' said Mrs. Pemberton.

Mrs. Marly, her cigar clenched firmly between her teeth, regarded Mrs. Pemberton with a surprised and calculating eye. 'You've got more brains than I thought,' she said, a little grudgingly. 'It took me nearly a year to find that out. But it wasn't a joke for all that!'

'If it weren't for the Sultan and Mr. Kershawe, I mightn't be here,' said Mrs. Pemberton with deep feeling in her voice; and turned to see the Sultan coming towards them, balancing a glass on a silver tray.

'I intercepted the steward who was bringing you this,' he told Mrs. Marly, 'and I begged the pleasure for myself. But why have you deserted the party?'

'We came up for a breath of fresh air.'

'It's hotter here than in the saloon. Far hotter.'

'We've been talking about you,' said Mrs. Pemberton with innocent happiness.

'It's a fascinating subject, but you'll have to postpone it.

There are young men down below who want to talk about themselves, and you ought to be listening to them. We can discuss my unfailing charm for the next two weeks.'

'For the next two weeks!' exclaimed Mrs. Marly. 'I thought you were going to Singapore?'

'So we are,' said the Sultan, 'and Emily is coming with us.'

'William wanted to stay in Maipani, and go on tour with Mr. Kershawe, so I left him there. I'm an abandoned woman,' said Mrs. Pemberton, proud of her independence and her joke.

'Pemberton will go to Singapore when he's finished his work here, and Emily decided that a sea voyage would be pleasanter than waiting for him in Port Philip.'

'I jumped at the chance,' said Mrs. Pemberton.

'Well,' said Mrs. Marly, 'it will be a change from the ordinary sort of honeymoon. There's that to be said for it.'

'One of the advantages of marriage,' said the Sultan, 'is that one's wife can immediately become a chaperon.'

'It's an inducement I haven't heard before.'

'Not an inducement,' said the Sultan. 'Just a reward.'

'Does anyone know you're going?' asked Mrs. Marly.

'Only Mr. Morland. I haven't told anyone else.'

'It's odd he didn't tell me. He came to lunch with me. But Jim, of course, thinks himself above gossip.'

She put down her glass and looked about her in what appeared to be a sudden access of uneasiness. 'Have you seen my bag anywhere?' she asked.

'You left it below, I think.'

'In the saloon? Yes, of course. How stupid of me. I think I must go and get it.'

She made a little bow to excuse herself, and walked with impatient purpose to the companionway, leaving on the still ocean of the air a thin wake of smoke.

'She will be the first with the news,' said the Sultan. 'That will give her great pleasure.'

'At this moment I couldn't grudge any woman her pleasure. I'm so happy, I can afford to be extravagantly generous.'

'Is that unusual?'

'To be happy?'

'To be generous.'

'I think it is. I think I was more generous a year ago, before I got married. Because William has never noticed when I'm being generous, and that has discouraged me. He always expected to get his own way.'

'Family life is like religion,' said the Sultan. 'The more we look at it, the more improbable it seems that it was meant for us. But like religion it has to be accepted, because there's nothing else. All we can do is to mollify its hardships.'

'By going abroad?'

'That's one of the better-known devices.'

'I haven't enjoyed it as much as I expected—not till now, I mean—because we flew straight to Singapore, and the first thing I really *felt* was that I was eight thousand miles from home. And that was disconcerting.'

'It's the reward of travelling, to feel far from home. When you're packing your suitcases you should never include tender memories of domestic life.'

'But you can't forget things as easily as that.'

'Don't try to forget them. Stop thinking about them; that's all. Use your eyes, use your imagination, think only about what you can see, and make up your mind to enjoy it because you may never get such a chance again.'

'I still feel rather *daunted* to think I'm so far away.'

'That's an excellent foundation for enjoyment. It shows imagination, and when imagination acquires confidence it becomes the best of company—and never lacks enjoyment.'

'I used to be confident about everything. But that was before I knew very much.'

'And early experience was discouraging?'

'Terribly discouraging.'

'It often is, I'm afraid. But when you regain your confidence, it's really worth something. And I'm not flattering you when I say you start with certain natural advantages.'

'Oh, I'm pretty, I know that, if that's what you mean,' said Mrs. Pemberton. 'I've been told that hundreds of times. But it doesn't help as much as people think it should. In some ways it makes things more difficult—and much harder to understand.'

'My dear Emily, we're going to have the most enchanting conversations! And I can promise you this: that when you're at sea, on the deck of a small ship at sea, in the tropics, you'll breathe an air that will resolve all the problems you've ever imagined.'

'I shan't bother about problems when I'm at sea. I love sailing—well, I used to sail a dinghy, and I loved that. And I expect this will be even better.'

'Yes,' said the Sultan gravely, 'you'll find this more comfortable than a dinghy, for a long voyage.'

There were now several pairs and trios of the wedding guests strolling on deck, and most of the Sultan's Palace friends had gathered to listen to the Constabulary band; which, having spent its early exuberance, was playing with gentle melancholy excerpts from *The Gondoliers*. Her Highness came up the companionway with Dr. Playfair, and the Sultan, going to meet her, took her by the hand.

'Emily,' she said, 'you must go down and talk to some of those young men. They're desperately looking round for pretty girls, and there are only five on board, in the most charitable judgment.'

'Off you go,' said the Sultan, 'but don't tire yourself. They won't expect you to say anything, you'll only have to listen.'

'I'm used to that,' she said. 'I really do know how to manage young men.' And with an assumption of confidence that charmed the Sultan, went cheerfully below.

'She's got her wits about her,' he said admiringly.

'I hope so indeed,' said Her Highness. 'But do you know this? Poor Dr. Playfair is going to be bored to death in Port Philip. He has finished his work, and now he's got nothing to do but wait for the boat to Singapore.'

'I've written a learned, monumental, and utterly unreadable account of the hookworm, its distribution, its intimate life and its pernicious habits,' said Playfair, 'and I've finished a private *opus* of infinitely greater value and extraordinary charm. I've done my job and exhausted my will to work. And for the next couple of weeks I've nothing to look forward to but drinking myself into a stupor at the Yacht Club.'

'Do you play bridge?' asked the Sultan.

'I would, if there was anyone here who could still face the rigours of the table. But they've all taken to a new heresy, a sort of sophisticated nursery game, that's neither honest gambling nor the pure science of the cards.'

'We are bridge players,' said the Sultan, 'and we need a fourth. Would you like to come to Singapore with us? We're sailing at ten.'

'Sir,' said the doctor, who had enjoyed the buffet as much as anyone, 'you are a great man, as I recognized at our first meeting.'

'When you saw me in an unusual aspect,' said the Sultan.

'I saw your courage in adversity,' said the doctor, 'and I shall be honoured to sail with you. I shall also take your money at the bridge-table. And now, sir, may I send a message to the shore and tell my absurdly inefficient servant to pack for me?'

He bowed, and left them with a light-hearted, almost skipping step.

'I'm glad you asked him,' said Her Highness. 'I thought you might like to have another man on board.'

'To give me conversation late at night?'

'Or to talk to me.'

'How a promise of divorce has sweetened you!—No, don't leave me, there's something I want to say.'

'I have my duty now. A duty to our guests.'

'You've done it admirably. I stood in pride beside you. But tell me this—it's something I ought to have asked you before, but we've never talked of such things—and don't be shy about it. I'm not trying to parade my generosity when I say that before I divorce you I'll have to make some provision for you. That's only good, traditional, Mahomedan custom. But I want to know if you have any money of your own? Any money at all?'

'Not very much.'

'How much?'

'I have a small investment. It's worth about £800, I think.'

'Is that all?'

'Yes.'

'What is your money in?'

'The Church of England Building Society.'

'That can't give you much return?'

'No.'

'My predecessor, your late husband—Tratteanu—didn't he leave you any money?'

'He had none. He lived on an allowance from his elder brother.'

'So your career has never been very profitable?'

247

'I have never begged,' she said, 'and never chaffered.'

'My dear Elizabeth! How woefully you've been miscast.'

'And you?' she asked.

'No, not miscast. Only de-synchronized.'

Mrs. Marly returned to them, leading in her muscular hand a reluctant Mrs. Pemberton, and said with boisterous confidence, 'I know perfectly well that you don't want to see me again, but I had to come and ask you: is it true that Jim Morland went out, at the risk of his life, to save Mr. Pemberton?'

'I've told her he did,' said Mrs. Pemberton, 'but I said it was all William's fault—'

'What does that matter?' asked Mrs. Marly.

'Morland did his duty, according to his own conception of it, as he always has done,' said the Sultan. 'He showed considerable bravery in going to look for Pemberton.'

'I knew it!' exclaimed Mrs. Marly. 'I knew it was true as soon as I heard it. Jim did a first-class job at Maipani, and I hope you'll see that he gets recognition for it.'

She thrust her sturdy arm under the Sultan's, and led him apart. 'There's something else I want to ask you—in confidence, of course—and with the freedom, if you'll allow it, of a very old friend.'

'That I could never deny you.'

'Well, then. There was that trouble in Fairweather. She broke her bail, didn't she? And now, apparently, she's going scot-free. Well, was it Jim who made that possible? Did he smooth things over?'

'I think it would be an exaggeration to say that.'

'Then who's given her permission to go to Singapore?'

'I have,' said the Sultan. 'As my wife, she is free to go anywhere.'

'Oh ho!' said Mrs. Marly in triumph. 'So that's why you

did it! I've been racking my brain, but I just couldn't think why you'd married her.'

'I married her, my dear Maggie, for the conventional reason: because I love her.'

'Yes, I'm sure you do. And you always marry them, don't you? But what I'm beginning to ask myself now is whether it wasn't Jim who put the idea into your head.'

'Indirectly, and after a fashion, that's true, I suppose.'

'I knew it! I guessed it at once. Jim's a wonderful man, and I'm very proud of him.'

'He is, perhaps, all a government official should be.'

'I'm so glad to hear you say that! You've made me a very happy woman. Very happy indeed.'

They rejoined the others, and Mrs. Marly said, 'I must have another drink. I'm so proud I want to float.'

'Whisky and soda?' asked the Sultan. 'I'll get it for you.'

'Isn't there a steward who can go?' asked Her Highness.

'The stewards are busy with our guests, all of whom are very thirsty,' said the Sultan.

Mrs. Marly, her blue eyes lustrous with emotion, visibly adored the strong movement of his retreating figure. 'The most charming man east of Singapore!' she exclaimed. 'As I know well. Oh, who better? But he still needs looking after, doesn't he? I always found that, and he hasn't changed a scrap.'

'I think your memory must be failing,' said Her Highness. 'In the short time I've known him, I've been deeply impressed by his all-round competence.'

'Yes, on the surface. That's what everyone thinks when they first meet him. But when you get to know him better you'll find he's just a boy at heart, and irresponsible as a boy.'

'He's far kinder than any boy could be,' said Mrs. Pemberton.

'Nor, in my experience,' said Her Highness, 'has he shown any sign of emotional immaturity. Though in your day that was to be expected, of course.'

'In my day,' said Mrs. Marly, 'we didn't analyse our emotions. We simply admitted them, and gave way to them.'

'And plunged recklessly into the shallow end of a municipal swimming bath?'

Mrs. Marly's face grew a little pale, a little flaccid under the shock of insult. Not for many years had anyone spoken so rudely to her, and her consternation was aggravated by her inability to think of an appropriate answer. She threw the butt-end of her cigar to the deck, and trod on it angrily; and an unexpected music rose from the saloon to divert attention from her discomfiture.

Someone was playing the piano with ponderous, uncertain, but party-spirited fingers, and a chorus of ill-tuned voices sang with noisy enthusiasm:

> 'For he's a jolly good fellow,
> For he's a jolly good fellow. . . .'

All on deck turned amused or inquiring heads towards the raucous jollity, and Mrs. Pemberton said impulsively, 'I'm so glad! They're cheering the Sultan!'

They moved towards the companionway and met the Sultan coming up, again bearing a glass on a small salver.

'If the oil-wells of Te Aku run dry,' he said, 'I shall go to California and become a butler.' And with a small obeisance he presented her whisky and soda to Mrs. Marly.

'But you shouldn't be here,' said Her Highness. 'You mustn't leave them when they're singing to you.'

'They're not singing to me,' said the Sultan.

'But who else is there?'

'Why, Morland. Morland has become the hero of the party.'

'I thought as much!' exclaimed Mrs. Marly. 'I felt it as soon as they began singing. Is he going to make a speech, do you think?'

'I've no doubt he will.'

Mrs. Marly had just withdrawn, from the leather case she carried, a new cigar. She held it in her right hand like a sceptre, in her left she clutched her whisky glass like an orb. Her bearing became regal, her bosom rose like the shoulder of a deep-sea wave, and as she turned to glance triumphantly at Her Highness a thin beam of the sun, penetrating a gap in the awning, lit like a crystal a drop at her nose. 'I must go and listen to him,' she said, and went majestically below.

'But why, why?' demanded Her Highness. 'Why should anyone think Morland a jolly good fellow?'

'He did nothing but interfere with you and Mr. Kershawe,' said Mrs. Pemberton indignantly.

'Is he going to get the credit for what happened?'

'I expect he will; or most of it. He was, after all, the senior official there. And that's what counts.'

'But it's monstrous!'

'It's wicked!'

'No, no, you mustn't exaggerate,' said the Sultan. 'It is, if you want a precise description, gently ironical. And why should we complain of that? Irony, or the recognition of it, is one of the major graces of a decent life. Without irony history would be quite intolerable.'

'But it's so unfair,' said Mrs. Pemberton.

'When we're going sailing, in perfect weather, and the most that Morland can expect is a C.B.E.? Don't grudge him that, Emily.'

Plump and rosy and excited, walking as though the deck were elastic beneath his hurried feet, Dr. Playfair returned to them and exclaimed, 'I've made all my arrangements, sir; or at least, I hope so. I'll go ashore and pay my bill at the Club, and pick up my luggage, and be aboard again about half-past nine. Will that be all right?'

'Come a little earlier if you can.'

'I will, sir. I'll have to wait for Dr. Marshall, that's all I'm worrying about, because he's got that paper I've written. The one I told you about.'

'The history of the hookworm?'

'No, bless your heart, nobody will ever waste time on that. That's just for the government. It's the beautiful life-story of a little, thin worm I'm thinking of. A little worm I discovered in a poor pig suffering from swine-fever, and the noblest work I've ever done. You'll read it, sir, and your heart will sing like the celestial spheres.'

'About a worm?' asked Mrs. Pemberton.

'I'm the Hans Andersen of parasitology,' said Playfair, and wiped his ruddy, sweating forehead with a yellow silk hand-kerchief. 'I found her feeding on the poor pig's tears. The pig's eye, in its fever, was dripping like a honey-comb, and what do you think was the attraction of the tears? I studied the life of the little worm to find out, and plotted its history from alpha to omega. And the secret was that she couldn't get the satisfaction of fertility—she couldn't reproduce her kind—till she'd been stimulated by grief! By the grief, and a strong dose of salt, in the pig's tears. Oh, it's a beautiful story, and it's given me a new faith in life.'

'In human life?' asked the Sultan.

'I discovered it, and I'm a man,' said Playfair. 'But worms, pigs, or humans, what's the difference? Fearfully and wonder-fully are we made. Will you dance with me, Your Highness?'

The band of the Namuan Constabulary had begun to play, slowly and carefully, 'The Blue Danube'; and the wedding guests were leaving the buffet, coming up from the saloon, and moving under a canopy of busy voices to the broad and open part of the deck. The light was deepening as the sun more rapidly declined, and the evening breeze had begun to blow.

The Sultan and Mrs. Pemberton stood by the rail, at the after end of the deck, and listened to the lap of moving water. Throughout the hot afternoon the sea had slept quietly under the hull of the yacht, but now in the wind that came before the darkness it wakened, and with a small, hard, musical noise it clapped and chuckled against the steep side of the ship as though gossiping of flying-fish, and islands below the horizon, and the ocean-lanes.

'I think,' said the Sultan, 'I can palliate my sense of guilt. This morning, in Maipani, I disappointed a young man who deserved better of me. Perhaps he expected too much, but I gave him nothing at all. I thought of sending him some small present—the usual thing: a watch or a pair of cuff-links—and it has just occurred to me that I have something he would probably like better. And I really don't see why I should keep it. Come down with me, and I'll show you what I'm thinking of.'

They went down into the saloon, now empty of guests but still redolent of their cigarettes and perfumes, and the Sultan told a steward to bring him a small screw-driver.

'You remember what that is? I told you about it the first time you came aboard.'

They stood before a little oval gilt frame, set into a bulkhead, in which, behind glass, a sprig of what had once been white heather, but now was brown as tea-leaves, was fastened to faded blue velvet by an old-fashioned diamond tie-pin.

'Mrs. Disraeli,' she said, 'gave your grandfather the white heather, and Queen Victoria gave him the diamond pin and called him her Faithful Ally.'

He took the screw-driver from the steward and slowly,

laboriously, detached the frame. 'Don't you think Kershawe would like to have it?' he asked.

'Are you going to give it him?'

'I'm sure he deserves it, and I'm inclined to think he has the better claim to it. I shall have it packed and sent off before we sail.'

He put it into his pocket, and looked at the disfigured bulkhead.

'It leaves a gap,' said the Sultan. 'I must do something to conceal it.'

On the deck above, the band of the Namuan Constabulary began to play again, by request, 'The Blue Danube'.

'Give me,' he said, 'the consolation of the waltz.'

The Gods and their Machines

'Completely fantastical yet totally relevant'

Eoin Colfer,
author of the *Artemis Fowl* trilogy and *The Wish List*

*'A pacy, action-filled plot with very real characters
facing gripping dilemmas'*

Mark O'Sullivan,
Reading Association of Ireland award-winner